"I'm not here to make friends."

Dillon's voice was firm. "I'm here to save a sinking ship."

Don't let her get to you, he thought. *Just make her understand.* In many ways she was naive and too idealistic for her own good.

"And one of my first rules," he added, carefully avoiding her eyes, "is that bleeding hearts have no place in business. And neither do personal feelings—not if you want to sleep nights."

"I'll try to remember that." Adrienne's voice dripped with sarcasm. "But sleeping nights has never been a problem for *me.*"

Dear Reader,

Four more fabulous WOMEN WHO DARE are heading your way!

In May, you'll thrill to the time-travel tale Lynn Erickson spins in *Paradox*. When loan executive Emily Jacoby is catapulted back in time during a train wreck, she is thoroughly unnerved by the fate that awaits her. In 1893, Colorado is a harsh and rugged land. Women's rights have yet to be invented, and Will Dutcher, Emily's reluctant host, is making her question her desire to return to her own time.

In June, you'll be reminded that courage can strike at any age. Our heroine in Peg Sutherland's *Late Bloomer* discovers unplumbed depths at the age of forty. After a lifetime of living for others, she realizes that she wants something for herself—college, a career, a *life*. But when a mysterious stranger drifts into town, she discovers to her shock that she also wants *him!*

Sharon Brondos introduces us to spunky Allison Ford in our July WOMEN WHO DARE title, *The Marriage Ticket*. Allison stands up for what she believes in. And she believes in playing fair. Unfortunately, some of her community's leaders don't have the same scruples, and going head-to-head with them lands her in serious trouble.

You'll never forget Leah Temple, the heroine of August's *Another Woman*, by Margot Dalton. This riveting tale of a wife with her husband's murder on her mind will hold you spellbound...and surprised! Don't miss it!

Some of your favorite Superromance authors have also contributed to our spring and summer lineup. Look for books by Pamela Bauer, Debbi Bedford, Dawn Stewardson, Jane Silverwood, Sally Garrett, Bobby Hutchinson and Judith Arnold...to name just a few! Some wonderful Superromance reading awaits you!

Marsha Zinberg
Senior Editor

P.S. Don't forget that you can write to your favorite author

> c/o Harlequin Reader Service,
> P.O. Box 1297
> Buffalo, New York
> 14240 U.S.A.

Anne Logan

TWIN OAKS

Harlequin Books

TORONTO • NEW YORK • LONDON
AMSTERDAM • PARIS • SYDNEY • HAMBURG
STOCKHOLM • ATHENS • TOKYO • MILAN
MADRID • WARSAW • BUDAPEST • AUCKLAND

Published June 1993

ISBN 0-373-70550-6

TWIN OAKS

ABOUT THE AUTHOR

In *Twin Oaks,* says Anne Logan, "I wanted to create a hero and heroine who possessed the kind of love that perseveres even when the odds are stacked against it."

Twin Oaks is Anne's second Superromance novel. She and her husband live in Luling, Louisiana, and are looking forward to their role as new grandparents.

Books by Anne Logan

HARLEQUIN SUPERROMANCE
507—GULF BREEZES

Don't miss any of our special offers. Write to us at the following address for information on our newest releases.

Harlequin Reader Service
P.O. Box 1397, Buffalo, NY 14240
Canadian address: P.O. Box 603,
Fort Erie, Ont. L2A 5X3

With thanks to all my friends at O.C.C.
And a special thanks to Evan Marshall

CHAPTER ONE

"MISS ADRIENNE, is it true? Is Mr. Reynolds's son coming back home to run things?"

"His son?"

Eva Sanders nodded. "Mr. Dillon Reynolds, Franklin's son."

Adrienne Hamilton shook her head and rolled her eyes toward the ceiling.

"I know who Franklin's son is, Eva." *Great. The grapevine at Twin Oaks Country Club strikes again.* Just what she needed to end a perfect week, she thought sarcastically. Then, noticing that Eva's Swedish accent seemed more pronounced than usual, a sure sign she was truly upset, Adrienne tried to make light of the waitress's concern.

"Rumors fly around here worse than golf balls on the driving range. But that's all they are—rumors. Why, just the other day, I heard one of the other waitresses say that the club is going bankrupt. I've never heard anything so ridiculous in all my life."

Eva frowned. "One of the members said that when a new manager comes in, he cleans house."

"Eva, I'm the assistant food and beverage manager. Don't you think that I would know if we were getting a new boss?"

"But if young Mr. Reynolds does come in and clean house, I'll be one of the first to go, since I was hired just a month ago. Waitressing jobs aren't easy to come by— at least good ones aren't, out here in the suburbs. I can't afford to drive into Houston, not with my old man out of work because of his back."

"I know how you feel," Adrienne said sympathetically. "Believe me, I need my job just as much as you need yours, and you're right. Decent jobs aren't easy to come by, but..." She reached out and gently patted Eva's arm. "The club can't operate without its employees, especially good waitresses like you. January and February are always slow months. Everyone's on edge. Even Pierre is worse than usual."

At mention of the quick-tempered Frenchman, Eva grinned. "Yes, I heard about that. Did he really threaten to dump a plate of fettuccine on Mr. Tanner's head because he'd complained it was served cold?"

Adrienne chuckled and nodded. "I had to do some fast talking to placate him and Mr. Tanner." After a moment, she took a deep breath. "The point is, we've been in tight spots before and survived. If everyone pulls together and does their job—"

"I do my job," Eva interrupted. "But sometimes that doesn't matter."

The sound of her name being paged over the intercom was a good excuse to end the no-win conversation. Adrienne gave Eva an apologetic look as she began backing toward the door. "As far as I know, we are not getting a new manager, but we'll talk more later."

She walked briskly toward the door that led upstairs to the business office. There was really no use agonizing over what might or might not happen, she decided. If there was one thing she had learned in her thirty years of living, it was that nothing stayed the same forever. And not all changes were necessarily bad, she reminded herself as she climbed the stairs.

The moment she stepped through the doorway, Joanne Thompson, the receptionist, gave her a look of relief and a meaningful nod toward the manager's office.

"He's going to stroke out if someone doesn't calm him down," she said.

"What now?"

Joanne grimaced expressively. "He got another call from Ms. Langley a few minutes ago. She claims yesterday's buffet gave her an upset stomach."

"Probably because she ate so much of it," quipped Adrienne. "I swear, the woman went back for a fourth helping of everything."

Joanne snickered, then sobered. "No kidding. When I paged you, he was in the middle of a tirade about Ms. Langley, but another call came in and he seems to have calmed down some."

At that moment Joanne's desk phone rang and she turned to answer it. Adrienne took a deep breath and walked to the closed door labeled Manager. She knocked softly and entered.

Franklin Reynolds was still talking on the phone, but motioned for her to come in and sit. Adrienne smiled at the distinguished, gray-haired man she'd come to respect and admire, but she couldn't help noticing that his pale face was covered with a fine film of perspiration.

She hated seeing him in such a state. Normally he had an easygoing, laid-back demeanor and rarely got upset over anything. Deep down, she suspected more was wrong with him than he was letting on. She knew he'd had several doctor's appointments lately, but he'd shrugged off her concern, telling her it was time for his annual checkups, that men his age always had one thing or another wrong with them.

Adrienne studied Franklin's face more closely. Some of the color was beginning to return, and by the patient, loving tone of his voice, she knew his caller had to be his wife. If anyone had the power to calm him down, it was Myrna.

Adrienne had heard time and time again how Franklin's wife had encouraged and supported him during their early years of building the small, exclusive Twin Oaks community. She'd also heard rumors that he'd tried his hand at managing a couple of businesses but had lost them. Then he'd taken a chance and bought property no one else wanted. Adrienne knew that, over a fifteen-year span, he had not only succeeded in developing what some would consider a suburban paradise, he'd also built up one of the most prestigious and respected country clubs in the Houston area. Oil millionaires, senators, and even a governor had, at one time or another, been listed on the membership rolls.

When several minutes passed and there was no sign of Franklin ending the call, Adrienne glanced at her watch. The lunch buffet was already set out. Two of the bus help hadn't showed up for work yet, and Adrienne knew that Eva would be having fits if she didn't get someone in.

Wondering who on her list could get there the fastest, Adrienne impatiently tapped her fingers against the padded chair arm and recrossed her legs. Just as she'd decided she couldn't wait any longer, Franklin hung up the phone.

"That was Myrna," he said, his voice full of nervous excitement. "I've got some great news. She talked with our son and he's finally agreed to come home and help manage Twin Oaks."

All thoughts of the lunch buffet fled and Adrienne felt her insides knot with apprehension. Eva had been right.

"That's—that's wonderful, but I thought he was managing a successful club in Florida."

Franklin nodded. "He is, but his talents are wasted on that small club. Besides, he's been away too long. He belongs here, with his family. He's giving notice and should be arriving within a couple of weeks."

From time to time, Adrienne had heard some of the other employees talk about Dillon Reynolds and speculate as to why he never visited his parents. She'd gotten the idea that there had been a rift between Franklin and his son, but no one seemed to know what their quarrel was about.

Even though Adrienne felt uneasy about Franklin's announcement, she forced a smile. "Maybe now you can take Myrna on that vacation she's always wanted to go on. Lord knows, with all the crazy hours you put in, you both deserve one."

"I have to be honest with you." Franklin couldn't seem to look her in the eyes. Instead, he lowered his gaze to the papers stacked in front of him. "A couple of years back, I had to sell everything but the country club and a worthless piece of undeveloped acreage that no one wanted."

"Everything?" Adrienne was shocked. "What do you mean, everything?"

"The new residential section—Pinetree Village—and most of the commercial reserves. And even with all of that gone, it will still probably take both of us to get the club back on its feet. I borrowed some operating money and I've only been able to make the interest payments. The bank has given me two months to come up with what I borrowed or they're calling in the loan...in full." His gravelly voice was suspiciously gruff. "Everything I have is tied up in this club. If I don't pay off that loan," he continued, "I'll lose it all."

Adrienne felt a chill go through her. Were all the rumors true? she wondered as she stared at Franklin.

For the first time in the six years she'd known him, she found herself really angry with him. Franklin had always been too easygoing for his own good. He didn't like unpleasant confrontations and avoided them as much as possible. The only reason the Twin Oaks development and the club had survived at all, she suddenly realized, was because, up until the past two years, there had been plenty of cash rolling in.

Now, with even the wealthiest members moving out because of the recession, the financial padding was gone. Why hadn't Franklin seen this coming and taken some steps to counteract the damage?

She forced herself to relax. There was no use getting angry at him. Besides, who was she to question his unorthodox way of doing things? After all, she reminded herself, he had taken a chance on her when she'd desperately needed a job six years earlier.

"I'd just as soon the rest of the employees don't learn about this quite yet," he continued.

Adrienne shrugged. "I think it's a little late to worry about that. Word—according to the grapevine—is that Twin Oaks is going bankrupt."

Franklin groaned. "How on earth . . ." He shook his head. "No, don't tell me. I swear, sometimes I think this office is bugged."

Adrienne felt a smile tug at her lips. "If you think that's something, wait until you hear the latest."

Franklin raised his eyebrows.

"Eva just asked me if your son was coming back to run things."

For several seconds, Franklin simply stared at her, a look of utter disbelief on his face. Then he grimaced and shook his head again. "Unbelievable. But after all this time, I should know better. Tell you what. If the grapevine figures out a way to come up with the extra money we need, let me know. One thing's for sure." He picked up a pile of folders and shuffled them into a neat stack, placing them on the corner of his cluttered desk. "It's going to take a miracle to get us out of this mess."

"What about going to the members—at least to the ones who own stock? If each of the four hundred stockholders were assessed . . . say, three or four hundred dollars . . . wouldn't that be enough? If they knew—"

Franklin shook his head. "No! Not this time." He raised his chin a notch. "Once, years ago, I might have taken the easy way out, but not anymore. If we can't save it without going begging, then I have no business running it in the first place."

Two weeks later, on a Friday afternoon, Franklin Reynolds called a staff meeting. He announced that his son would be taking charge of Twin Oaks, and that there would probably be some changes made.

ON TUESDAY MORNING, Adrienne stood in her living room waiting impatiently for her daughter. Usually the first one dressed, Kristen seemed to be taking an inordinate amount of time this particular day.

Adrienne glanced at her watch and resisted the temptation to go see what was taking so long. Instead, she walked over to the sofa and straightened the throw pillows, moving them strategically to hide the more threadbare spots. She had hoped to buy a new couch, but now . . .

She sighed. There were worse things in life than having worn-out furniture. She should be grateful to have a roof over her head. The only thing she'd been able to depend on from her ex-husband, with his unstable job record, was the house payment. At least they wouldn't be out on the streets if she got laid off.

"Kristen," Adrienne called as she grabbed up her handbag, unzipped one of its compartments and searched for an elusive tube of rose-colored lipstick. "We're going to be late if you don't hurry." She spied it hiding beneath her checkbook and fished it out just as her daughter wheeled through the doorway.

"My legs are squeaking again," the young girl complained, giving the arm of her wheelchair a frustrated slap with her hand.

Adrienne frowned, then turned toward the wall mirror and carefully applied the rich pink color to her lips. The secondhand wheelchair had seemed like a bargain when she'd bought it, but the contrary thing had proved to be nothing but trouble. Still, it was all she could afford at the time, and as much as it pained her, Kristen would have to make the best of things.

Rubbing her lips together to smooth the color evenly, Adrienne inspected her reflection, then moved away from the mirror and slipped the tube back into her purse. "Remind me this afternoon and I'll ask Uncle Louie to oil it again," she offered.

Usually just the mention of Uncle Louis brought a smile to Kristen's lips. Since Adam Louis Johnson had showed up on the doorstep six months ago, the sixty-eight-year old and his great-niece had developed a special relationship. Kristen seemed delighted to have a man in the house and Adrienne had to admit that having a great-uncle around had been good for the girl.

But today Kristen was not smiling.

"He just oiled them," Kristen answered sullenly. "My old one never squeaked."

But you outgrew your old one, Adrienne argued silently, knowing better than to say it out loud. She could tell by the stubborn look on her daughter's face that she was just itching for a quarrel, and that was the last thing Adrienne wanted to deal with this particular morning.

According to Franklin, his son was due to arrive today. And according to the chef, Dillon Reynolds was worse than the plague. It seemed that Pierre had worked for him in Florida a few years back.

The day Franklin had announced that his son would be taking over, Pierre had cornered her. "The man is a ruthless *bâtard,*" he'd declared, his expressive hands slicing the air with each word. "Do not trust him as far as you can throw him."

Adrienne had patiently listened to the Frenchman, but as always, she had already made up her mind to reserve judgment for herself. If Dillon Reynolds could come in and save Twin Oaks and her job, she would support him one hundred percent. And since he was scheduled to arrive at noon today, she wanted to be calm and clearheaded when she met him for the first time.

Adrienne turned her attention back to her daughter. "I like the way you fixed your hair," she said, hoping to change the subject and diffuse a potential argument. Kristen had used hot rollers, and her normally straight blond hair curled gently around her smooth, oval face.

Kristen ignored the compliment. "I'm not going to that snooty school with this thing squeaking. Everyone will look at me."

Pretending to search for her car keys, Adrienne turned away to hide the smile on her lips. Kristen had been in a wheelchair since she was five and had adjusted amazingly well to her disability, accepting it as a simple fact of her young life. Adrienne knew that her daughter's remark had nothing to do with being self-conscious of her handicap, but was typical of any other twelve-year-old girl who would rather die than call undue attention to herself.

Adrienne slipped on her jacket. "They're not all snooty, and if they look, just smile," she said.

"They *are* snooty. Ever since Susan moved, nothing's been the same."

"She's only been gone a week. Give it some time. You'll make a new friend, but just remember you have to be a friend to have one." Adrienne turned, heading for the front door. Kristen had met Susan in the hospital after her accident. They'd both been in therapy together and had been inseparable ever since. Their friendship was one of the reasons Adrienne had stretched her budget to the limit so that Kristen could attend the exclusive private school in the first place. At the time, she'd felt her daughter needed all the support she could get.

She heard Kristen let out a sound of disgust, but she continued walking. At the door, she paused and turned. Kristen hadn't moved. She was sitting with her slender arms tightly crossed against her chest, her sweater dangling from the chair arm.

Adrienne silently counted to ten, telling herself to keep calm and be firm. "If we don't leave now, you and I are both going to be late."

"That's all you care about! It doesn't matter to you if this stupid thing squeaks."

"Kristen," Adrienne warned, "please keep your voice down. Uncle Louie is still sleeping. Besides," she said, trying to keep a reign on her temper, "that's not true, and you know it. Now get your sweater on and get rolling, or you'll be grounded this weekend."

For several moments Kristen didn't move, and Adrienne held her breath as she reminded herself that it was normal for girls her age to be a little rebellious. When her daughter finally lowered her arms, pulled on her sweater and wheeled herself toward the doorway, Adrienne breathed a sigh of relief. She hated these confrontations. Lately, her usually sweet daughter had turned into an obstinate stranger, and the only thing that seemed to gain her cooperation was the threat of being grounded.

Kristen remained stubbornly silent during the short drive to school. Even when Adrienne pulled into the circular driveway, the young girl simply sat and stared straight ahead. When she finally spoke, her voice had lost its defiant edge. "Has Daddy called yet?" she asked.

So that's what this is all about, Adrienne thought as she turned to face her. Not only had her best friend and confidante moved away, but Kristen was anxious about her planned outing with her father. Silently condemning her ex-husband for disappointing their daughter so many times, she found her heart melting at the apprehensive look on Kristen's face.

"No, honey, he hasn't called yet," she said softly.

"Do you think he'll keep our date this weekend? He missed the last one."

Adrienne swallowed the sudden lump in her throat and forced a smile. "I'm sure he'll do the best he can, sweetheart."

Minutes later, Adrienne pulled the wheelchair from the back seat, unfolded it and held it steady while Kristen slid over into it. As Kristen wheeled herself up the walkway, Adrienne stood and watched. After the doors of the school closed behind her daughter, she walked back around the car.

Slipping inside, she thought about Kristen's parting remarks. Jack was supposed to have her two weekends each month, but once every two months had been his average. It hadn't been so hard to explain when Kristen was younger. But as she'd gotten older, she'd begun to notice his absences more and more, and she'd begun to question his excuses.

Adrienne offered up a silent prayer that, for once, Jack Hamilton would keep his promise to his daughter instead of backing out as he usually did. Why couldn't he see beyond the wheelchair and realize what a bright and beautiful child he had? And why couldn't he pay her more attention?

Because he can't get past his own selfishness and guilt over the accident came the unbidden answer.

Adrienne shifted into drive and pulled onto the street. As always, any time she thought about Jack, she felt a familiar tightening in her chest. For Kristen's sake, she'd tried to fight the bitterness she felt, but Jack's unwillingness to face up to his responsibilities was becoming harder and harder to explain or excuse.

She slowed to a halt at a red light. She was the one who saw to Kristen's every need. She was the one who was there for her daughter, no matter what. How ironic that she was the one who weathered the brunt of Kristen's resentments. Even though Jack disappointed his daughter time and time again, Kristen never spoke a word against him and would do almost anything to spend time with him.

The red light changed to green and Adrienne released the brake and accelerated. Why did life have to be so unfair? she wondered for the thousandth time. And why did it have to be so darn complicated?

She pulled her ancient Toyota into the parking lot behind the club and shut off the engine. Gathering up her briefcase and handbag, she got out and locked the door. As she entered the club through the kitchen, she was immediately assaulted with the aroma of onions and garlic being sautéed, with the noise of pots and pans clanging and dishes being stacked. The cooks were already busy preparing the noon buffet, and waitresses were scurrying about, setting up one of the small meeting rooms for a midmorning business function.

Adrienne loved the stately elegance of Twin Oaks and she loved her job. She didn't want to think about the possibility of losing the only security she'd known since her parents' death. The money she earned was a necessity, but she didn't work here just for the money. For the past six years, the club had been her home away from home. She paused at the coffee station and glanced at her watch. Frowning, she poured herself a cup to take with her upstairs to her office. As assistant food and beverage manager, she didn't normally come in until about ten-thirty, but with Franklin's son arriving, she'd wanted to finish up some loose ends before he got there.

DILLON REYNOLDS sat in the veranda area of Twin Oaks's elegant dining room and nursed a cup of luke-warm coffee. Spread out in front of him were the pages of the latest financial statement on the club, and to his trained eyes, it was a disaster. Half the membership accounts were more than ninety days overdue and the payables were an accountant's worst nightmare. On top of that there was evidence of a large short-term loan his father must have recently taken out—one he'd neglected to mention.

Dillon shook his head, feeling his frustration mounting. How on God's earth had his dad let things get into such a mess? As far as he could calculate, there was no way in hell they could pay the loan back when it was due. Two months just wasn't long enough. If he'd known, if he'd realized . . .

What would you have done—refused your own mother? a little voice taunted. Dillon briefly closed his eyes, then opened them. He knew he'd still have come. There was no way he could have refused his mother's quiet plea. She'd been hurt enough in the past.

A flash of midnight blue suddenly caught his attention, and he looked up in time to see a woman stride past, with a gait that reminded him of a thoroughbred strutting to the starting post. Confidence, he thought. Now there was a self-assured woman who knew where she was going. She was balancing a cup of coffee in one hand and juggling her handbag and briefcase in the other, all with ease and poise. When she reached the doorway, she stopped to talk with one of the waitresses.

The low, husky cadence of her voice reached out to him, and he watched her for a moment longer, admiring her sleek good looks. Her hair, a sunlit brown color, was styled in a sophisticated twist. She had a creamy complexion, dark, flashing eyes and full, pouty, rose-colored lips. She was tall and slim, but well endowed with womanly curves and long, shapely legs.

Shifting in his chair, Dillon turned his attention back to the sheaf of papers before him and began to gather them into a stack. By the looks of the woman's trim, two-piece suit and matching heels, she was more than likely a salesperson or office personnel.

Enough, he thought, shuffling through the printouts until he found the general administrative sheet. He needed to keep his mind on the business at hand. He definitely couldn't afford the kind of distractions a woman presented. Any minute now his father was going to walk through the door; facing him again was more than enough to worry about. And if what he'd observed so far about the club proved true, he had a hell of a mess to straighten out.

As ADRIENNE CLIMBED the stairs to the office, she wondered about the lone man she'd seen sitting on the veranda. There was something about him that was vaguely familiar, and that puzzled her. A man with his kind of startling good looks, the type of looks that had Virile Male stamped all over him, wouldn't be easily forgotten. In vain she tried to place where she might have seen him before.

He could be a new member, but she didn't think so. She made it a personal priority to meet each one as soon as he or she was approved by the executive council. Since he was wearing a sport coat, she finally decided that he was more than likely an early arrival for the business function scheduled in the lounge.

Midway up the stairs, she hesitated, tempted to re-
trace her steps and find out exactly who the dark-haired
stranger was. It was rare, but sometimes people ventured in, thinking the restaurant was open to the public.

Adrienne gave a slight shrug and continued up the
stairs. Franklin's son was due to arrive around noon,
and if the intriguing stranger didn't belong there, Eva
or one of the other waitresses would take care of him.
Besides, there were still three party sheets that needed
completing, as well as the work schedule for the upcoming week. With her job at stake, she couldn't afford to have Dillon Reynolds catch her shirking her
duties.

Adrienne rounded the corner, then jerked to a halt
just inside the reception area. Her sudden stop caused
the coffee in her cup to slosh over the rim onto the carpet, just barely missing her shoes.

The place looked like a Texas twister had been
through it. File boxes were stacked everywhere; the
phone was ringing off the hook. And in the midst of
everything, Joanne barked out instructions like a drill
sergeant to two burly male employees. "Hurry up,
guys! Get this stuff back up into the attic. It's almost
eight and I don't want members coming in and seeing
this mess."

When Joanne spotted Adrienne, she gingerly picked
her way through the stacks of files to where Adrienne
stood. "He's here," she whispered, her eyes darting
around as if the devil himself might appear at any mo-

ment. "I came in a few minutes early and he was already in here, digging through the files."

Adrienne didn't have to ask who *he* was. She suddenly felt her stomach flip-flop and she almost groaned out loud as the image of the dark-haired stranger flitted through her mind. She didn't have to ask why the place was being turned upside down, either.

No wonder he'd looked so familiar, she thought. The man making himself at home on the veranda had to be none other than Franklin's son, Dillon Reynolds.

Adrienne took a deep breath and tried to ignore the ripple of apprehension that ran through her. She thanked her lucky stars that she hadn't approached him...at least not yet, not without being more prepared.

As she stepped through the maze of file boxes, she shook her head. The day wasn't starting out at all like she had planned. "Murphy's Law," she mumbled, wondering if it was a preview of things to come.

CHAPTER TWO

THE MINUTE HE ENTERED the veranda, Franklin Reynolds spotted Dillon seated at a table next to the large plate-glass window, his dark head bent over a stack of financial statements.

For the moment, Franklin was content to simply stand and feast his hungry eyes upon his only son. No longer a fresh-faced college graduate, Dillon had become a man—a successful man, by all accounts. He certainly looked the part. Yes, Franklin thought with quiet pride, his son had come a long way from that headstrong young man who'd been so impatient with life and its complexities. Franklin had hoped that time would heal the differences between them. But too much time had passed, as far as he was concerned. And deep down, he had known better. During their last phone conversation, it had taken Dillon only a few minutes to flatly refuse even discussing the possibility of him managing Twin Oaks. Franklin was ashamed and a little peeved to have to admit that it had taken a call from Myrna to persuade their son to finally come home.

Myrna understood part of the problem between father and son but not all of it, he knew. Nor had Dillon ever told her the real reason why he'd suddenly left, and why he always had an excuse to stay away. Franklin didn't blame his son completely. After all, his son was a chip off the old stubborn, pigheaded block.

Still, he had hoped that his son's homecoming was a positive sign. With only intermittent phone calls, the past seven years had been lonely... too lonely.

Franklin took a deep breath and let it out slowly. It was time to get on with it, to finally face his son.

"I see you got here earlier than we expected. Welcome home."

Dillon looked up when he heard the familiar voice, but he couldn't speak, so he simply nodded. Memories of the last time he'd seen his father and of the accusations he'd hurled at him reeled through his mind, and he felt every muscle in his body tighten in response. Making a conscious effort to relax, he took refuge in assessing his father's looks. Other than being a little overweight and appearing a bit pale, his father hadn't changed much. But there was something about the look of his eyes that wasn't quite right that worried Dillon.

As his father drew nearer, Dillon shoved his chair back and stood. Maybe he was overreacting. After all, it had been a long time. His father was seven years older.

Finally face-to-face, each man regarded the other with a steady, if reserved, gaze. Neither made a move toward the other. After several long seconds, Dillon drew in a deep breath and stuck out his hand. Franklin immediately reached out and clasped it, and Dillon thought that, for a moment, some of his coolness seemed to falter. He had the sudden urge to pull his father forward and embrace him, but the moment quickly passed. Instead, he briefly tightened his grip, then withdrew his hand.

Dillon waited until his father sat down before he dropped back into his chair.

"Well? What do you think so far?" Franklin asked, motioning toward the papers.

Dillon hesitated only a moment, glad to have something other than his churning emotions to focus his attention on. "I'll reserve final judgment until I've gone over everything, but from the financial statements, I think we've got serious problems." Dillon was careful to keep his voice low and even. "Short of winning a lottery, you—*we* haven't got a prayer. Twin Oaks—"

He broke off as he saw a waitress heading toward their table. At this point he didn't want anyone, least of all the employees, speculating on Twin Oaks's future or his plans to try and change that future.

When the woman had poured Franklin a cup of coffee, she offered to fill up Dillon's cup.

He shook his head. "No, thanks. I've had too much already."

For a moment she stood there, coffee pot in hand. Dillon figured she was waiting for his father to introduce him. When the older man looked up, Dillon gave a slight shake of his head. He wasn't ready to meet the staff yet, not until he went over their employee files.

"That's all for now, Eva," Franklin said, smiling to take the sting out of the dismissal. "I'll call you if we need anything else."

When the waitress finally walked away, Franklin let out a sigh, then turned his attention back to his son. "It's bad, huh?"

"You know it is," Dillon answered, thinking of the short-term loan. "Why didn't you tell me about the loan, and how on earth did you expect to pay it back?"

Franklin took a swallow of coffee, then shifted in his chair before he answered. "Ted Jamison sits on the club's board of directors and has been a member for several years. He assured me his bank would grant an extension if I needed one. But now that I need it, the bank won't allow it."

Dillon felt his composure slip as a stab of annoyance flashed through him. Some people never changed, he thought. Franklin Reynolds was too damn trusting for his own good. "Like I said, I need to go over everything before I form any concrete opinions or plans. Just remember..." he paused for emphasis "...this time we do it my way. That was the agreement."

"Have you seen your mother yet?"

The abrupt change of subject caught Dillon off guard. But then, except for the last time they'd been face to face, his father had always done his best to avoid unpleasant confrontations. He was also adept at avoiding financial matters, leaving such things up to whatever accountant he happened to employ at any given time. And there had been several, Dillon knew. Usually they became so frustrated with his father's lack of interest and guidance that they lasted only a couple of months.

"No," he finally answered. "I got in too late last night. I dropped by this morning, but no one answered the door. I figured she was either in the shower or maybe playing golf."

"She and I played an early round. She'd be at home now."

Dillon stared at his father as a sudden thought hit him. Maybe something was wrong with his mother: maybe that was the real reason she had almost begged him to come home. He frowned. "Is Mom okay?"

"If you mean physically, then yes, she's fine." Franklin lowered his gaze, focusing on the steaming coffee. "But inside, she's hurt—"

Dillon stood abruptly. "I know she's hurt, but that's not entirely my fault," he said, his voice defensive and sharp. "I intend to go see her this afternoon." When his father didn't reply, Dillon leaned down and began to shove the scattered papers into a lopsided stack. "I need to get on with my assessment."

Franklin stood slowly, feeling every one of his sixty-eight years. Nothing had been forgiven or forgotten, he realized sadly. Dillon was still defensive. Maybe with more time...

"Joe Blount, the food and beverage manager, isn't in today, but I'll have his assistant show you around. She knows the score about the club, and she's a bright young woman who can answer most any questions you might have.''

Dillon nodded, already regretting his outburst. When he'd finally agreed to come home, he'd made himself a promise to try—to really try—to put the past where it belonged. Perhaps in time... ''Under the circumstances, maybe that would be best.''

''Yes. Maybe it would,'' Franklin agreed in a low, resigned voice.

Thirty minutes later, Dillon glanced at his watch. His father had called the woman who was supposed to assist him, but she had yet to show up. And being cooped up in the office with his father was beginning to get on his nerves. Too many painful memories of the last time he had worked at Twin Oaks were trying to surface.

He drew in a deep breath and tried to hang onto the little bit of patience he had left. Where was the woman?

ADRIENNE HESITATED outside of Franklin's closed door and glanced at her watch. She was late. Fifteen minutes late.

Right after he'd buzzed her to come to his office, she'd gotten a phone call from a member who was anxious to set a date for her daughter's wedding reception. The call had taken longer than she'd expected, but she hadn't worried. Franklin would understand.

She reached up and knocked lightly, then entered. Franklin was seated behind his desk, and at first glance, he appeared to be alone. But as she stepped into the room, she noticed a movement to her right. The man she'd seen earlier seated on the veranda was standing there, his arms crossed against his chest. One look at his face told her he wasn't used to being kept waiting.

Before she had time to apologize and explain, Franklin rushed around his desk and put his hand on her shoulder. It was a friendly, comforting gesture, one that she and the other staff were used to. "Adrienne Hamilton, I'd like you to meet my son, Dillon."

Adrienne could feel her neck grow warm as she faced Franklin's son. She offered up a quick, silent prayer of thanks again that earlier she had ignored her instincts to question his right to be in the club.

Up close, he was every bit as good-looking as he had been from a distance, she decided. Taller than she'd imagined. For reasons she couldn't begin to fathom, making such an observation at this particular moment irritated her.

She thrust out her hand, and belatedly wondered if he would notice how sweaty her palm was.

She needn't have worried. His handshake was brief and cool, almost as cool as the look in his clear green eyes, which seemed to stay glued to his father's hand still resting lightly on her shoulder.

Noticing the direction of his son's gaze, Franklin removed his hand, almost self-consciously, Adrienne thought as she watched him retreat to his chair. Maybe it was just her imagination, but for a moment, Franklin had seemed almost intimidated by his son. But then, she felt a little intimidated herself, so she decided she was probably overreacting.

Her mind was still on the disturbing, silent scenario that had just transpired between father and son when the latter's words forced her attention back to him. "My father tells me you're available to show me around."

"If you'll give me a few minutes to finish up the work schedule, I'll be happy to do that." Adrienne attempted a smile.

"What I need to see won't take long," he said. "You can finish the schedule later."

Momentarily taken aback, Adrienne stared at him. The man certainly didn't lack brass or self-confidence. In two short sentences he had succeeded in dismissing her work as irrelevant and unimportant, and for a minute she wondered if she should be insulted . . . or worried.

"If that's convenient," he added belatedly, almost as if he'd read her mind.

Adrienne decided to give him the benefit of the doubt. *Who knows?* she thought. *Maybe he's nervous, too.* Somehow she doubted it, though. If anything, he seemed irritated.

He motioned toward the door. "I'd like to start with the pro shop and golf course," he said. "After that, we'll inspect the kitchen. You do keep weekly inventories in the kitchen, don't you?"

Left no choice but to do as he wanted, Adrienne took a second to glare at Franklin, who refused to look at her, before she headed toward the stairwell.

"Well?" Dillon persisted as they descended the stairs.

"Oh, the inventories. No, we don't take weekly inventories, but we do keep monthly ones."

"From now on, I'd like inventories done weekly, and I'd appreciate it if you could make sure I get them each Tuesday morning."

Adrienne rolled her eyes. The chef was going to just love that bit of news, she thought, already dreading the tirade she knew was coming. The high-strung Pierre would more than likely hit the ceiling . . . with anything he could get his hands on.

Twenty minutes later, after a whirlwind inspection of the pro shop, Adrienne stepped into the electric golf cart Dillon had commandeered for their tour of the course. Her first impression of him had been right on target, she decided. He definitely had more than his share of self-confidence and he exuded a certain charisma.

It had amazed her to watch the transition in Mick Starky, the golf pro. Mick, who was usually so cock-sure of himself, stood eye-to-eye with Dillon and outweighed him by fifty pounds. But before Dillon was done with him, Mick had been reduced to "yes, sir" and "no, sir."

The whir of the golf cart stopped abruptly. Without a word, Dillon stepped out and walked several yards off the path. He knelt down and ran his hand over the grass, then stared ahead toward the open fairway. Adrienne followed his gaze.

It had been a long time since she'd been out on the course and she had forgotten how peaceful it could be. Stretching almost as far as she could see were lush green fairways still sparkling with dew and small ponds banked by oaks and pines and low, flowering shrubs. The smells of crisp, clean air and fresh-cut grass were almost as soothing as the pleasant warmth of the mid-morning sun on her face. It was hard to believe other parts of the country were experiencing winter snows. Once again she was glad she lived in south Texas, where winters were mild enough for flowers to bloom almost year-round.

Adrienne's gaze returned to Dillon. Getting out on such a beautiful day would have been perfect, she thought, if she could somehow get over the feeling that Franklin's son didn't much care for her. The man was strictly business. He'd yet to ask her one personal question.

In fact, if anything, his attitude bordered on rude-ness...at least toward her. What made her more un-easy was knowing that her job might depend on the impression she made on him.

At that moment, Dillon turned his head and looked directly at her. His shrewd expression told her he'd known she'd been staring at him. Adrienne felt her face grow warm and she quickly looked away.

"At least something seems to be right about this place," he said as he stood up and walked back to the cart. "Of course, I'll have to play a few rounds, but as far as I can tell, the course appears to be in tip-top con-dition."

Adrienne felt the slight dip of the cart as he seated himself, but she still couldn't bring herself to look at him. "Craig Johnson does a great job," she offered quietly.

"I presume Craig is the greens superintendent."

Still staring straight ahead, she nodded. When he jerked the cart into gear, she braced herself. Relief flowed through her when she realized they were speeding along the cart path back toward the clubhouse. The sooner they reached it, the better, she decided. Being isolated with Dillon Reynolds was making her as nervous as a cat that had used up eight of its nine lives.

Within minutes, they skidded to a halt outside the golf shop. Adrienne followed Dillon through the shop and down the hallway leading to the main lounge. For once in her life, as she matched him step for step, she was glad the good Lord had seen fit to give her long legs.

He didn't slacken his pace until he reached the kitchen. Adrienne was about to suggest that she introduce him to the staff when she heard her name being paged. She immediately excused herself and headed for the nearest phone, located in the snack bar.

By the time she had hung up the phone, Dillon was standing a few feet away from her, that same look of impatience he'd had earlier in Franklin's office on his face.

Too bad, she thought, raising her chin. "That was the secretary at my daughter's school. My daughter isn't feeling well, so I have to go pick her up. Unless I find that she's seriously ill, I should be back within the hour." Without waiting for his permission or his response, she hurried toward the office to grab her purse.

THE MINUTE KRISTEN settled in the car, she crossed her arms tightly around her stomach and leaned her head back against the seat. After glancing sideways at her mother, she closed her eyes and gave a little groan.

Adrienne studied her daughter and frowned. "Where does it hurt? Do you feel like throwing up?"

"A little," she whispered.

"Maybe I should take you straight to the doctor."

At that, Kristen opened her eyes. "Oh, no...I mean, it's probably just something I ate."

"Kristen, you didn't eat anything but a bowl of cereal and some toast for breakfast."

"Oh, yeah, I forgot. Well, maybe it's just a bug, one of those twenty-four-hour things that go around."

Adrienne narrowed her gaze. "Sure it is, and maybe I'm the tooth fairy."

Kristen winced at her mother's condescending tone. Now she'd had it for sure, she figured. But they were almost home, and if she could just stall until they got there, Uncle Louie would take her side.

"Okay. Out with it. What gives?"

Kristen delayed answering as long as she dared. One more block and they would be home. "I don't feel good," she finally said when she caught sight of their house.

Adrienne pulled into the driveway and shut off the engine. She turned to face her daughter. "How come I

don't believe you?" She waited a few seconds, but
Kristen refused to look at her. "If you're really ill, that's
one thing, but if you pulled me away from work just so
you could skip classes the rest of the day, you're in big
trouble."

Kristen glared at her mother. "Oh, yeah, Mom.
That's right. Don't even believe your own daughter."

Adrienne frowned. "I don't think I appreciate your
tone of voice."

"Well, I don't appreciate being called a liar," Kristen shot back.

"Okay, that's it." Adrienne jerked open the car door,
slid out, then slammed it behind her. Once she'd retrieved Kristen's wheelchair from the back seat and unfolded it, she helped her daughter into it. Without a
word, she marched to the front door of the house,
opened it and waited. Seconds later, Kristen whizzed
past her, heading toward the hallway.

"Not so fast, young lady." Hands on her hips, she
braced herself. "We're going to have a little talk first."

Kristen stopped but didn't turn around. "I really
don't feel good, Mom." This time it wasn't a lie. Each
time she fought with her mom, it made her sick. But
lately she just couldn't seem to help herself. "All I want
to do is go to bed. Please," she added, hoping that
would do the trick.

Adrienne's insides churned with indecision. Her gut
instincts told her Kristen was faking, but a tiny voice
whispered that her daughter might be telling the truth.
After all, Kristen had had her share of physical prob-

lems. They had missed her last scheduled checkup, too. "Go lie down for now, but I'm calling Dr. Tom. Maybe he can work us in this afternoon."

Kristen wheeled around and glared at her mother. "Okay, Mom. You win. I'm not sick, so there's no reason to call Dr. Tom." Geez, the last thing she needed was the doc poking and prodding her.

Adrienne sighed. "Then why did you call me? You knew today was an important day for me."

How could she tell her mother she needed to be home...just in case her dad called? He usually phoned on Tuesdays or Thursdays, but always when she was at school. She'd figured that if she were home and answered the telephone, maybe he wouldn't back out this time. Besides, she thought, sometimes she suspected her mother was purposely trying to keep her away from him.

"I'm waiting for an answer."

"Hey, what's all the commotion about in here?"

Adrienne turned as her uncle sauntered into the room. Dressed in his standard khaki pants and plaid shirt, he smelled of Old Spice and soap. Tall and lean, with his wealth of iron gray hair slicked back, he was still a striking figure for a man his age. "You'll have to ask Kristen," she said. "I can't get anything out of her that makes sense, and I've got to get back to work."

"Uh, oh. Trouble, eh, kiddo?" Louie pinched Kristen's cheek and winked, which made her almost smile. Then he walked over and patted Adrienne on the arm. "Don't worry about a thing, darlin'. Me and the kid will get it all straightened out. You run along back to work and I'll fix you a special treat for dinner tonight. I was thinking about something Chinese.''

At that, even Adrienne almost smiled. Her uncle's version of sweet-and-sour chicken was her idea of heaven. "Thanks, Uncle Louie. I'll try not to be late."

With one more searching look at her daughter, who refused to make eye contact, Adrienne shook her head and left.

Even Louie's offer of her favorite dish didn't distract her thoughts for long as she drove the short distance back to Twin Oaks. Somehow she had to find a way to reach out to her daughter, to bridge the ever-widening gap that seemed to plague them the last few months.

The minute Adrienne walked into her office, Dillon was at the door. "How's your daughter?"

Even though his tone seemed sincere, Adrienne doubted he was really concerned with Kristen's welfare. Still, out of fairness, she felt she needed to explain. "She's okay. It was a false alarm. I'm sorry if I've delayed you, but having a twelve year old can sometimes be a trying experience."

"Does this happen often?"

Adrienne stared at him for several seconds. "No," she finally answered. "Most of the time she's the picture of health."

"Hmm, that's good to know. Now, I'd like to continue with where we left off, if you don't mind."

And what if I do? Adrienne thought. But she knew better than to voice the question out loud. Instead, she clamped her mouth shut and strolled past him out of her office.

The kitchen tour lasted an hour—an hour in which Dillon inspected everything from the walk-in freezer to the dumpster area outside the back door. Adrienne found it odd that the chef had suddenly disappeared, but in a way, she was relieved. At the moment, she had all she could handle with Dillon Reynolds.

When Dillon requested that she make a note of each health violation he found, Adrienne grabbed a handful of paper napkins and borrowed a pen from one of the waitresses.

The next area he insisted on looking at was the liquor storeroom, and by this time the club was in full swing for the lunch crowd. As she followed him through the bar, Adrienne glanced worriedly over her shoulder toward the entrance of the dining room. As far as she could tell, Eva and the other two waitresses had managed to seat the members and wait on them, but from the sour look on Eva's face, Adrienne knew she would get an earful before the day was over. She wondered who was keeping an eye on the buffet table. There was nothing that irritated the members more than having to stand around and wait for the bowls and platters to be replenished. Most of the clientele were there for a quick business lunch and had time restraints.

"This place is a mess," Dillon said as he shoved open the door to the storeroom. Sidestepping boxes stacked haphazardly throughout the room, he opened one of the cabinets lining the walls, then several more, shaking his head each time. "Make a note for the bartenders to clean out these cabinets and get this place organized." He kicked at a stack of boxes with one foot. "Tell them to put this stuff away. I don't see how the hell anyone can take inventory or tell what needs ordering."

Adrienne scribbled a note and stuffed yet another napkin into her jacket pocket. She bit her lip but refrained from telling him that she had voiced the same complaint to both his father and to Joe Blount, but neither had seemed too concerned over the matter.

By the time Adrienne returned to her office that afternoon, she had about an hour left to catch up on all her phone messages and finish the schedule she'd started that morning. It was only when her stomach growled that she realized she'd been so busy she hadn't eaten lunch.

Her phone buzzed and she snatched up the receiver. It was Eva. "We have a problem in the lounge. Could you come down?"

"In a minute—" The firm click of the phone cut her off midsentence. Adrienne held the receiver away from her ear and glared at it. What now? she wondered.

By the time she walked into the lounge, the problem was more than evident. "Why me, and why today?" she groaned. Several of the ceiling tiles had fallen smack in the middle of the long row of tables set up for a dinner party scheduled for that evening. She turned to Eva. "Was anyone in here when it happened?"

Eva shook her head. "No. We'd just finished setting up and had walked out the door."

"Thank God," she murmured, but before she could question Eva further, Dillon rushed in.

"How did this happen?" he demanded, glaring at her as if the whole mess were her fault.

Out of the corner of her eye, she saw Eva edge closer toward the door. *Coward,* she thought as she glared right back at Franklin's son. "Unless I miss my guess, the drain has plugged up again."

"The drain?"

Adrienne nodded. "The laundry room is located directly above the lounge, on the second floor. Once before the drain to the washing machine stopped up and overflowed, apparently, causing the ceiling tiles to loosen and fall. But it hasn't happened since I've been here."

"Right. I'd forgotten about that. The laundry room should have been moved years ago." Dillon shook his head with disgust. "Tell Joanne to call the plumber and get him out here today. And for Pete's sake, tell the laundry staff to turn off the washing machine." He walked toward the center of the room. Kicking a broken tile out of his path, he stopped, placed his hands on his hips and peered up into the gaping hole in the ceiling. "Who's our maintenance person?"

His totally masculine stance drew Adrienne's attention to his broad shoulders, and at first his words didn't register. At some point during the day he'd discarded his coat and tie, rolled up his shirtsleeves and unbuttoned the first three buttons of his shirt. A sprinkling of bronzed hair peeked out from the V of his shirt and liberally covered his tanned, sinewy forearms.

"Ms. Hamilton?"

Adrienne blinked, then met his penetrating gaze. That he'd caught her staring again was downright humiliating. *Get a grip, Adrienne. The man is going to think you're a flake.* "We don't have one... a maintenance person, that is. Not full time, anyway. Craig lends us one of his men whenever we need something done."

"Well, get him over here. I want this mess cleaned up and the ceiling repaired before tonight's event."

Adrienne glanced at her watch. It was four-thirty. "It's too late. They've all gone home by now."

"What do you mean, they've all gone home?"

"Craig's men come in around six each morning and leave about two-thirty."

Dillon reached up and shoved his fingers through his hair. "Oh, yeah. That's right."

Adrienne took heart. The man actually sounded a little weary and frustrated. Maybe he was human, after all.

He turned and faced her. "Got any suggestions?"

His question surprised her, since not once during the day had he asked her opinion about anything. She quickly considered their options. "Maybe one of the private dining rooms would work. The Governor's

Room is the largest, but it only holds twenty people for a sit-down dinner.''

"How many are booked for this party?''

"Twenty-four, but I'm sure we can squeeze them all in.''

"Any other options?''

Adrienne shook her head. "Only the ballroom. The rest are booked.''

"No, the ballroom's too big.'' He sighed and rubbed his neck. "Guess the Governor's Room is it. Tell the maître d' to explain and apologize, and give them a couple of bottles of champagne on the house.'' He tried unsuccessfully to cover a yawn, then shook his head. "Sorry. Guess I'm more tired than I thought. I'm calling it a day. Joanne has my hotel number if anything else comes up.''

Adrienne nodded and made a mental note to call her uncle and tell him she'd be late for dinner. The way things were stacking up, she'd be lucky to get home at all.

BY THE TIME she did pull up to the house that evening, she'd decided that the chef was right. Dillon Reynolds was a royal pain in the rear.

Adrienne slipped off her shoes at the door and groaned with pleasure as she flexed her toes. Tomorrow she'd wear lower heels. Many more days of following Dillon Reynolds around, and she would need roller skates.

Laughter from the kitchen and the wonderful aroma of food drew her attention. When she passed through the dining room, she noticed the table was set and ready, but it held four place settings instead of three. Eyeing the extra plate with irritation, she continued on to the kitchen. Company for dinner was the last thing she wanted tonight.

For a moment, neither Kristen nor her uncle noticed her. Louie was at the stove, stir-frying an array of vegetables, and Kristen was sitting at the counter, drying spots off the glasses.

"Hey, folks. Guess who's finally home?"

Louie turned his head and grinned. "Well, hello, darlin'. Had a rough day?"

Adrienne groaned. "Please don't remind me. I didn't even have time for lunch and I'm starved." She glanced at her daughter. "Are you feeling better?"

Kristen only shrugged and picked up another glass to dry.

Adrienne silently counted to ten, willing herself to have patience. Right now she was just too hungry and too tired to deal with Kristen. Later, after she'd eaten and rested a bit, would be time enough.

"By the way, we're having a guest for dinner." Louie lifted the wok from the stove and set it on the counter. Wiping his hands on the dish towel tucked into his belt, he turned to face Adrienne. "He called just a few minutes ago to talk with you—something about a golf tournament that's scheduled for next week."

Warning bells went off in Adrienne's head as she listened to her uncle.

"I told young Mr. Reynolds that you weren't home yet," Louie continued. "And since he sounded like such a nice young man, and he needed to talk with you, I told him to come on over, that I'd cooked plenty."

"Oh, Uncle Louie, please tell me you didn't!"

The self-satisfied look on her uncle's face faded. "Aw, hon. I'm sorry if I did something wrong, but I didn't think you would mind, since you work with him."

For a moment she was tempted to tell her uncle just how much she did mind. Dillon Reynolds was the last person on earth she wanted to see again tonight. And why would he—almost a perfect stranger—accept such an invitation?

But Louie's anxious look and his hurt tone made her ashamed of herself and her outburst. Her uncle, she'd learned from experience, had a soft heart at times that was just too big and too generous for his own good.

She walked over to him, wrapped her arms around his waist and hugged him tightly. "No, I'm the one who's sorry for being such a grouch. You did fine…just fine."

CHAPTER THREE

"WELL, IT'S ABOUT TIME you showed your face around here."

Dillon eyed his attractive, well-groomed mother, noting that she looked just as fit and trim as ever.

He grinned and held out his arms. "Come here, shortie." He pulled her into his arms for a long hug, savoring the warmth of her. He'd missed her, missed her sassy smile and her bossy ways. Telephone calls were a poor substitute for the real thing.

She patted him on the back. "Ohh!" She squeezed him tightly. "It's so good to see you." She pulled away to peer up at him, a frown forming on her face, then reached up and tugged at his ear. "You look tired."

Dillon yawned. "I always look this way after a nap."

His mother's eyebrows rose in speculation. "A nap?"

"Just a short one." Dillon gave her a sheepish smile. "The long drive yesterday finally caught up with me. I sneaked away from work a few minutes early."

"Humph! You should have rested up for a few *days* before going to the club. I was hoping you'd stay with us...at least till you got settled."

"Mom, we discussed that on the phone. It's really not a good idea."

"Well, come on in and relax a few minutes. I've just made a fresh pot of coffee and some of those sugar cookies you always liked so well."

Yes, he'd missed her, he thought with a pang of guilt, following her back to the kitchen. But what he'd missed most was the kind of love and concern that only a mother could give. None of his problems with his father were her fault, but yet he'd punished both her and himself by staying away so long . . . too long.

"Your dad said you came by this morning." She glanced over her shoulder as they entered the kitchen. "We didn't expect you till noon, so I let him talk me into a round of golf."

"I didn't decide until the last minute to drive in last night." Dillon snitched a cookie from the plate in the center of the table. "By the time I got in, it was too late to phone." He seated himself and glanced around. He bit into the cookie, savoring the sweet confection all the more because his mother had made them especially for him. Except for a new refrigerator, everything looked exactly as he remembered it.

His mother placed a mug of coffee in front of him, then settled across the table from him. "You are staying for dinner, aren't you?"

Dillon shook his head. "Not tonight, but I'll take a rain check."

"And just why not tonight?"

Dillon grinned at the indignant look on her face. He reached over and squeezed her hand. "I'm having dinner at Adrienne Hamilton's house." When her eyebrows shot up in speculation, Dillon quickly added, "Business, Mom. Strictly business."

"Too bad," she quipped. "Now there's a fine young woman."

Dillon took a sip of coffee. "She seems capable enough."

"Humph! More than capable. And pretty, too."

For reasons he couldn't discern, Dillon felt uncomfortable with the turn of the conversation. He reached for another cookie. "Anyway," he continued, "I got railroaded. I called to leave a message for her and I got her uncle." Remembering the one-sided conversation, Dillon smiled. "I couldn't get a word in edgewise. And before I knew what had happened, I found myself agreeing to go over and have dinner."

Dillon's mother chuckled. "That sounds like Louie, all right. But he means well and he's a nice man. Just a bit too generous at times."

"Humph!" He shot back. "Look who's talking."

AN HOUR LATER Dillon pulled into Adrienne's driveway and switched off the engine. When his father had conceived the idea of the Twin Oaks development, he'd subdivided it into several residential villages, each providing an array of architectural styles and with a different range of price options.

The village where Adrienne lived was the most modest. The house itself was one of the smaller ones, but, except for needing a coat of paint, it looked very pleasant, he decided as he glanced around.

Someone—probably the uncle, he figured—had attempted to make some repairs. He could tell that the fascia board beneath one of the corner eaves had been replaced recently; the wood was still bare. From what his mother had told him, it seemed unlikely that Adrienne's ex-husband had done the work.

Thinking back on his conversation with his mother, he still felt uncomfortable. She had been more than eager to fill him in on the details of Adrienne's life. According to her, the woman was a genius and a saint rolled into one. But then his mother had always seen the best in everyone.

Dillon eased open the car door and slid out. He eyed the short ramp leading up to the front door. Thinking of Adrienne's uncle, he wondered why a man capable of doing carpentry work needed a ramp. Maybe he'd been wrong. Maybe the uncle hadn't done the repairs on the house, and she'd hired someone.

Dillon walked up the ramp.

He shouldn't have come, he thought, slowing his steps. He should have simply said "no, thank you" and left a message for her to call him, or he should have waited until tomorrow to talk with her. And he would have, regardless of her uncle, if he hadn't been so curious... and if the picture of his father's hand resting so easily on her shoulder hadn't stuck in his mind. There was still a tiny part of him that had to know, that had to make sure, one way or the other, about Adrienne's relationship with his father....

He reached up and knocked on the front door. No, he shouldn't be here, but what the hell. Besides, the dinner invitation had been a good excuse to leave before his father got home. And it sure beat going back to a lonely hotel room.

The minute the door swung open, Dillon forgot every reason why he shouldn't have come. For long moments, all he could do was stare at Adrienne.

She'd removed the pins from her hair and it fell in glorious disarray around her shoulders. She'd also removed her suit jacket, and the clear outline of a lacy slip peeked through the filmy cream-colored blouse she wore. He let his gaze roam downward, past her trim waist and over her rounded hips, then up again.

Dillon slid his hands into his back pockets. Her face was flushed and it was plain to see that his once-over had embarrassed her. He mentally kicked himself for his obvious lapse of good manners.

"I hope I'm not intruding," he finally managed to say.

"Ah . . . no. Of course not."

She gestured for him to come inside, but the look she gave him clearly said he wasn't an especially welcome sight.

"Dinner is almost ready," she continued. "And Uncle Louie always cooks more than we can possibly eat."

Dillon stepped into the house, and to keep his eyes and thoughts from straying, he cast a brief look around. The living room had a certain homey appeal about it even if some of the furniture had seen better days.

"Would you like something to drink? A soda or tea?"

He glanced over at her. "I could really use a beer, if you have one."

"Sorry, I don't keep liquor in the house."

He was momentarily taken aback by her cool tone. Then he remembered something his mother had said when she'd been extolling Adrienne's virtues, something about her ex having a drinking problem. "A glass of tea would be fine."

"Lemon and sugar?"

Dillon shook his head. "Neither. Just plenty of ice, please."

With a polite little smile, she nodded, motioning toward the sofa. "Make yourself comfortable and I'll be right back."

Dillon watched her walk out of the room, his gaze zooming in on the gentle sway of her hips. Shapely hips...

When she disappeared through the doorway, he strolled over to the sofa and seated himself. Considering the fact that she worked at a place where social drinking was a normal, day-to-day occurrence, he wondered how she was able to separate her job from her personal feelings. Yet she handled her work with a quiet efficiency that seemed to command the other employees' respect.

Dillon frowned as he stretched out his arm across the backrest and crossed his ankle over his knee. His father was certainly smitten with her. Why, the old man couldn't seem to keep his hands off of her.

You're making mountains out of molehills... again.

"Damn," he whispered between clenched teeth. Coming here *had* been a mistake, a big mistake.

As the low murmur of voices from another room filtered through the open doorway, Dillon looked around, again searching for some sort of distraction. Several small pictures were grouped together on an end table. The center one, of a young girl, caught his eye.

The child's blue eyes seemed to glow with some mischievous secret and the teasing expression on her pixie face made him want to laugh. Except for her creamy complexion and oval-shaped face, she bore little resemblance to her mother.

A rhythmic squeaking sound drew his gaze toward the doorway. Though he tried to hide it, the sight of the same girl seated in a wheelchair came as a shock. No one had bothered to tell him... the ramp... of course she would need a ramp. But what had happened to her? And why hadn't anyone mentioned it? he wondered as she rolled up to him and thrust out a sweating glass filled with tea and ice.

"Mom said to bring you this."

Dillon accepted the glass but hesitated to thank her. It was clear from the sullen look on her face that she'd been coerced into bringing him the drink.

"You must be Kristen."

"Yeah." She glared at him.

He decided to ignore her rudeness. "My name is..."
Dillon's voice trailed off as she suddenly spun the chair
around and headed back toward the dining room. So
much for pictures of sweet young girls, he thought.
"Dillon's my name," he called out. "Nice to meet you,
too." Wheelchair or no wheelchair, the girl needed some
lessons in being polite.

Seconds later, he could hear low, angry voices and
then Adrienne appeared in the doorway and walked toward him. Her face was flushed and her lips were com-
pressed into a tight line of anger. "Sorry about that.
She's usually not that disrespectful. I, ah...dinner is
ready."

Dillon stood up. It was evident she wasn't used to
apologizing for her daughter, and it was even more evident that she was precariously close to tears. That he
wanted to somehow comfort her came as a complete
surprise.

"Hey, no problem," he offered and smiled. "Kids
can have good days and bad days, too."

For a moment, she looked as if she wanted to say
more, but with a shrug of her shoulders, she motioned
toward the door. "This way."

Dillon followed her into the dining room. An older
man—the uncle, Dillon presumed—walked in carrying
a steaming dish of food. The enticing aroma reminded
him that he hadn't eaten all day.

"You must be Dillon," he said as he set the bowl in
the middle of the table. "I'm Louis Johnson. Uncle
Louie to the folks around here."

Louie fixed his shrewd, knowing eyes on Dillon as he wiped his hands on the towel tucked under his belt. Only a moment passed, but in that moment Dillon felt as if the old man was sizing him up, like a prime bull at a county auction.

Louie suddenly grinned and stuck out his age-worn hand. "Glad you could make it."

Dillon shook his hand, noting that the fellow still had a grip to be reckoned with. The amusing thought that he'd passed inspection went through his mind, and he grinned back at Louie. "It was nice of you to invite me."

Louie chuckled, the sound low and raspy. "Nice had nothing to do with it. I hate eating leftovers. Never learned how to cook just a little bit. But here now." He pulled out the chair at the head of the table. "Have a seat and dig in while I go and get the kid. Sweet little thing, isn't she?"

Dillon gave him a startled look, but Louie just winked and laughed. "We're still working on manners." He turned away, then hesitated. "I'll leave you to get to know my niece better."

"Uncle Louie!"

Dillon almost dropped his glass. He glanced quickly at Adrienne. Her face was crimson with embarrassment, but the tight line around her mouth had softened, and he felt a smile tug at his own lips.

"Now, darlin'. No need to get all worked up. Dillon knows I'm just kidd'n' around." He looked back at Dillon, his eyes twinkling with mischief. "My niece takes life a little too serious at times. Doesn't take my teasing too well yet, but she's learning. Yep.'' He glanced at his niece, and there was blatant affection shining in his eyes. "She's coming along nicely."

As soon as Louie left the room, Adrienne seated herself at the opposite end of the table. For a second, she refused to look at Dillon and made a show of unfolding her napkin. Then, as if the words had to be choked out of her, she said, "I hope he didn't embarrass you. My uncle is—"

Dillon grinned. "Quite a character. But a likable one," he hastened to add.

She finally looked up at him. "Yes, he is, but there are times—"

"Here we go," Louie's booming voice interrupted. With his hands placed firmly on the back of her wheelchair, he pushed a solemn-faced Kristen into the room. "I think you owe our guest an apology. It's not his fault you and your mom are on the outs." Louie glanced at Dillon. "Kristen and her mother had a little disagreement earlier," he said by way of explanation. "But I'm sure she didn't mean anything personal." He patted Kristen on the shoulder. "Huh, kiddo?"

Dillon gazed steadily at the young girl. When she raised her chin, he noticed that her lower lip was quivering, and he felt a tug of compassion for her.

"Sorry," she whispered. "Uncle Louie's right. I shouldn't have been rude."

He nodded. "Apology accepted."

Louie patted her on the shoulder again, then pushed her up to the table. "Now then. Don't you feel better, sweetheart?"

Kristen looked up at her uncle and smiled. It was obvious to Dillon the girl adored Louie.

ADRIENNE PUSHED HER FOOD around her plate with her fork and was careful to keep her gaze from straying to the opposite end of the table. To give him his due, Uncle Louie was doing a great job of entertaining her new boss. Dillon didn't seem bored in the least by Louie's stories.

Of course, no one was ever bored by her uncle. He had spent his life working on a construction crew that built dams all over the world, and he had a colorful way of making ordinary things seem exotic. Adrienne loved hearing of his adventures, and any other time she would have been intrigued by his stories, too.

But not tonight.

She cast a sideways glance at her daughter and sighed. Kristen was eating even less than she was. Something was obviously troubling her, but Adrienne felt helpless when it came to finding out what. She'd tried ignoring the temper tantrums and the rudeness, and she'd tried talking with her, attempting to draw out whatever was eating away at her. But lately, talking to her daughter was like talking to a steam cooker simmering with pressure and ready to blow at any moment.

A loud knock at the front door interrupted her somber thoughts. She started to rise.

"No, don't get up." Louie wiped his mouth with his napkin and stood. "Finish your dinner, hon. I'll see who it is."

Adrienne watched him hurry toward the living room. Seconds later, he returned. "Sorry to leave you, Dillon, but a friend of mine dropped by to see if I wanted to go out for a while."

Dillon stood up. "Dinner was great. Thanks for inviting me."

"Feel free to stay as long as you like." He chuckled suggestively. "I won't be home till late."

Adrienne was speechless when her uncle turned toward her, a grin splitting his face. "Don't wait up, hon. And don't worry about the dishes. Kristen promised to clear the table and go to bed early. I'll do them tomorrow. You and Dillon just enjoy the evening."

Without further ado, he sauntered out of the room.

Adrienne felt frozen to her chair. She knew Louie meant no harm, but this was carrying things too far. What must Dillon think?

Seconds later, she was startled to hear a female giggle coming from the living room, followed by the distinct click of the front door being shut. The next thing she heard was the roar of a car squealing out of her driveway.

And then there was nothing but stillness, occasionally punctuated by the scrape of Kristen's fork against her plate.

Adrienne looked across the table at Dillon and their eyes met. His steady gaze held hers and his green eyes seemed to pierce right through her, searching . . . for what? For a split second, all she could think of was the way he'd looked at her earlier, at the front door, and she couldn't seem to tear her gaze away. She felt as if her blood was suddenly racing through her veins, raising her body temperature dangerously close to the hot-and-bothered stage. Too dangerously close for comfort.

Adrienne stood up abruptly. Other men had given her the once-over before, but she couldn't remember ever being so sexually stirred by a simple look.

"Would you like some coffee?" she blurted out. She didn't give him time to answer. "My uncle said you wanted to talk about the golf tournament scheduled for next week."

Dillon wiped his mouth, then laid his napkin on the table. "Why don't I help Kristen clear the table first? It's the least I can do after such a great meal."

Before Adrienne could protest, Kristen spoke up. "Thanks, but that's one of my chores." She smiled sheepishly. "Uncle Louie keeps score and if you help, I won't get my allowance." She took a moment to glare at Adrienne. "And then I'd have to go to bed even earlier. Mom's idea of punishment for being rude," she added.

Dillon looked bemused. "Aha. I see." He grinned. "In that case, I definitely won't touch a thing."

A sly, mischievous smile from Kristen was his reward. It was the same expression he'd seen earlier in her photograph on the table in the living room.

BALANCING A TRAY complete with a pot of coffee, cups and saucers, Adrienne entered the living room. Except for the occasional rattle of dishes from the dining room and the ever-present squeak of Kristen's wheelchair, the house was quiet…too quiet, she thought as she walked over to the small table in front of the sofa. The cups and saucers rattled ominously as she set down the tray, and she silently willed her shaky hands to be steady.

Louie had said Dillon wanted to question her about the golf tournament scheduled for the following week, but the man had yet to mention it. So why had he come? She couldn't imagine anything so pressing that it couldn't have waited until the next day.

Her back was to Dillon, but she could feel him staring at her. She quickly poured two cups and moved so that she faced him. Adrienne didn't like feeling out of control, and she figured the sooner she got down to the reason for Dillon's visit, the better. She motioned toward the tray. "There's cream and sugar."

Dillon gave a slight shake of his head and reached for a cup. "Just black is fine."

Adrienne bent over and added a spoonful of sugar, picked up her own cup and saucer, then sat in a chair facing the sofa. "What do you need to know about the golf tournament?" she asked, slowly stirring her coffee.

"How long have you worked at Twin Oaks?"

Adrienne shot him a puzzled look, then took a deep breath. Discounting his brief inquiry about her daughter, not once during the long, grueling day had he made an attempt to be very friendly. Had the tournament just been an excuse? But an excuse for what? "Six years," she answered, placing the spoon beside her cup on the saucer. "About the tournament—"

"Were you hired as the assistant food and beverage manager?"

Something about the way he asked the question made her think he already knew the answer. So why was he asking? "No. I was hired as a waitress and promoted later."

"Hmm." He paused as if giving the matter great thought, then took a sip of coffee. "Who promoted you? My father?"

The question seemed innocent enough, but a frisson of unease stirred in her stomach. Why did she get the feeling she was being grilled like some sort of criminal? "Yes," she answered in a clipped voice. "Your father promoted me."

The cool, assessing look he gave her only added to her discomfort.

"That's interesting. The club never needed an assistant before . . . until you came along. I wonder why the old man felt the need for one." Then, more to himself than her, he muttered, "Why didn't he hire someone qualified?"

Adrienne stiffened her back. "I beg your pardon?"

By the startled look he gave her, she knew he hadn't meant to actually say the words out loud.

"Nothing personal," he hastened to add, confirming her suspicion. "But to take a waitress and put her in charge of—"

"I worked hard for that promotion. I—"

"I'm sure you did," he interrupted.

The tone of his voice and the knowing look on his face belied his words, and Adrienne didn't like the implication one bit. But why would he even think such a thing? she wondered as she studied his closed expression. Then she suddenly remembered the scene in Franklin's office earlier that morning and the way Dillon had stared at his father's hand on her shoulder. The longer she thought about it, the more furious she grew.

Under other circumstances, she might have blasted him for his innuendo. But after all that Franklin had done for her, she felt she owed it to him to set his son straight.

Adrienne took a deep breath, hoping she could control her temper. "Just for the record, my promotion came at a time when the executive council was pushing for more outside events. Members were resigning at an alarming rate and the club was having a cash-flow problem. The council's solution was to book as many events as possible. Joe Blount was working seven days a week, ten hours a day, not to mention the time your father was putting in. As far as my qualifications, I was and still am working on a management degree. If there's anything else you need to know, I suggest you consult my personnel file or ask your father."

Dillon met her indignant gaze with a knowing look, his eyes never wavering. "All of that's very commendable, and I'm sure the raise you received with your promotion helped a great deal."

His sarcasm wasn't lost on Adrienne, and she had the sudden urge to scream. Was the man that dense? She ground her teeth, feeling the tenuous hold on her temper slip even more.

"For the first three months, I worked for the same salary as before," she informed him. "I suggested the arrangement so I could prove myself." *Put that in your narrow-minded pipe and smoke it..*

He had pushed too hard, and for that, Dillon was sorry and ashamed. After seeing her with her daughter and her uncle, he'd realized his earlier suspicions seemed ludicrous. Deep down, he'd known all along that her relationship with his father was based on friendship and nothing else. But some perverse part of him had needed to make sure.

Dillon felt embarrassed heat creep up his neck. Why couldn't he let go of the past? He'd never had any proof of his suspicions anyway...not real proof. He'd never given his father the opportunity to explain. And anyway, it was ancient history. None of it concerned Adrienne. There was no way she was involved with his father.

But was she involved with anyone else? And why did the thought of her being involved with someone else even matter?

"Mom?"

The sound of Kristen's voice startled Dillon. He hadn't realized that she'd come into the room, and he wondered just how much of their conversation the girl had overheard.

To give credit, Adrienne composed herself enough to give her daughter a tight smile. "Are you through cleaning up?"

Kristen nodded. "I—I just came in to say good-night."

Adrienne glanced at her watch and then shot Dillon a meaningful look. "It *is* getting late." To Kristen, she said, "Thanks for clearing the table."

Kristen lifted one shoulder in a shrug that indicated it was no big deal, then wheeled over to Adrienne, stopping beside her chair. Adrienne leaned over and Kristen gave her a kiss on her cheek. "Night, Mom." She turned to Dillon. "Good night, Mr. Reynolds."

"Call me Dillon," he corrected. "Mr. Reynolds makes me feel like an old man."

His reward was a shy smile before Kristen wheeled herself toward the hallway. As soon as she was out of sight, he took a hasty swallow of coffee and returned his cup and saucer to the tray. "It is getting late." He stood. "Guess I've overstayed my welcome."

Adrienne stood but didn't say anything. But the look in her eyes spoke volumes, and he felt like a heel all over again. She hadn't deserved what he had dished out, and he wanted to somehow make amends, to somehow... "She's really a beautiful young girl." And he meant it.

Adrienne nodded her thanks and the tightness of her lips seemed to soften.

"And so well mannered."

For a moment she studied him, as if trying to decide what he was up to now.

"That was supposed to be a joke," he said. A stupid one, he thought, feeling more nervous as each minute passed. He sighed. "I'm sorry...for staying too long." *And for being such an ass,* he added silently. "You've got to be exhausted after the day we put in."

When she still didn't respond, Dillon walked to the door. "Be sure and thank Louie again for me. He's one hell of a cook. And one hell of a persuasive man," he added with a chuckle. "If I were you, I'd watch out. He'll have you fixed up with someone before you know it."

Adrienne rolled her eyes toward the ceiling. "I hate to ask, but just what did he say?"

Dillon grinned, glad to see something on her face besides anger. "When I called, the first thing he asked was if I was married. He has a way about him that you can't take offense and before you know it, you've said yes to whatever he's asked. Maybe I should hire him to head up a membership drive."

Adrienne groaned and shook her head. "He really does mean well, but he sometimes goes overboard with his enthusiasm."

Dillon put his hand on the doorknob. "Don't worry about it. And don't be too hard on him. He's a good man." He paused, and then in an almost wistful tone, added, "It's clear he loves you and your daughter very much."

With that, he turned the doorknob and opened the door. "Thanks again. And I...earlier, I didn't mean to offend you. From what I've seen so far, you're more than qualified for your position."

When Dillon closed the door behind him, Adrienne walked over and secured the lock. For several moments she stood there, her hand still on the knob. When she tried to conjure up her earlier anger, the expressive look in Dillon's eyes when he'd spoken of her uncle's love kept getting in the way.

She finally pushed away from the door, gathered the empty coffee cups and tray, and took them to the kitchen. For long moments she stood in front of the sink, thinking about Dillon Reynolds. Something about him, about his visit, just didn't make sense. And the way he'd grilled her made even less sense.

Adrienne headed toward Kristen's room. Part of her, the part that wanted to bury her head in the sand and pretend everything was just fine, hoped her daughter was asleep. But another part, the part that recognized Kristen was crying out for help, hoped she was still awake.

Surprisingly, Kristen was already sound asleep. For a moment, Adrienne stood by her daughter's bed and gazed at her. Kristen had long ago conquered many of the day-to-day things that most twelve year olds took for granted—things like dressing herself and getting into bed at night. Her self-sufficiency and her small victories over her handicap were amazing and, as Adrienne was well aware, hard fought for.

Adrienne reached down and smoothed back a lock of her daughter's blond hair. In sleep, she looked almost angelic. She leaned over and brushed her lips against Kristen's forehead. It was at times like these, late at night, when Kristen lay sleeping, that she pitied Jack Hamilton. Her ex-husband had no idea of the simple joys he was missing.

Later, after she'd changed into a satin gown and matching robe—a birthday gift from Louie and Kristen—and she'd carefully cleansed her face, she returned to the living room and switched on the television. As she settled herself on the sofa, she hoped she could stay awake until Louie returned.

It was past time they had a little talk about his attempts at matchmaking. Tonight had been embarrassing and awkward, and she was determined that it wouldn't happen again. She had enough to deal with. Somehow, without hurting his feelings, she had to make her uncle stop interfering.

As the ten o'clock news droned on and on, Adrienne again thought of Dillon...and Franklin. What had happened between the men to cause such a strained relationship? No one at the club seemed to have a clue, but of course, except for one or two of the golf-course staff, no one had been working there long enough to have remembered Dillon.

Adrienne slid down a little farther on the sofa and stretched out her legs. The wistful look on Dillon's face right before he had left kept reappearing in her mind, and somewhere deep within, the woman in her wondered if there was something she could do to make that look disappear.

CHAPTER FOUR

DILLON PULLED into the crowded parking lot of the Southern Stomping Grounds. For a moment, he sat and stared at the flashing red neon boots that appeared to be dancing on the billboard above the double entrance doors.

Each time the doors swung open and a fresh batch of customers entered, he could hear the rowdy sounds of laughter and country music spill into the evening air. Even at ten o'clock on a Tuesday night, the place was hopping.

Bracing himself, he removed the car keys, opened the door and stepped out onto the pavement. As long and as grueling as the day had been, he'd dreaded the thought of returning to the hotel. After spending the evening surrounded by the warmth and genuine affection of Adrienne's family, walking into a lonely hotel room held little appeal. Maybe it wouldn't be so bad once he'd moved into his own place. He'd noticed that there were several available condos within walking distance of the club. Tomorrow he'd make a point of checking them out.

For a moment he thought longingly of the cozy beach house he'd left behind in Florida. There, when the self-

imposed isolation from his family had begun to over-
whelm him, he'd been able to jog along the warm sandy
beach. He'd come to depend on the soothing sounds of
the Gulf waters to comfort his lonely soul.

There were no beaches or sounds of waves lapping at
Twin Oaks, but there were acres of forest, streams and
lakes. And there were miles of greenbelts with paths for
bicycling or jogging. The sooner he got out of the hotel
and into the Twin Oaks area, the better, he thought.

Suddenly, the doors of the lounge swung open again,
and another burst of boot-stomping music followed
several laughing couples outside.

Dillon smiled. He would miss the beach house and
the friends he'd made, but the old adage "there's no
place like home" still held true. It was good to be back
in the Houston area. Good to be back at Twin Oaks,
where he belonged.

Dillon pocketed the car keys and strolled toward the
double doors. He knew from talking with the waitress
everyone called Eva that many of the club employees
congregated at the Southern Stomping Grounds after
work.

Employee files didn't tell him anything about per-
sonalities, and most of the staff were pretty uptight at
the club, especially if they saw him standing around
observing them. If he was going to learn anything about
them on a personal level, this was the place to do it. He
knew from experience that after a few beers and a few
rousing turns on the dance floor, inhibitions seemed to
disappear and tongues loosened.

When Dillon stepped inside the huge, rectangular room, the smell of smoke and stale beer assaulted him. He hesitated a second to let his eyes adjust to the dim lighting and his ears adjust to the noise level. Along one end of the barnlike structure was a gleaming bar that stretched the length of the room. At the opposite end was an elevated stage. Small round tables were scattered along the other two sides, forming a semicircle that outlined the dance floor.

He'd just wrapped his hand around a cool beer when the fast-paced music ended and the band immediately went into a slower tempo. Dillon recognized the melody as an old Hank Williams favorite, and an image of Adrienne in his arms formed in his mind. How would it feel to have her so close, pressed against him?

Don't even think about it.

He gave a little shake of his head, banishing the image. And while the singer lamented about a lonesome whippoorwill, he tried to ignore the surge of melancholy that rose within him. Willing himself to concentrate on why he'd stopped at the bar in the first place, he scanned the crowded dance floor again.

Just as he'd decided he was wasting his time and he might as well go to his room and get some sleep, the band swung into a rousing rendition of the "Cottoneyed Joe." He smiled at the dancers' enthusiasm each time they yelled out the standard "Bullshit!" that was required by the tune. Still smiling, he turned to signal the bartender for a beer. One more wouldn't hurt.

When he turned back toward the dance floor, a familiar face caught his attention, and he stared in disbelief.

Uncle Louie.

The old man had a grin as big as Texas on his face. Looking as spry as any twenty year old, he was kicking up his heels, keeping perfect time with the lively beat. The attractive woman he had his arm wrapped around looked familiar, too, and Dillon recognized her as one of the part-time waitresses at the club. He was sure she wasn't much older than Adrienne.

"Why, that sly old coot," Dillon murmured, laughter rumbling in his chest. So that's who his "friend" was.

Just before the end of the song, Louie looked over and spotted him. Dillon smiled, held up his beer mug and made a mock salute. Louie looked startled and his grin faded. Within seconds, the old man was shoving his way through the crowd with a worried frown on his face. The woman he'd been dancing with was tagging close behind and seemed a bit disconcerted.

By the time he reached the bar, Louie's frown had been replaced by a stiff smile. "Hey, Dillon," he called out in his booming voice. He shook Dillon's hand and quickly glanced around. Seemingly satisfied about something, he grinned. "You're by yourself." It was a statement more than a question.

When Dillon nodded, the old man seemed to sag against the bar with relief, and it suddenly dawned on Dillon that Louie had been worried that he might have brought Adrienne with him. Why would that worry him?

Louie held up two fingers. "Two beers," he shouted at the bartender. Then he pulled the woman standing behind him around to his side. "Carol, you know Dillon, don't you?"

The dark-haired woman nodded and gave Dillon a flashy smile.

"Now don't be shy, darlin'. Dillon won't bite."

Dillon suspected that shy was about the last thing Carol was, but he just nodded back at her, took a sip of his beer and waited to see what Louie would say next.

He didn't have to wait long. Louie picked up the beers he'd ordered and handed one to Carol. He turned to Dillon. "I'd appreciate it if you wouldn't mention to my niece that you saw me here."

When Dillon shot him a puzzled look, the old man seemed almost embarrassed. "It might ruin my image as the kindly, elderly uncle," he explained. "That niece of mine would think I'm too old to be carousing about." He draped his free arm around Carol and gave her a lewd wink, causing her to giggle. Then he turned back to Dillon. "Adrienne has some funny ideas about things." He held out his beer. "Especially about this stuff." He shrugged. "But then, who could blame her after all she went through with Kristen. Big responsibility, raising a kid all by yourself."

Dillon tilted his head and frowned. "All that she went through?" he questioned. "You mean with Kristen being crippled?" What did beer have to do with Kristen?

he wondered. He remembered again that his mother had mentioned that Adrienne's ex had a drinking problem. Had Kristen's father been an abusive drunk? Even the thought of such a thing caused his stomach to tighten in a knot.

Louie was looking uncomfortable. "Aw, hell." More to himself than Dillon, he mumbled, "I thought you knew."

"Knew what?"

Louie glared at his beer mug. "Adrienne's right. All this stuff is good for is to loosen tongues . . . and cause accidents." He looked up at Dillon. "When Kristen was about five, Jack—that's Adrienne's ex-husband—was supposed to pick her up from kindergarten. He'd had one too many, ran a stop sign and . . ."

Louie stared down at the floor for several seconds. He cleared his throat, and when he glanced up, Dillon was sure the old man's eyes were watery from more than just the smokey room. "Jack walked away without a scratch. Kristen didn't."

Dillon felt as if he'd been gut-punched, and every preconceived idea he'd formed about Adrienne went right out the window.

Louie cursed again. "Guess I've had about enough for one night." He slammed his mug down on the bar. "Don't get me wrong. I think what Jack did to that baby was criminal, but I've lived long enough to know that once in a while, a person needs to loosen up and live a little. And I'm not talking about drinking, if you get my drift. Adrienne's coming along nicely, but she has a ways to go and I intend to help her get there. If only I'd been here..." He shook his head. "Never mind. Don't pay any attention to an old man's ramblings."

Trying to follow Louie's train of thought was like solving a crossword puzzle, Dillon decided. But it was clear he had his reasons for wanting to keep his outing from his niece—whatever they were. "Don't worry, I won't let on I saw you here tonight."

Louie gave a curt nod. "Thanks, I appreciate it." He turned to Carol. "Well, darlin', it's time you took me home. These old bones have had about enough jarring for one night." He suddenly wiggled his eyebrows, à la Groucho Marx. "A little jarring of another kind wouldn't hurt, though."

Carol snickered. "Now I know it's time to take you home."

LOUIE WAVED GOODBYE to Carol from the front porch and watched until she pulled out of the driveway. Nice lady, he thought, watching the taillights disappear down the street. And a lot of good old-fashioned fun.

A faint sound from inside the house caught his attention. He turned and cocked his head, listening at the door. The TV was on, so Adrienne must still be awake.

Uh-oh, he thought. He must be in for a lecture. But after the stunt he'd pulled, inviting Dillon over and all and then running out on her, he couldn't really blame her. Of course, he could always hope that she was simply too keyed up to sleep. What with her job, Kristen and dealing with her ex-husband, Lord knew she had enough on her mind lately.

He unlocked the door and stepped inside. She was lying on the sofa, curled on her side and fast asleep. She didn't stir when he softly closed the door or when he walked over to stand beside her.

Favors her father, he thought, staring down at her. And as always, when he remembered his only brother and the tragic way he and his wife had died, Louie's throat grew tight. He'd been off helping build a dam in the jungles of South America when the accident had occurred. It had taken two months for the message to reach him and for him to arrange to come home. By then, his brother and sister-in-law had been long buried. He'd arrived just in time to see Adrienne marry Jack Hamilton.

And he'd blamed himself ever since. If only he'd been there when she'd lost her parents, maybe she wouldn't have turned to Hamilton for solace. Maybe she wouldn't have gotten pregnant and ended up having to get married.

Louie gave a slight shake of his head. He'd learned a long time ago that regretting the past was wasted energy. There wasn't a damned thing you could do about what had already happened. Only the present really mattered. And he was here now…for however long she needed him or for however long the Good Lord saw fit to allow him to remain on earth.

Louie turned and tiptoed to the television. Glancing down, he smiled as he recognized the old black-and-white movie playing on the screen.

Casablanca. He flicked off the TV.

He picked up a folded afghan and gently spread it over Adrienne's legs. No use in waking her, he decided. She'd had a long, rough day. He stepped over to the lamp, switched it off, then tiptoed to his bedroom.

WHEN ADRIENNE ENTERED the club the following morning, she stopped off at the coffee station on her way to the office. She emptied two packets of sugar into a white mug, and as she stirred the steaming liquid, she rotated her head from side to side. All she'd gotten by trying to wait up for her uncle had been a stiff neck from sleeping on the sofa all night. She had no idea what time he'd come in, and when she'd left the house around ten to come to work, he'd still been asleep.

Halfway up the stairs, Adrienne heard her name being paged. She groaned, wondering if Dillon had some kind of radar that told him the minute she entered the club. But that was silly. *You're just being paranoid.*

But who wouldn't be? The man held her future in his hands. And after some of the insinuating comments he'd made last night about her job... She let out a little sigh. No use thinking about it now. Besides, for now he needed her. For now...

As Adrienne rounded the corner, Joanne looked up from her word processor and smiled. "Good morning," she chirped. "You're just in time to see the boss."

"Which one?" Adrienne grumbled.

Joanne motioned toward Franklin's office and Adrienne almost sighed with relief. "Where's the other one?" she asked.

"Dillon?" When Adrienne gave a curt nod, Joanne shrugged. "Haven't seen him yet."

Adrienne headed for her office down the hallway. "If we're lucky, maybe we won't," she muttered.

After she had deposited her briefcase and handbag, she picked up her coffee and walked back to Franklin's office. She knocked lightly on the door. Hearing his muffled, "Come in," she entered.

Franklin looked up from the notepad he'd been writing on and motioned for Adrienne to be seated. Placing his elbows on the desk, he leaned forward, twisting his pen between his fingers.

"So how's it going?" he asked, his voice seemingly casual.

"Okay," she answered cautiously, unsure of exactly what he meant.

"Did Dillon finish his inspection yesterday?"

"We went over just about everything," Adrienne answered.

"Did he seem . . . ah . . . satisfied?"

Adrienne studied the intense expression on Franklin's face and wondered what he was getting at. She finally shrugged. "I—I guess so. We really didn't talk much." It wasn't the complete truth, but for some inexplicable reason, she didn't feel comfortable telling Franklin about her confusing evening with his son. She didn't think he wanted to hear about the unorganized liquor storage room or the health violations in the kitchen, either. She wondered if he knew that the ceiling in the lounge had fallen in. Since she already had instructions to take care of those problems, there seemed no reason to give him more to worry about.

She took a sip of coffee. Glancing at Franklin over the rim of the cup, she noticed that he was frowning, and she thought she detected a hint of disappointment in his eyes. She searched for something positive to say, something that would take away the gloomy look on his face. "He did comment about the greens being in good shape," she offered.

Franklin let out an impatient sigh. "But did he say what his plans were...I mean, what he plans to do—you know, cutbacks and finances?"

Adrienne narrowed her eyes. Why, the old sly fox, she thought. He was pumping her for information, information that he was too chicken or too prideful to ask Dillon for himself. Then she remembered Dillon's pointed questions about his father, and for a second she felt like groaning with frustration. Two grown men acting like children.

"Well? Did he?"

"No, but don't you think it's a little early yet? After all, this is only his second day back."

Franklin let out a long sigh. "You're right." He dropped his pen and sat back in his chair. "Of course it's too early, but..." He paused, as if considering his words. "I would like you to keep me updated on what he's doing. I promised him I wouldn't interfere, and I won't—at least not directly. But occasionally I might have a word of advice that you could pass along. I wouldn't be breaking my promise and he wouldn't have to know about our arrangement."

For a moment, Adrienne wasn't sure she'd heard him correctly. "Like a go-between?"

Franklin nodded.

Adrienne hesitated, then decided to plunge right in. "That puts me in a pretty precarious position, don't you think? And I'm not sure I want to be in the middle." *Nor do I appreciate you suggesting such a thing in the first place,* she refrained from adding. She owed Franklin. But she was not going to spy on the son and report to the father. Surely there was some diplomatic way of handling this without offending her old boss.

Looking a bit uncomfortable, Franklin lowered his gaze to the desktop. "It's really no big deal. It's just that every time I open my mouth, Dillon becomes defensive."

"It's obvious you and Dillon don't...get along. Has it always been that way?"

Franklin waved a dismissing hand. "It's no secret we've never seen eye to eye on much of anything, but that's mostly my fault. I wasn't around much when he was growing up." He gave her a pointed look. "Work, just like anything else, can be addictive to the exclusion of everything—even your family. And before you know it, it's too late. You just make sure that doesn't happen to you."

A slow, knowing smile pulled at Adrienne's lips and she felt duly chastised. Since the day she'd been promoted to assistant food and beverage manager, Franklin had been at her constantly to ease up, to spend more time with her daughter. It was a friendly point of contention between them.

She started to comment, but the office door swung open and Dillon stuck his head inside.

"Sorry to interrupt." He gave his father a cursory glance, then spoke directly to Adrienne. "If you've got a minute, I'd like to go over some files."

Depositing her empty coffee mug on a nearby counter, Adrienne followed Dillon back to the chef's office. As she walked in, she noticed that the room had been rearranged to accommodate an additional desk. She also noticed that the chef's desk, which was usually cluttered and totally unorganized, had been cleared until nothing remained but a solitary pile of neatly stacked papers, a blank notepad and a pen.

Dillon closed the door and walked behind his desk. "I didn't want any interruptions, so I told Joanne to hold your calls and take messages . . . unless, of course, it's an emergency."

"That's fine," she replied, eyeing the large stack of files sitting in the middle of Dillon's desk. She recognized the white, pocket-style folders as the ones used exclusively for employees' files.

Dillon pulled a chair over next to his and gestured for her to sit down. He picked up the first file on top of the stack. "As you're probably already aware, my father made a loan that's due in a few months. The only way we can possibly pay it is to trim waste. Unfortunately, along with other measures I've decided to take, that means cutting back on staff. And even then I'm not sure the cuts will be enough.''

A trickle of alarm shot through her, and Adrienne almost groaned out loud. ''We're already understaffed,'' she blurted out without thinking.

Dillon held up his hand. ''I disagree.''

Adrienne could feel her insides begin to churn. He'd only been there one day and already he professed to know what they did and didn't need.

''That's one of the reasons I want you to go over these files with me,'' he continued. ''I'm hoping you'll give me some insight to each person's abilities—whether they'll be willing to go the extra mile or whether they'll balk at being asked to do something that might not exactly be in their job description.''

''Take this one for instance.'' He opened the file. ''Tell me about Eva.''

Adrienne hesitated. She didn't like what he was asking her to do one bit. And she certainly didn't consider it within *her* job description to rat on fellow employees. She didn't hire them or fire them. Joe Blount was the food and beverage manager; that was his job. She was only the assistant. So why wasn't he asking Joe these questions?

''Well?'' he asked impatiently.

Adrienne swallowed and slowly raised her chin. "Wouldn't you rather wait and talk with Joe about this?"

"Joe's not here," he pointed out. "And I'd like to get through these files as soon as possible."

Still staring at him, Adrienne remained silent, trying to control the growing resentment she felt. First Franklin, wanting her to be a go-between for him and Dillon, and now Dillon, wanting her to put the finger on her fellow employees.

Suddenly, Dillon slapped the file closed and abruptly rose to his feet. "Do you think I like taking jobs away from people? Believe it or not, I don't like this any more than you do. However, as the old saying goes, it's a dirty job but someone has to do it."

Tension increased, silent moments that seemed to drag on forever, and Adrienne wondered if he could hear her heart pounding. In all the years she'd worked for Franklin, she'd never heard him raise his voice at an employee. But Dillon wasn't Franklin, she reminded herself. And just because Dillon appeared cool and unfeeling on the outside didn't necessarily make him so. She'd seen evidence of deeper feelings the night before.

As Dillon stared down at Adrienne's head, he realized he'd overreacted, and regretted it instantly. After coming up empty last night at the Southern Stomping Grounds, he'd decided this was the best way to find out what he needed to know. But dammit, when she'd looked at him with those wide brown eyes as if he was some sort of monster...

He sat back down. "Ask yourself this," he said in a more reasonable tone. "What's more important—saving a few at the expense of all? Or saving all at the expense of a few?"

Adrienne could tell from the sound of his voice that he was still struggling for control of his emotions. Much as she hated to admit it, he was right.

She raised her head and met his gaze head on. "I—I guess I hadn't thought of it like that. I'm sorry. Of course I'll help you if I can."

During the next hour, Adrienne told Dillon what she knew and what she'd observed about each employee during the time she had worked at the club. And she tried to the best of her ability to answer each question he posed. She was relieved when he picked up the last file.

Being confined with Dillon was beginning to wreak havoc with her nerves. For one thing, the combined mixture of the leather-scented cologne he wore and his own unique, manly odor was fast becoming intoxicating. Several times she'd caught herself taking a deeper breath than usual.

And then there was that certain way he had of looking at her with those cool, green eyes of his. At times she couldn't help but remember the night before, when she'd first opened the door to let him in. Even now, she felt her neck grow warm just thinking about her own inappropriate reaction . . . and overactive imagination.

"Well?"

Adrienne blinked several times. "Well what?" She blurted, painfully aware that she'd been caught daydreaming.

"What about Pierre Deville?"

"Oh, Pierre." She cleared her throat and made a show of glancing over the chef's file. Then she remembered what Pierre had said about Dillon. With a puzzled frown, she glanced up. "Didn't you work with him at a club in Florida?"

Dillon nodded. "Yes, but that was some time back, and . . . I'd like to think he's changed—for the better. I want another opinion, so to speak."

At least he's trying to be fair, Adrienne thought, but she had a sneaking suspicion that Pierre hadn't changed one iota. "He is an excellent chef. Everyone loves the exotic dishes he creates."

"But," Dillon prompted.

Adrienne hesitated only a moment. Dillon was far too astute to be fooled, so she might as well tell the truth. "He—he's not much when it comes to economizing, and his—his temper sometimes gets out of control, but—"

"What about the other cooks?" he interrupted. "Could they survive without a chef's supervision . . . for a while?"

Adrienne shrugged. "We were without a chef for two months before he came, and even though it wasn't an ideal situation, the food was still excellent. We had only one or two complaints from the members."

Dillon studied the file a moment longer, mulling over what Adrienne had said. The past hour had been enlightening... in more ways than one. If nothing else, he'd learned that Adrienne was impartial and equitable in her assessment of employees. And from the little he'd observed, he'd concluded that she had a definite gift for honing in on the strengths and weaknesses of each person.

Maybe his mother was right. Maybe Adrienne was a genius and a saint, all rolled into one.

Dillon slapped the file closed. Who was he kidding? No woman was perfect. So what if he found her attractive and easy to be around? So what if she was intelligent and warm, and sexy in an understated way that made his blood heat to the simmering stage? Didn't he have enough on his mind without adding complications?

He glanced up to find her looking at him with a strange expression on her face, an expression he recognized as something close to desire. When her cheeks suddenly flushed and she quickly glanced at her watch, he knew he was right.

She stood. "If there's nothing else, I need to go check on the buffet," she said, already easing toward the door.

"There is one other thing. Early tomorrow morning I'd like to hold a staff meeting. Would you ask Joanne to set it up?"

"Sure," she called over her shoulder.

As Adrienne hurried down the hallway, she offered a quick prayer of thanks that she hadn't made a complete fool of herself. Staring at him like some sort of starry-eyed adolescent was bad enough, but blushing like a simpering southern belle was totally embarrassing.

Maybe Uncle Louie was right. Maybe she did need to get out more—go out with some men. It had been a long time since she'd been so attracted to anyone. But of all the men to be attracted to, why did she have to pick Dillon Reynolds?

CHAPTER FIVE

WHEN ADRIENNE ENTERED the conference room on Thursday morning, she glanced around. Amazing, she thought. Not once in the six years she'd worked at the club had so many staff members showed up for a meeting.

She did a quick mental roll call. It seemed that everyone but Pierre and Franklin was seated around the huge oak table. That Franklin was absent didn't surprise her. She knew Dillon hadn't invited him. And she understood why. If Dillon was to have a fighting chance of saving Twin Oaks, he had to establish up front that he was calling the shots. Still, she missed seeing Franklin sitting at the head of the table.

Adrienne noticed two empty chairs, one at the far end and one just beside Dillon. As she made her way toward the former, Dillon held up his hand and signaled for her to come to the head of the table.

As she walked toward him, she felt Dillon's piercing look clear to her toes. It lasted only for a moment, but it reminded her of the way he'd stared at her the night he'd come to dinner. And it had the same heated effect on her body now as it had then. Then, in a flash, he looked away.

When she slid into the empty chair beside him and he didn't bother to look at her, she decided she'd been wrong, that her imagination had been working overtime…again. Just because being near him made her feel more feminine than she'd felt in years was no reason to assume there was some sort of mutual attraction.

Several seconds passed, and still Dillon didn't start the meeting. Adrienne glanced around the table and noticed that she wasn't the only one beginning to get a little edgy. Next to her, her boss, Joe Blount, had stopped doodling and was staring at the ceiling. Across from her, Mick Starky was tapping out an impatient rhythm with his fingers.

Adrienne figured Dillon was waiting for Pierre to show up, but how long did he intend to wait? When he touched her arm, she jumped. Just his touch set off tiny tingles over her skin. Steeling herself not to react, she leaned closer.

"Where the hell is Pierre?" he snapped in a low voice meant for her ears only.

But the murmurs of the rest of the staff immediately ceased, and Adrienne became conscious of everyone's gaze directed at her. Did they think it was her fault the chef hadn't showed? She pulled back and glared at Dillon. "I—I don't know," she answered with chilly politeness. "He was given a notice just like everyone else."

"Well, find out!"

His voice seemed extra loud in the suddenly quiet room. Keeping a tight reign on her temper, Adrienne pushed away from the table and hurried from the room.

As she rushed down the stairs, she fumed. Now was not the right moment, she kept telling herself. Later, after everyone had left, then she would tell Dillon Reynolds what an arrogant jerk he could be at times.

As Adrienne marched through the dining room, she could hear frenzied shouts coming from the kitchen. "Oh, wonderful," she moaned. Just what she needed right now. On top of having to cope with Dillon's unpredictable moods, it sounded as if Pierre was having one of his famous tirades.

Adrienne grimaced. Chefs were known for their temperamental natures. The combination of constant heat in the kitchens and their own natural creativity was to blame, or so the experts said. But Adrienne suspected Pierre carried his temperamental tantrums to the extreme.

One glance around the dining room told her it was empty, and she breathed a small sigh of relief. As she pushed her way through the kitchen doorway, she recalled enough college French to know that Pierre was cursing for all he was worth. From what she could gather, the dishwasher had called in sick and one of the cooks had phoned to say he would be late. The irate chef was taking out his frustrations on anyone in his path.

When Adrienne entered the kitchen, she couldn't believe her eyes. Pierre had two of the cooks and the salad lady hemmed in a corner by the walk-in freezer. All three were cowering in fear. And with good reason, she decided as she got a better look. In his hand, Pierre was brandishing a meat cleaver, waving it wildly above his head.

Adrienne knew that Pierre was all growl and no bite. Still, what he was doing was definitely cause for legal action if one of the frightened employees decided to file a complaint—which they never had before.

"Pierre!" she shouted.

The sound of her voice seemed to surprise him, and for a moment he halted his tirade. Then he turned and slowly walked toward her. "What's going on here?" she demanded.

Adrienne stood her ground as he came even closer, but she didn't like the wild look in his eyes one bit. For the first time since she'd entered the kitchen, a shiver of unease ran down her spine, and she wondered if maybe his ranting was more than just frustration, that maybe he was strung out on something.

Out of the corner of her eye, she noticed that the minute Pierre turned his attention on her, the cooks and the salad lady had scurried away.

And still Pierre came closer, the meat cleaver still clutched tightly in his hand.

"Drop it and back off. Now!"

Adrienne started at the harsh sound of Dillon's voice behind her. But rather than reassuring her, his presence only served to increase her uneasiness. She could feel the blood rushing through her veins at an alarming rate. Pierre had let it be known from the beginning that there was no love lost between him and their new boss. She could only pray that the chef had sense enough to listen to reason. What if he attacked Dillon?

Adrienne watched as Pierre's eyes narrowed and honed in at a point beyond her shoulder. Even though she couldn't see him, she could feel Dillon slowly approaching from behind.

"If you move so much as one step closer to her, I'll take that cleaver away from you and hack you into little pieces."

Dillon's voice raised goose bumps along Adrienne's arms. Evidently, it seemed to have the same effect on Pierre. With one last, hateful glare directed first at Dillon, then at her, the chef released the meat cleaver and it clattered to the floor.

Without a word, he yanked off his apron and hat, threw them on the nearby counter and stalked out the back door of the kitchen. The screen door banged in his wake.

Adrienne felt her knees begin to buckle. She reached out, grabbed the counter to steady herself and took several deep breaths.

"Show's over, folks." Dillon's voice was calm and even. "Everyone take a five-minute break, then get back to work."

Adrienne stiffened when she felt his hand at her waist.

"Are you all right?"

For a moment she wanted to throw herself into his arms and take the comfort he seemed to be offering. But only for a moment. Aware that the others were still around and that every eye was on them, she shrugged and moved away from his touch.

All she needed was for everyone to start gossiping about her and the new boss. Not that she wasn't grateful for his interference—she was. But now she would never know if she could have handled Pierre by herself. And if she ever expected to be a manager, coping with employees was part of the requirements of the job.

Adrienne turned to face Dillon. "He wouldn't have actually hurt anyone. He never has before."

Dillon's mouth dropped open. "My God, you mean he's done this before?"

Adrienne gave a tiny shrug. "Not exactly. I mean, he never had a meat cleaver before—"

"And you didn't fire him?"

It was on the tip of her tongue to tell him that Joe Blount had made it clear from the beginning that she didn't have the authority to hire or fire anyone, but she caught a movement in the doorway. It was one of the cooks. "Could we talk about this later?" she asked pointedly.

Dillon followed the direction of her gaze and gave a curt nod. "At least now I won't have to justify firing him," he muttered. "Everyone's still waiting upstairs, and I still intend to have a meeting."

"I'll be there in a minute. With Pierre gone, I need to talk to the cooks about lunch."

"Go ahead. I'll wait."

Several minutes later, after reassuring herself that even without Pierre, the noon buffet would be ready on time, she followed Dillon back upstairs. When they reached the reception area, Dillon stopped long enough at Joanne's desk to instruct her to call the police and file a report of what had happened.

Adrienne halted in her tracks and whirled around. "Do you have to do that? You know how fast news travels in this business. He'll never work anywhere in the Houston area again if you bring in the police." She knew for a fact it wouldn't matter how good a chef Pierre was if a manager knew he'd had a run-in with the law.

Dillon gave her a cold, hard look. "He doesn't deserve to work anywhere around Houston again."

"The board won't like that kind of publicity," she warned. "And neither will the members."

"They would like it even less if he killed someone."

"That's ridiculous. Pierre wouldn't—"

Ignoring her, he turned back to Joanne. "Call the police."

For the next hour, Adrienne tried to concentrate on what Dillon had to say during the staff meeting, but the incident with the chef, along with Dillon's decision to call in the police, had shaken her more than she'd been willing to admit. And sitting beside him, as he had insisted she do, was, in her opinion, much too close.

Unlike his father, Dillon believed in laying his strategy on the line. He told each department head that they were to cut back spending, that they were to order only supplies absolutely necessary for the club to operate.

Although there was some grumbling, their protests were nothing compared to the outburst when he informed them that effective immediately, there was a freeze on salaries and on hiring. For several minutes he allowed them to vent their objections, then with three sharp raps of his knuckles on the table, he signaled that the discussion was over.

"Before I end this meeting," he said, "there's one other thing I want to add." He waited until every eye in the room was directed at him. "I know these seem like harsh measures, and believe me, I don't like them any more than you do. But the survival of the club depends solely on our abilities to tighten our belts. I have to have your full cooperation, and I want this to be a team effort. But..." He paused. "Any staff members who refuse to go along with the policies I've just laid out can consider themselves free to look for another job."

Adrienne swallowed hard. So much for her earlier visions of telling him what she thought of his high-handed actions, she thought. She dropped her gaze to the yellow legal pad in front of her. Who was she kidding? After his last statement, there was no way she could complain about anything. She'd be lucky to keep her job.

By the time the meeting ended, there was still a lot of grumbling, but not as much resistance as Adrienne had thought there would be.

Dillon stayed seated until almost everyone had filed out of the room. Intent on heading straight to her office, Adrienne followed close on the heels of Mick

Starky. She had almost reached the door when Dillon called her back.

"Adrienne, could you hold up a minute? And shut the door...please."

Mick gave her a knowing look and a smug smile, then made a grand production of stepping out and closing the door behind him.

Great, she thought. Not only would the kitchen staff have something to speculate about after the incident with Pierre, but from now on she'd have to put up with Mick's teasing as well.

"How do you feel the meeting went?"

The sound of Dillon's voice next to her startled her. She hadn't noticed he'd moved closer. She backed up a step and clutched her notepad to her chest. "I—I think it went well."

Dillon looked at her oddly. "Is something wrong? Are you still upset about Pierre?"

"No, I'm fine," she answered. At the moment, Pierre was the last thing she was thinking about. But there was no way she could confess her real thoughts.

Dillon felt the tension in the room, could see it in Adrienne's face. He figured that, contrary to what she'd said, she was still upset about the incident in the kitchen. And contrary to his good intentions of keeping her at arm's length, he had to admit that the reason he'd asked her to stay behind had nothing to do with the meeting.

"If you're worried he might try to—"

Adrienne shook her head. "Pierre is all talk and no action. He'll go off and pout a while, then he'll be back, begging everyone to forgive him . . . although this time, I guess it won't do him much good."

"You're right. It won't." Dillon had his doubts about what Pierre might or might not do, especially after seeing the glazed look in the chef's eyes. The man was a menace. Even now the thought of what could have happened was enough to make him break out in a cold sweat. At the time, all he had thought about was protecting Adrienne.

He'd argued with himself that he would have done the same for anyone, and he knew he would have. But if he was truthful, he also knew that had it been anyone but Adrienne, he wouldn't have overreacted like he had. And that was crazy. Why, he barely knew the woman, had only been around her for a couple of days.

"Well, if you're sure you're okay . . ."

A knock on the door made him pause. Irritated at the intrusion, he snapped his head around just as Joanne peeped inside.

Joanne raised her eyebrows. "Sorry to interrupt, but the police are out here. They'd like to talk with you." She turned to Adrienne. "Jack called. He said to tell you he has to go out of town this weekend, so he won't be able to keep his date with Kristen."

Adrienne silently counted to ten as instant fury raced through her. The bastard! He'd done it again! Tightening her lips against the scathing things she wanted to say, she curtly excused herself and headed straight for the nearest phone. Once there, she punched out Jack's number and waited.

From the next room she could hear the murmur of male voices, and she worried that Dillon would decide to press charges against Pierre. But that was his prerogative, she reminded herself. And at the moment, getting in touch with Jack Hamilton before he left for the weekend took priority.

The coward, she thought, listening to his answering machine click in. Adrienne slammed down the phone. He always had some kind of excuse. And he always left it up to her to have to deal with Kristen's disappointment.

"I tried to get him to hold until you could come to the phone."

Adrienne turned to face Joanne. "I know. Don't worry about it. It's just that . . . that—"

"Kristen will be devastated . . . again."

Adrienne nodded, glad to have someone who understood. "She was really looking forward to seeing him— although, for the life of me, I'll never figure out why."

"Hey, I've got an idea. Why don't you and Kristen come with Katie and me to the mall Saturday afternoon? We can make an evening of it—you know, shopping, pizza and a movie."

Joanne's daughter, Katie, was fifteen, and Adrienne knew that Kristen would be thrilled at the chance to be around the teenager. Since Susan had moved, Kristen had stayed mostly to herself. Maybe the prospect of spending the day with Katie would help ease some of the disappointment of the canceled outing with her father.

It was Joe's turn to work this weekend, so Adrienne was free to join Joanne. But with money being a bit short, she had to consider the cost of such an outing. Then she thought about her daughter and she nodded. Somehow she'd come up with the money.

"Are you sure Katie won't mind having a mere twelve-year-old tagging along?"

Joanne shook her head. "Are you kidding? Katie's saved up fifty dollars and it's burning a hole in her pocket. Let her loose in a mall with that much money and she won't care who tags along. Besides, she really likes Kristen. But then, who wouldn't?"

Adrienne sighed. It seemed that everyone liked Kristen, everyone except the one person who meant the most to her daughter.

AS SHE CLIMBED the stairs to the office on Friday morning, Adrienne was still smiling from the joke Eva had just told her. But her smile was merely an added reflection of the relief and happiness she felt inside.

She'd finally worked up the courage to speak to Kristen about Jack the night before. And just as she'd expected, Kristen had been disappointed. It had nearly broken Adrienne's heart to see the hurt and disillusionment on her daughter's face. Then she'd sprung her surprise about their trip to the mall, and although a trace of hurt still dulled her normally bright blue eyes, Kristen was soon worrying about what she should wear, and wondering if Uncle Louie would give her an advance on her allowance.

As Adrienne stepped into the reception area, the sound of raised voices coming from Franklin's office stopped her in her tracks.

Dillon and Franklin.

She gave Joanne a searching look. Joanne rolled her eyes toward the ceiling. "They've been at it for almost an hour now," she explained in a hushed voice.

"Over what?"

Joanne shrugged. "I'm not sure, but whatever it is, I've never heard Franklin so upset."

With a worried frown, Adrienne turned toward the closed door. A picture of Franklin, pale and perspiring, flashed through her mind. Didn't Dillon realize that his father was not a well man?

Suddenly, the office door burst open, and without a word or so much as a glance toward either woman, Dillon stormed out of the room and down the stairs.

Adrienne and Joanne exchanged puzzled looks. Adrienne hesitated only a moment before she squared her shoulders and stepped over to the open doorway of Franklin's office.

He was so preoccupied with what he was doing that he didn't seem to notice her standing there. Adrienne frowned when she saw how flushed his face was, and she watched quietly while he shook out a pill from a small vial and carefully placed it under his tongue.

Adrienne cleared her throat. "May I come in?"

He gave her a startled look, then shoved the vial into his coat pocket. "Just the person I wanted to see." He motioned with his hand. "Come in and shut the door."

Adrienne closed the door behind her and seated herself in front of Franklin's desk. Placing her elbows on the arms of the chair, she leaned forward. "Is everything okay?"

Franklin smiled, but she could tell it was forced. "Of course it is. Dillon was just blowing off a little steam."

Adrienne shook her head. "That's not what I meant. What was that pill you just took?"

Franklin waved his hand. "Oh that—that's nothing. What I want to know is how the meeting went yesterday. Did they give Dillon much trouble?"

For several seconds, all she could do was stare at him. If he was so interested in how the meeting went, why hadn't he asked Dillon himself? Unless, of course, he was just trying to change the subject. Well, it wouldn't work this time, she decided.

"Franklin, are you ill?"

He shot her an irritated look, then sighed heavily. "Haven't you got enough to worry about without mother-henning me, too? I'm just fine. End of subject. Okay?"

Knowing he'd left her little choice, Adrienne glared at him. "Okay, but why the big deal if taking a pill is 'nothing'?"

"There's no big deal. When you get to be my age, you have to take a pill now and then. Doctors are always shoving them at you. Now..." He paused. "I have a few ideas I want you to pass along to my son, then I want you to tell me what went on in that meeting.''

Adrienne groaned in protest. "I don't think I want to hear this," she said.

Franklin ignored her. "With Pierre gone, that's one less salary to pay. With simpler menus, Dillon can get by with just the cooks for a few months until we get past this financial crunch.''

As she listened to Franklin go over menu items that could be cut, Adrienne didn't bother to tell him she suspected that Dillon had already thought of that possibility.

ADRIENNE WAS SEATED at her desk that afternoon, trying to concentrate on the final details of a wedding reception scheduled for the following weekend. Joe had assured the bride's mother that the club could furnish anything her daughter wanted, but every time Adrienne added up the numbers, the cost went over the price Joe had quoted the woman. Once again she began adding the figures, but the numbers seemed to run together, and halfway through she threw down her pen.

It was no use. No matter how hard she tried to stop thinking about Franklin and Dillon, and no matter how much she tried to focus her attention on something else, the picture of her old boss swallowing that pill wouldn't go away. Something was wrong with him, and each time he got upset, he seemed to get worse.

She considered discussing the matter with Dillon, but then decided it really wasn't any of her business. After all, they were grown men. If Dillon couldn't see that his father was ill, and if Franklin refused to...

Adrienne groaned and picked up her pen. Being caught in the middle was driving her crazy. *Forget it and do your work.*

She glared at the banquet sheet before her, and the numbers seemed to dance before her eyes. Thanks to Joe's rash promises, by the time they rented enough long white tablecloths and furnished two swan ice carvings, there was no way they could stay within the budget he had agreed to. The club would lose money, again. And Dillon would blow his stack....

The sound of raised voices outside her door interrupted her thoughts. When they grew louder, she stood and walked to the open doorway. Just as she stepped into the hallway, Pierre came out of Franklin's office.

Oblivious to everything around him, he stood just outside the door, shaking what looked like a check at Franklin.

"This is an outrage," he shouted. "Your son, he has never liked me. He was just looking for an excuse. You owe me vacation pay and...and how you say, the severance pay, too."

DILLON COULD HEAR Pierre ranting at his father all the way down in the foyer. Cold fury made his heart pound in his chest.

After their argument that morning, Dillon's suspicions had been confirmed. His father was ill, and any confrontation seemed to make his condition worse.

That's why he'd had to walk out. Even after everything that had happened in the past, he sure as hell didn't intend to cause his father more stress. Nor did he intend to allow anyone else to upset him, either.

Dillon hurried toward the door off the foyer marked Offices. He jerked it open and took the stairs two at a time, reaching the top and rounding the corner that opened into the reception area. To his left was the door to his father's office, standing wide open. Franklin was beside his desk, Pierre Deville in front of him.

"Hold it right there, Deville," Dillon ordered. Out of the corner of his eye, he saw Adrienne standing in the hallway. The minute she'd seen him, she took a step backward. Would she have taken on the irate chef herself if he hadn't appeared?

Pierre whirled around to face him.

"This is between you and me," Dillon snapped. "My father has nothing to do with it."

Pierre's eyes narrowed and he lifted his chin. "You owe me vacation pay."

Still standing in the doorway, Dillon kept his eyes trained on the chef. "Joanne, have payroll draw up a check."

Joanne scurried past Dillon down the hall to the accountant's office. Within minutes, the club's accountant, followed closely by Joanne, walked out with a check.

Dillon took the check, hastily scrawled his name on it and held it out to the chef. "Now get out. And if I ever see you here again, I'll have the cops throw you in jail for trespassing.''

With a hate-filled glare, Pierre snatched up the check, brushed past Dillon and disappeared down the stairs.

The look that Dillon gave the accountant and Joanne sent them scurrying back to the computer room. Then he focused on Adrienne, who was still standing in the hallway, her hands on her hips, her feet spread apart as if ready to do battle.

Dillon ignored her and turned to his father. He lowered his voice, but he knew Adrienne could still hear him.

''I asked you to call me if he showed up, and I asked you not to interfere. From now on, let me handle things... like we agreed.''

Adrienne glared at Dillon as her blood began to boil. ''It wasn't his fault,'' she blurted. ''There wasn't time to call you or anyone, so don't go blaming your father.''

''I wasn't blaming him. I—''

''And another thing,'' she continued as if he hadn't spoken. ''No one is trying to interfere with you running the club. *Everyone* knows you're the boss now.''

Franklin held up his hand. ''Adrienne, it's okay. I appreciate your concern, but I'm sure Dillon didn't mean anything.''

Adrienne looked first at Franklin, then back at Dillon. After a moment of hesitation, she whirled around and stomped back to her office.

Whatever had made her think she could keep the peace between the two men? she wondered, shutting her office door none too gently. From now on, as far as she was concerned, they were on their own. And if Dillon wanted to fire her, then let him.

Adrienne sighed and leaned against the door. Who was she kidding? She had to think of Kristen. If she didn't have this job, she couldn't keep Kristen in the private school. And with only a few more semesters needed to get her management degree, she couldn't afford to stop now.

Besides, whatever happened between father and son was none of her business. She was just an employee— nothing else.

DILLON STARED at the empty space where Adrienne had been standing. The look of disgust she'd given him had not escaped him.

But why, he wondered, did it matter if she approved or disapproved of what he did, how he acted? She didn't understand—none of them understood—that he had no choice. Not if Twin Oaks was to survive.

Maybe it was time he had a little talk with her, to set her straight on a few matters.

Later that afternoon, he stopped by the dining room, where he spotted Adrienne immediately. She was on the opposite side, talking to Eva. He glanced at his watch. It was almost time for her to leave. If he was going to talk to her, it had to be now.

Dillon waited several seconds, figuring she was giving Eva some last-minute instructions about that evening's function in the ballroom. When Eva leaned over and whispered something in her ear, Adrienne grinned, and even across the room he could hear her throaty chuckle.

The sultry sound did strange things to his insides, stirring up unwelcome feelings he'd thought he had under control. For a moment, he regretted having to play the heavy. If circumstances were different, he might even be tempted to break his self-imposed rule about fraternizing with employees.

Since the episode with Pierre earlier today, he'd sensed Adrienne had done her best to avoid him. When their eyes had met, all he'd gotten from her were cool, tight-lipped looks of disapproval.

Enough was enough. Had it been anyone else, he wouldn't have bothered trying to explain himself. But somehow Adrienne wasn't that easy to ignore, and he found himself even more determined to set things straight.

Dillon waited until Eva walked away before he approached Adrienne. ''I'd like to talk to you...in my office.''

She glanced up from the banquet sheet she'd been staring at. From the look on her face, he could tell that talking with him was the last thing she wanted to do. ''Can it wait? I have a class tonight—''

''This won't take long.''

Looking decidedly uncomfortable, she nodded curtly and slipped the banquet sheet out of the clipboard. "As soon as I post this, I'll be up."

Dillon returned her nod, pivoted and headed for the office.

As Adrienne tacked the sheet on the kitchen bulletin board, she tried to shake off her uneasiness. He'd said talk. About what? If Pierre was expendable, didn't it stand to reason that she was, too? Especially after her little tirade. Adrienne took a deep breath and turned away from the bulletin board.

Don't look for trouble until it hits you in the face. But the old saying did nothing to alleviate the sick feeling in her stomach, or the simmering anger she had tried to control for the past two hours.

A few minutes later, in his office, Dillon motioned for her to be seated in a chair in front of his desk. "Okay. What's the problem?"

"Problem?"

Dillon leaned his hip against the edge of the desk and crossed his arms over his chest. "Ever since that little scene with Pierre, you've had something on your mind. So now's the time to spit it out."

He wasn't going to fire her.

Adrienne felt herself almost sag with relief. But fast on the heels of relief came anger that had been building all afternoon. She glared up at him. With the threat of losing her job hanging over her head, how could he expect her—or anyone else, for that matter—to be open and honest about anything?

"The only thing on my mind is doing my job," she said with chilly politeness. "Anything else, including who you hire or fire, is none of my business."

"But you're obviously angry."

"If I am, I'll just have to get over it," she retorted. "After the policies you laid down at the staff meeting—" she straightened her spine "—I quote, 'Any staff members who refuse to go along with the policies . . . can consider themselves free to—'"

"Okay, okay. Enough." Dillon stared up at the ceiling and gave a long, frustrated sigh, then he looked at her again. "I only said that to make a point. You and I both know that Mick Starky has a reputation for doing things his way, come hell or high water. Craig Johnson hires and fires at the drop of a hat. And Joe Blount hasn't stayed within his budget since the day he started working here."

Dillon reached up and rubbed the back of his neck, then dropped his hand and gripped the edge of the desk. He leaned forward slightly, giving her a piercing look. "I was trying to bring it home to all three that their past behavior would no longer be tolerated.

"Don't misunderstand," he added. "Mick, Craig and Joe are each experts at what they do. And those three have the makings of a fine team. My father's business practices may not always be sound, but with few exceptions, he knows people, knows how to spot potential.

"But what I said in the meeting had nothing to do with you. It wasn't coincidence that my father picked you to update me on things around here. Like I said, he knows how to spot potential. And after observing you even for a short time, I find I have to agree with his choice.''

Caught totally off guard and grappling with what he'd just said, Adrienne stared at him. After four days of watching *him,* she figured his little speech was as close to a compliment as he was capable of giving.

''Don't you see?'' he continued. ''My father knows a manager can't be everywhere all the time. He trusts you, so he chose you to be my eyes and ears when I'm not around.''

On the surface, that all sounded good, but Adrienne still had the niggling feeling that the only reason Franklin gave her the extra responsibility was to spy on his son.

Dillon recrossed his arms over his chest, and she detected a hint of a challenge in the way he was staring at her. ''Now that we've got that straight, are you going to tell me why you've been giving me go-to-hell looks all afternoon?''

Adrienne seized upon the first thing that popped into her mind. ''I realize that incidents like the one with Pierre shouldn't be tolerated, but—''

''Pierre! My God, you're not going to defend him, are you?''

Adrienne felt her insides begin to churn. She had no intention of defending the crazy chef's actions, but since he'd asked, she intended to tell him how she felt about his interference with her doing her job. "I just think that—"

"The man is a menace." Dillon's voice rose. "Besides that, he's incompetent and extravagant. He was costing the club money it could ill afford. And whether you like it or not, business is business."

Adrienne felt her temper rising. "Could I get a word in edgewise?" She glared at him for several seconds, daring him to interrupt again. When he didn't, she continued. "You undermined what little authority I had when you interfered this morning down in the kitchen. I could have—should have—had the chance to handle the situation."

When Dillon opened his mouth to protest, she held up her hand. "I also don't appreciate being embarrassed in front of my co-workers, especially about something that I had absolutely no control over."

Dillon frowned. "Sorry, but you just lost me."

"In the meeting," she reminded him. "When you sent me after Pierre."

She could tell by the change in his expression that it had never crossed his mind that he had done anything amiss.

"Anything else?"

Adrienne continued to scowl at him. Now was the time to tell him her suspicions about Franklin's ill health. But from the look on his face, she wasn't sure she had the nerve to, so she shook her head.

After several silent, tension filled seconds, Dillon took a deep breath. To Adrienne, he suddenly looked as weary as she felt. "Look," he said. "I know I can be overbearing at times, and unlike my father, I'm not always diplomatic about things. But I'm not here to make friends. I'm here to try and save a sinking ship. And to do that, I need all the help I can get. I'm warning you now that there are going to be more changes."

He paused. How could he make her understand? In many ways she was naive and too idealistic for her own good...just like his father. If she didn't toughen up, she would never make it in the cutthroat world of business.

"And one more thing," he added. "One of the first rules you learn in management is that bleeding hearts have no place in business. Neither do personal emotions—not if you want to sleep nights." The minute the words were out, he knew he'd hit a nerve. Adrienne stood, her flashing eyes reflecting her inner turmoil. "I'll try to remember that from now on." Her voice dripped sarcasm. "But sleeping nights has never been a problem for me. Now, if you'll excuse me, I have a class and I'm already late."

Dillon watched as she marched out the door. For a moment he wanted to call her back, tell her...tell her what?

He stood and walked over to the window. Acres of lush, expertly manicured greens stretched out before him, but did little to soothe the churning inside his stomach.

Adrienne Hamilton was getting to him. There was something about her that turned him inside out. He knew she thought he was being hard-nosed, and he knew he came across as uncaring. But too much was riding on the next two months for him to back down. From now on, every penny counted. He would do everything he could to save Twin Oaks, because without the place, his father and mother would be left with nothing.

That damned loan.

Dillon sighed and mentally reviewed what he'd dug up on Ted Jamison. The slick banker had a reputation for being single-minded when it came to profit. And Ted Jamison, apparently, never did anything without an ulterior motive.

Since everyone knew that no one got rich from running a country club, and Ted had no experience with clubs other than sitting on the board of directors, Dillon could only conclude that Ted had something in mind other than running the place himself if the loan wasn't paid and the bank foreclosed. But what?

The next thing Dillon intended to do was check out the council records. It was a long shot, and from experience, he knew it would be pretty dull reading, but maybe there was something in the minutes that would give him a clue as to why Twin Oaks had been steadily going downhill, especially when Ted Jamison just happened to be chairman of the finance committee. Dillon couldn't believe that *all* of Twin Oaks's financial problems were his father's fault.

CHAPTER SIX

JACK HAMILTON STARED bleakly at the phone on his desk. It was only Thursday, and already his gut felt as if it was full of broken glass.

What reason could he use this time? Going out of town on business usually worked, but Kristen might not believe the same tired excuse again.

He reached out and picked up the framed photograph he kept next to the phone. His daughter was too intelligent for her own good at times.

He slowly traced the outline of her face with his forefinger. The smiling picture was a head-and-shoulder shot, and if he concentrated on just her face, he could blot out the telltale outline of the wheelchair she was sitting in.

He felt his chest tighten. God, she was beautiful, a daughter that any father would be proud of.... Any father but him, he thought with disgust. It wasn't that he didn't love her—he did. But facing her, facing what he'd done—even just on an occasional weekend—was more than he could cope with. Especially knowing that if it weren't for him, she would be a whole person, able to walk, to run...

The ache inside him spread, and the dreaded craving came over him with a vengeance. Jack set down the picture and reached for the phone. Without hesitation, he punched out a phone number. It was picked up on the third ring.

"It's Jack," he said. "God, I need a drink."

Jack closed his eyes as he listened to the gruff voice over the line tell him all the reasons he shouldn't go buy a bottle and get plastered.

No matter what the hour, day or night, Ray had been there for him during the past six years. Once, when he'd called Ray from outside a neighborhood bar, the older man had showed up and talked him into going home instead of going inside. And for six years, he'd listened and heeded the encouragement Ray had given, and he'd stayed dry.

But there was still one thing Ray harped on that he just couldn't seem to do, and that was forgive himself. Ray, like the rest of the group he met with once a week, kept telling him he needed to learn to forgive himself. If he didn't, how could he expect to be forgiven?

But how could he forgive himself when every time he saw Kristen, he was reminded that because of him, his baby was serving out an irrevocable life sentence in a wheelchair? He didn't deserve forgiveness.

ADRIENNE STUDIED the proofs for the new dining room menus. With Pierre gone, they'd cut some of the more exotic dishes.

It seemed impossible that two whole weeks had passed since Dillon had fired the chef. So much had happened in that short time that she felt like she'd been swept up on a merry-go-round that she couldn't get off of. The more she was near Dillon, the faster it seemed to turn.

One thing she had learned since their last clash: Dillon had been right when he'd said he wasn't always as diplomatic in dealing with people as his father was. But he had a fair and honest, aboveboard approach that she'd grown to respect over the past few days.

In fact, after watching Dillon deal with disgruntled members and complaining employees, she'd drastically revised her initial holier-than-thou attitude. His polite but firm demeanor was devoid of emotion, yet he didn't seem as hard and cynical as she'd first thought.

A light knock at the door interrupted her thoughts. Adrienne glanced up as Dillon entered her office. He was wearing navy slacks and a crisp, pale blue shirt with the cuffs rolled back almost to his elbows.

A smile tugged at her lips. Dillon usually started out each morning wearing a tie and a suit—the perfect management image—but at some point during the day, he would discard the tie and coat, undo the top two shirt buttons and roll up his shirtsleeves.

He paused in front of her desk. "Are those the new menus?"

Adrienne nodded. "The proofs. Joanne just picked them up from the printer."

"How do they look?"

"Except for a couple of typos, they seem fine." She held out the sheaf of papers, but instead of taking them from her, Dillon walked around her desk and leaned over her shoulder to look at them.

The nearness of him, his scent—spicy, sharp and overwhelmingly male—set her pulse racing. He was talking about the menu, something about deleting one of the more costly specials, but Adrienne couldn't seem to concentrate.

He reached down to flip over the top page and his shoulder pressed against her back. She could feel the heat of his body. And when his arm brushed against her own, tiny shock waves from the skin-to-skin contact set off a quake of longing so strong that Adrienne tightened her fingers into a death grip around the pen she held in her hand.

The intercom buzzed, and her gaze flew to Dillon's face. By the smoldering look in his eyes, she suspected he had been just as affected as she had during the last few moments. That thought sent another wave of desire coursing through her.

But in an instant, the look was gone. He grabbed up the papers and backed away. Adrienne took a deep breath and picked up the receiver.

"Line one is for you," Joanne said. "It's your ex."

Adrienne felt like groaning out loud. "Thanks, Joanne," she finally murmured, glancing over at Dillon. Instead of stepping out while she took the call, he had seated himself in the chair in front of her desk and was flipping through the proofs.

Feeling slightly uncomfortable with him still in the room and dreading what she knew was coming, she punched line one. "Hello, Jack."

DILLON KEPT HIS EYES glued to the papers in front of him, but the words written there could have been Greek for all he knew. He should have stepped out while she took the call, but something in her voice, a certain tenseness, made him change his mind. And the moment he'd heard her identify the caller, he'd given in to temptation and let his curiosity and his concern for her override his good manners.

The longer the conversation went on, the more upset Adrienne seemed to become. Although she never raised her voice, Dillon could feel her frustration building with each word she spoke.

He looked up when she finally hung up the receiver. As she continued to stare at the phone, the anguish reflected in her eyes made him wish for a fleeting second that he could smash his fist into Jack Hamilton's face for causing her such pain.

"Is something wrong?"

She blinked several times and looked up. "No," she answered, clearly still distracted. "Everything's... fine."

"Sorry, I didn't realize your call was personal."

Liar.

Dillon ignored the tiny voice of his conscience. "I should have left you with some privacy."

Adrienne shrugged. "No problem."

"I couldn't help overhearing. That was your ex-husband?"

When she didn't answer, Dillon knew he should drop the subject, but he kept telling himself that he couldn't afford to have her upset, especially on the job. And the more he knew about her, the better they could work with each other.

And you're as full of it as a Thanksgiving turkey.

Dillon again ignored the aggravating voice. "I gather he called about Kristen."

She let out a sigh and gave a little nod. "Something like that."

"Sometimes it helps to talk about things." The words just seemed to spill out all by themselves, and Dillon couldn't believe he'd said them. By the surprised look on Adrienne's face, it was evident that she didn't believe he'd said them, either.

He couldn't blame her. Only two weeks ago he had told her that emotion had no place in business; yet here he was, breaking his self-imposed rule by inviting her to confide her personal problems.

Dillon shifted in his chair. The woman was definitely getting to him. He was slowly but surely losing his perspective where she was concerned.

But before he could think of some way to tactfully take back what he'd said, she began talking.

"Jack is supposed to have Kristen twice a month on the weekends. If he kept to the schedule, the arrangement would be ideal for me, since I usually have to work every other weekend and I'm off on Mondays. But as usual, he finds all kinds of excuses not to. Over the past six years he's averaged about one weekend every two months, and the past two years even less. The last time she saw him was three months ago. Oh, he calls every week to check on her, but it's not the same as spending time with her. When she was younger, she didn't make a big deal out of it." Adrienne sighed. "Now that she's older, she seems to so look forward to her time with her father that when he cancels, she spends the whole weekend moping. Now he's making excuses again."

Excuses, Dillon thought. And as the single word dredged up a bevy of emotions, Dillon ached for Kristen. His own father had always had excuses, too: excuses why he couldn't attend a Little League game, excuses why they couldn't take a family vacation, excuses for not coming home in the evenings.

Jack Hamilton was a fool, Dillon decided. The best years of his little girl's life were slipping away without him being a part of them. One day he'd wake up and realize what he'd done, what he'd lost. But by then it would be too late.

"Every week it's the same thing over and over," Adrienne continued. "He makes plans with her, then calls me at the last minute and cancels. Then I'm the heavy and she ends up taking out her frustrations on me."

"And you let her. And him," Dillon added.

Adrienne scowled. "What do you mean? What other choice do I have?"

"Stop being the heavy. Stop being the go-between. Your ex-husband's a grown man. Let him handle his own problems. And let Kristen learn to deal directly with her father instead of blaming you."

He was right. Adrienne knew it, deep down. And she had always known it. But knowing the right thing to do was quite different from doing it.

Adrienne shook her head. "You don't understand. There's more to it than that. Jack is . . . he has . . . problems. He doesn't handle pressure too well. And for Kristen's sake, I can't just turn my back." What Dillon didn't—couldn't—know was that Jack had his own demons to fight. One more pressure might drive him over the edge again. And there was no way she could be the one to push him over that edge. Kristen might never forgive her if she found out.

Dillon wanted to tell her that he understood about Jack's so-called problems. But he couldn't, not without betraying Louie's confidence. It was an enigma to him that she could still protect Hamilton after everything he'd done.

But Adrienne had a caring nature, he reminded himself. And she loved her daughter. More than likely she was simply trying to protect Kristen from being hurt. What she couldn't see, and what Kristen was trying to show her by acting out was that she couldn't keep her daughter forever cocooned from the realities of life. His own mother had tried it, and the results had been less than desirable.

The older he'd gotten, the more Dillon had come to realize just how much of her own life his mother had sacrificed by trying to substitute for his father. She'd tried doubly hard to make up for his father's neglect by giving more of herself. She'd made Dillon the center of her world, almost to the exclusion of everything else. And all she'd accomplished was to make him resent his father even more.

"Everyone has problems," he said bluntly. "But that doesn't make you responsible. Your ex and your daughter have to be accountable for their own actions. And no matter how hard you try to make things right, or make excuses, in the long run you'll be the one hurt." *Like my mother,* he added silently, thinking of that day seven years ago when he'd told her goodbye.

"And Kristen will only end up resenting you even more," he continued. "At some point, you have to let go and let Kristen face reality. She and her father have to find their own way."

Dillon's words stung. "That may be true if you're running a business," she shot back defensively. "But there's more to it when it involves family. Maybe you'd better stick to running Twin Oaks."

"Whether you want to admit it or not, the principles are the same," he said softly.

The gentleness in his voice was almost her undoing, and she was instantly ashamed of her outburst. But the truth hurt, and at times she felt as if she was walking an emotional tightrope. Nothing she did seemed to work. Although she'd tried to tell herself that her daughter's behavior was typical adolescent rebellion, she knew it went deeper than that. As each day passed, she could feel Kristen's resentment growing. She didn't want to lose her daughter…she couldn't. She'd already lost too much….

WHEN ADRIENNE ENTERED her living room that evening, she could hear Kristen and Louie laughing in the kitchen. For a moment she savored the happy sounds and wished with all her heart that she didn't have to tell Kristen that Jack had canceled out on her again.

Damn his rotten hide anyway, she thought, throwing her handbag onto the sofa. God, she was tired. Tired of making excuses, tired of being the scapegoat. Dillon was right. None of this was her fault, so why did she have to be the one to suffer the consequences? Maybe it was time she put a stop to it. Maybe she should talk to Jack—really talk to him.

Adrienne rolled her head from one side to the other, trying to loosen the bunched-up muscles in her neck. Already she could feel a headache developing at the mere thought of a confrontation with Jack.

Later, she decided. Maybe tomorrow she'd talk to him. But for tonight, she had to face Kristen. Tonight, for one last time, she decided with conviction, she'd make his excuses for him.

Adrienne straightened her shoulders and headed to the kitchen.

"Well, look who's here," Louie called over his shoulder. "Must have smelled my special all the way to the club."

Adrienne forced a smile for her uncle, who was taking a bubbling casserole from the oven. Kristen was at the table tearing lettuce leaves into a salad bowl.

"Whatever your special is, it smells great," Adrienne said, trying to inject enthusiasm into her voice.

"Special, my foot," Kristen quipped. "It's tuna casserole, and I found the recipe in one of your cookbooks."

Louie scowled and threw his niece a look of mock disgust. "Tattletale."

Kristen giggled and set aside the salad bowl. She picked up a dish towel and wiped her hands. "What time is Dad coming tomorrow? I thought I'd wear the new sweater that Katie helped me pick out when we went shopping."

Adrienne took a deep breath. "Something's come up. Your father called and said to tell you he's sorry, but he promises to make up for it next weekend."

For several seconds Kristen stared at her, the excited sparkle in her blue eyes dulling into disappointment. "When did he call?"

Adrienne lifted her chin. "This afternoon, just before I left to come home."

"What came up?"

Adrienne shrugged. "He didn't say, but I'm sure it was important. He sounded pretty hassled."

Kristen glared at Adrienne and threw down the dish towel. "Yeah. Sure," she retorted. With a sudden shove against the table, she turned her chair and wheeled past Adrienne, out of the room.

"Kristen—"

Louie reached out and grabbed Adrienne's arm. "Let her go," he said gently. "Give her a few minutes to herself."

Because she needed to get a hold on her own emotions, Adrienne allowed her uncle to lead her to a nearby chair. When she heard Kristen's bedroom door slam, she started to get up, but Louie gently pushed her back into the chair.

"Just sit for a while and give her, and yourself, awhile to cool off. I'll get you a nice glass of iced tea and you can tell me about your day while I finish up dinner."

Twenty minutes later, when she knocked on Kristen's closed door, Adrienne's stomach was still churning.

"Kristen, it's time to eat."

"Go away." She could barely hear Kristen's muffled reply. "I'm not hungry."

Adrienne twisted the doorknob but it refused to turn. She took a deep breath and tried to remain calm. "Unlock the door. We need to talk."

"I don't want to talk. Leave me alone."

"I'm not going to leave you alone, so you might as well open the door."

Several seconds passed before the door finally swung open. "Now, are you satisfied?"

Adrienne stared at her daughter's tear-stained face. Knowing the reason behind Kristen's hateful tone, she decided to ignore it for the moment. "Sweetheart, I know you're disappointed, but—"

"You don't know anything—how could you? All you think about is that stupid club and getting a degree. You don't care about me or Dad. If you did, you wouldn't have divorced him in the first place."

"I didn't..." Adrienne bit off the words and clamped her jaw shut. The churning in her stomach turned into a rolling turmoil. She wanted to scream that she wasn't to blame, that Jack had divorced her, had left them both, that he was the one who hadn't cared enough. But what purpose would it serve, except to foster more questions, questions she couldn't answer without hurting Kristen even more?

"I care about *you*," she finally said, trying to keep her voice even. "And right now, the dinner your uncle worked hard to prepare is getting cold, so get your butt in gear before I decide to ground you."

Kristen glared up at her for what seemed like forever. "I'm not hungry and I'm not eating. I'm going to bed." She wheeled her chair around and rolled it toward her bed.

Adrienne closed her eyes and counted to ten. It didn't help.

"Okay. Have it your way. Consider yourself grounded for the weekend. No phone calls and no visitors." She pivoted on her heel and stalked out of the room.

Dinner was a disaster. Adrienne tried, for Louie's sake, to eat, but with each tasteless bite she took, she could feel her anger building. She had to do something or explode.

Finally she threw down her napkin. "I have to go out for a while," she said to her uncle. "I won't be long, if you have plans this evening."

Louie shook his head. "No plans except to watch a little TV." The knowing, sympathetic look on his face spoke volumes, and Adrienne walked over to his chair and gave him a quick hug. He patted her back. "Take your time, hon. Just be careful."

Thirty minutes later, Adrienne pulled her Toyota up beside her ex-husband's Mustang in front of his apartment. *Good,* she thought. *At least he's home.*

All the way to his apartment complex, she'd debated on whether to wait until she'd calmed down or confront him while she had the courage. The longer she'd driven around, the more she'd thought about what Dillon had said. Maybe it was time she stopped letting Jack use her as his crutch. And maybe it was time he started taking responsibility for his own actions with Kristen.

She wasn't sure exactly what she was going to say to him. But one thing she was sure of: she had to get some kind of control over the situation. Tonight she'd almost slipped. She'd come close to telling Kristen the truth . . . too close.

She took a deep breath and knocked loudly on Jack's apartment door. After a couple of minutes, the door swung open.

"Adrienne. What are you doing here?"

From the look of him, she figured he'd just showered and dressed. Probably getting ready to go out, she thought, noticing his wrinkle-free shirt and neatly pressed slacks.

There had been a time when just the sight of him would have made her heart beat faster, but now she wondered what she'd ever seen in him. Thinking about the pathetic man he had turned into inside, she couldn't dredge up an ounce of anything but pity.

"We need to talk."

Jack frowned. "I was just on my way out—"

Adrienne pushed past him into the living room. "So you'll be a little late. I'm sure you can come up with a suitable excuse."

When she turned to face him, she was gratified to see a slight flush steal up his clean-shaven jaw.

"Look. If this is about Kristen, I already explained that I have to work tomorrow. I—"

"Cut the bull, Jack. You and I both know you don't have to work tomorrow. I just left our daughter so upset that she's shut herself up in her room without a bite of dinner. All because of your damned excuses. And I'm tired of it."

"Now listen here—"

"No." Adrienne shouted, jabbing him in the chest with her forefinger. "*You* listen. No more excuses, Jack. From now on, you deal with her. Whether you like it or not, whether you're ashamed of her or not, you're still her father."

Jack paled. "You know that's not true. I've never been ashamed of Kristen. It's myself I'm ashamed of, and you know why."

Suddenly weary, Adrienne felt her resolve weakening. Then a picture of Kristen's red-rimmed eyes flashed through her mind and she lifted her chin. "That's your problem, not mine. It always has been. And as of this moment, it's up to you to deal with it... and Kristen. From now on, you call *her,* not me. Do you understand?"

"Aw, come on, Adrienne. Don't be like that. You know I love Kristen, and I promise I'll try harder. Don't cut me out."

Adrienne stared at him for several seconds, wishing she could shake some sense into him. "I'm not cutting you out, Jack. You're cutting yourself out."

For some time after Adrienne stormed out the door, Jack continued to stare at it. He'd never seen Adrienne act so...so aggressive, so forceful. Something about her was different. Always before, he could depend on her. She was his link—at times his only link—to Kristen. She had always understood. Until now.

Jack backed up and sat down on the sofa. If Adrienne stopped taking his calls, if she stopped keeping him up-to-date on Kristen, how was he going to know what was happening in his daughter's life?

He reached up and fished a pack of cigarettes from his shirt pocket. He tapped one out, and with a shaky hand, lit it. Here he had been patting himself on the back for doing so well. He could handle once a month or once every six weeks, but more than that...

Jack sat forward and reached for the phone. He punched out the familiar number.

"Ray, have you got a minute?"

CHAPTER SEVEN

ON SATURDAY EVENING, Dillon stepped out of his car and reached back inside for a large paper bag and two video tapes. The clerk at the store had assured him that the tapes were suitable for a girl of twelve. And he wasn't too old to remember that hamburgers and French fries were always a hit with kids.

He straightened and for a moment stared at Adrienne's house. Something about it seemed different, and it took him a moment to realize that the trim had been freshly painted. Probably by Louie, he decided, appreciatively eyeing the robin's-egg blue color.

Slamming the car door, he walked slowly toward the ramp. He wasn't sure how Adrienne would feel about his surprise visit. But then, he hadn't made his decision based on whether she would or wouldn't welcome him, at least not entirely. He was here because of Kristen.

He'd tried to keep his distance, tried not to get involved with Adrienne or her family, but after his phone conversation with Kristen that morning, he'd decided he was fighting a losing battle.

He'd originally called to ask Adrienne about a luncheon booked at the club. There seemed to be a mix-up with the menu, and he'd suspected his father was interfering . . . again. Kristen had answered his call so quickly that he wasn't sure the phone had rung. When he'd asked to speak to her mother, she'd told him Adrienne had gone to the store. Then she'd confided that she'd been grounded. Dillon chuckled, remembering how indignant she'd sounded when she told him she wasn't even supposed to use the phone.

Curious, he'd asked why she was grounded, and surprisingly, she'd told him. They had talked for several minutes, and then he'd heard it—the distinct click of someone phoning in on the call-waiting mechanism. That's when Kristen had let it slip that she'd been talking with Katie, despite her mother's direct orders to the contrary.

Dillon was sure Adrienne had good reason for grounding Kristen, but that didn't keep him from sympathizing with the girl. Knowing that her father had canceled their weekend, he'd immediately read between the lines. It was a pattern he was all too familiar with, a pattern of his own past.

How many times had he purposely pulled some stunt, just to get his father's attention? It hadn't mattered that he would be punished, that he was getting the wrong kind of attention. All that mattered was that his father had finally taken notice of him.

At that moment, he'd felt an instant kinship with the young girl. And because he could relate to Kristen, because he could sympathize with her being rejected by her father and feeling rebellious, the girl, like her mother, was doing a number on his emotions.

Dillon walked up the small ramp to the door. Louie had picked up the phone the second time he'd called. Dillon felt a grin tug at his lips and gave a slight shake of his head. The old man was as manipulative as the devil himself. Louie had given him a song and dance about "poor Kristen" and how she and her mother were fighting again. Then he'd come right out and asked Dillon if he was busy that evening. "That's perfect," he'd said when Dillon told him he needed to speak with Adrienne. "I have plans to go out, so you can act as a mediator between Adrienne and Kristen."

Dillon knocked on the door. Even without Louie's invitation, he'd made up his mind to pay Adrienne and Kristen a visit. And it had nothing to do with the luncheon menu—he and Adrienne had dealt with that when she'd returned his call. But there was no harm in letting the old man think it was his idea.

ADRIENNE HEARD the car door slam, and for a moment, she hoped that Jack had changed his mind and had decided to surprise Kristen. When she peeped out the front window and saw Dillon, her heart picked up a beat and her stomach did a funny little flip-flop.

He was wearing faded jeans and a cream-colored pullover. Although she'd thought he looked handsome in a business suit, the sexy aura he usually projected was even more blatant in the snug-fitting sweater that defined his wide shoulders and muscular chest, and the body hugging jeans that, well, hugged every inch they covered to perfection.

Why was he here? she wondered. She'd already returned his call and answered his question about the menu. With all the bookings scheduled at Twin Oaks, she'd have thought he would be at the club working.

When his knock sounded at the door, Adrienne made a quick dash to the small wall mirror. At least she looked halfway decent, she decided. If he had showed up an hour earlier, he would have caught her smeared from one end to the other with blue paint.

Adrienne took a calming breath and smoothed her hands down the sides of her slacks. She opened the door.

"I hope I'm not intruding," he said, his eyes doing a quick inspection of his own. "But Louie assured me it would be okay to drop by. I wanted to somehow repay his dinner invitation...." He held out the sack and the videos, leaving her little choice but to take them.

He hooked his thumbs in his front jeans pockets. "I wanted to take all of you out to dinner and a movie, but your uncle said that Kristen was grounded. I know it's not much, but he assured me that he and Kristen love hamburgers, so..." He shrugged.

It was a lame excuse and he knew he was babbling, but it was the best he could come up with at the moment. "I noticed you had a VCR. The videos are supposed to be suitable for someone Kristen's age," he added.

Feeling every bit as flustered as he seemed, Adrienne allowed the politeness that had been grilled into her since early childhood to take over. She stepped back out of the doorway. "Come in," she said. Dillon's reasons for coming sounded legitimate enough, but she suspected there was more to it. Something to do with sneaky uncles, she decided, vowing yet again to have a little talk with Louie.

"I'm sure both my uncle and my daughter will prefer these to the leftovers I had in mind for dinner. They smell great."

Just then Kristen wheeled into the room. "Oh." She frowned. "It's you."

The instant he saw the wary look on her face, Dillon knew that Kristen thought he'd ratted on her. He gave a slight shake of his head and hoped that she got the message. "How are you, Kristen?" he asked.

Some of the suspicion faded. "Grounded," she answered flatly, throwing her mother a stony glare.

Adrienne grimaced and tried to hold on to her temper. "Dillon was kind enough to bring over hamburgers and videos," she said evenly. "Will you please go tell Uncle Louie for me?"

Kristen hesitated for a minute, then rolled her chair to the hall doorway. "Uncle Louie!" she shouted. "It's time to eat!"

Adrienne sighed. "That's not what I meant." When her daughter glowered back at her with one of her "so what" expressions, Adrienne felt her temper rise another notch. She pivoted and headed for the kitchen. "I'll get some plates," she muttered.

Left alone with Kristen, Dillon gave her a stern look. "What would happen if your mom knew you'd disobeyed her today?" Kristen frowned, but he didn't give her time to answer. "I imagine another day or two of being grounded would be in order. And since I have been known to use blackmail before, why don't you—for just this evening—give your mom a break and behave yourself?"

The smugness faded and Kristen's eyes widened. "That's not fair."

Dillon shrugged. "Life's not fair." For a moment he wondered if he'd pushed her too far. After all, he reminded himself, he was almost a stranger to her, an outsider. But from his own experience, he knew that kids, whether they admitted it or not, appreciated knowing just exactly what was expected of them. And usually they lived up to those expectations, good or bad.

Kristen thrust out her lower lip. "You sound just like Uncle Louie."

Dillon felt the tension in his gut ease a little with her comment. A comparison with her beloved great-uncle was about as close to a compliment—and acknowledgment of a truce—as he was going to get, he figured.

"Did I hear my name mentioned?"

Kristen and Dillon turned their heads in time to see the older man stroll into the room.

Kristen looked him over, from his slicked-back, steelgray hair to his booted feet. "Oh, wow! You look cool." She turned to Dillon and winked. "He only wears his snakeskin boots if he has a hot date."

Louie shook a finger at her. "That's no way for a young lady to talk."

"Ha!" She snorted. "Ladies have boobs, so I don't qualify...yet."

"Kristen!" Adrienne had walked back into the room just in time to hear the embarrassing remark.

"Oh, for Pete's sake, Mom. Uncle Louie and Dillon know women have boo—breasts."

Adrienne shot Kristen a stern look and hoped her burning cheeks weren't beet red. "I'm sure they do, but that doesn't mean it's polite to talk about...to say..." She glanced at her uncle and then at Dillon.

Louie had covered his mouth with one hand and turned his head to the side, but she could see the mirth dancing in his eyes. And Dillon—darn the man—was grinning from ear to ear.

Totally flustered, Adrienne whirled around and stalked off toward the dining room. "Come and eat," she grumbled. "The hamburgers are getting cold."

After the first few awkward minutes, Adrienne felt herself slowly begin to relax. The hamburgers, she'd learned, had come from a new specialty place that had just opened in the Twin Oaks community. And after the first mouth-watering bite, she figured the place would be a hit in no time.

Miraculously, Kristen was behaving. She seemed just as enthralled with the conversation between her great-uncle and Dillon as Adrienne was, especially when they began talking about old black-and-white movies.

"I get a kick out of watching them. In particular the silent ones," Dillon admitted. "And I've been able to collect videos of most of the classics."

Louie sighed. "They just don't make 'em like they used to. Nowadays, if they don't have sex, blood, guts and gore, no one wants to watch 'em."

"Now, that's my kind of movie," Kristen exclaimed. When all three adults cast frowns of disapproval her way, she rolled her eyes and shrugged. "Good grief, I was just kidding." Then she grinned and a glint of mischief sparkled in her eyes. "At least about all of it except the sex."

Adrienne groaned and Louie chuckled.

"I seem to remember being overly interested in that particular subject myself at your age," Dillon said, his grin growing wider.

Adrienne stood and briskly began to clear the table. No matter how liberated women were supposed to be and no matter how openly everyone discussed sex, she was never totally comfortable when the subject came up.

Jack had been her first and only experience. And it wasn't that she hadn't enjoyed the intimacy of it. On the contrary, she'd loved being touched and held. But after romanticizing about making love all throughout high school, the actual experience had fallen short of her expectations. She'd been left, time and time again, feeling as if she'd missed out on something.

As Dillon watched Adrienne clear the table, his grin faded. From observing her at the club, he'd learned that whenever she didn't want to discuss something, whenever she was uncomfortable, she had a habit of doing busywork. It didn't take a genius to conclude that their joking about sex was the reason for her discomfort. But why would a divorced woman who looked and dressed like she did, and who exuded sexuality be so uptight when the barest hint of the subject came into a conversation?

A car horn honked outside and Louie stood. "That's my ride," he said, giving Dillon a conspiratorial wink.

Adrienne was reaching for the empty hamburger sack and glanced up. "Your ride?"

Ignoring her questioning tone, Louie waltzed over and kissed her on the cheek. "I'll probably be late, so don't bother waiting up." With a quick kiss for Kristen and a handshake for Dillon, he left.

He'd done it again.

And from the amused look on Dillon's and Kristen's faces, Adrienne had a sneaking suspicion that everyone but her knew Louie had planned to go out. She snatched up the empty sack and marched off toward the kitchen.

"Why don't you go load the first video," Dillon suggested to Kristen. "I'll help your mom finish up in the kitchen."

"Do you think she's upset with Uncle Louie?"

Dillon smiled at the wide-eyed girl. "I think your uncle should have told her he was going out tonight."

"You wouldn't think so if you knew my mother better," she said. "She'd only get mad at him."

"For going out?"

Kristen shook her head. "Uh-uh. But she's accused him of trying to fix her up with men before, and she might think he was at it again." She pushed away from the table, then paused. "Is he?"

Dillon hesitated. By Kristen's concerned expression, he knew he needed to be careful how he replied. Like most children of divorced parents, she probably still secretly harbored hope that her mom and dad would one day get back together.

"Would you mind if he was trying to fix her up with me?" he asked softly.

For several seconds Kristen didn't reply, and he could see the turmoil of emotions playing across her face. Then she gave a noncommittal shrug. "It doesn't really matter if I mind or not," she answered. And before Dillon could deny what she'd said, she turned and wheeled herself out of the room.

Thoughtfully, Dillon picked up his plate and got to his feet. Stacking his plate on top of Kristen's and gathering up their forks and glasses, he carried the dishes to the kitchen. When he entered, Adrienne was standing at the sink with her back to him. She glanced over her shoulder.

"You don't have to do that," she said. "In fact..." She turned off the faucet and grabbed a dish towel. "If you want to leave, I'll understand. Uncle Louie means well, but he—he shouldn't have run out on you like that. I'm sorry if he's embarrassed you."

Dillon set the dishes on the cabinet. "Adrienne." He gently gripped her upper arms, and even though her skin was silky smooth, he could feel the tension in her taut muscles. His fingers itched to massage away the tightness. "Stop apologizing," he said. "I'm not embarrassed and neither should you be. I came because I wanted to come. And unless you object, I'm staying because I want to stay."

Because the urge to pull her against him was strong—too strong—Dillon released her and stepped back. He motioned toward the stacked plates. "That's the last of them, and by now Kristen should have the video set up. Should we wash them now or later?"

Adrienne smiled, and the mischievous look she gave him reminded him of Kristen. "Oh, I think we should leave them for my uncle to do tomorrow," she said. "Don't you?"

Dillon grinned and held out his arm. "Your wish is my command, madam."

Adrienne hesitated only a moment before she slid her arm within his and allowed him to escort her to the living room. She settled on the sofa and Dillon stretched out in a nearby chair. She could still feel the tingly aftermath of his touch.

Several times during the course of the movie, she had a hard time concentrating on the plot. It seemed her eyes and thoughts insisted on straying to Dillon.

The man was a total contradiction, she decided. Even though he was still strictly business while at the club, she had seen evidence that beneath his hard-nosed exterior lurked a softer, more compassionate man, a man who was more like his father than he wanted to admit.

Having a man other than her uncle in the house, stretched out near her, was a bit unnerving at first. But when Kristen began to tease and laugh along with him instead of pouting and picking a fight, Adrienne found herself laughing and enjoying herself, too.

After the first movie ended, Adrienne could tell Kristen was getting tired of sitting in her chair. Knowing how her daughter prided herself on her independence, she figured she might be a bit stubborn about admitting she needed help in front of Dillon. Keeping her tone matter-of-fact, Adrienne asked, "Would you like to stretch out, hon?"

Kristen's eyes cut to Dillon, but she nodded. As Adrienne tossed some pillows onto the floor, Dillon abruptly stood. Without a moment's hesitation, he lifted Kristen from her chair onto the pile of pillows.

"Thanks," Kristen said with a shy smile.

Dillon smiled back at her, and the look on his face held such profound tenderness that Adrienne suddenly felt tears spring to her eyes.

"Any time, sweetheart," he answered softly.

Adrienne blinked several times. She had never seen Jack look at his daughter in that special way. Unlike him, Dillon seemed totally comfortable with Kristen, treating her like any twelve-year-old should be treated. And unlike Jack, Dillon possessed an air of self-confidence that she couldn't help but admire.

By the time the second movie was over, Kristen had fallen asleep. Dillon pressed the remote-control rewind button, then turned to Adrienne. "Which way is her room?" She started to protest, but he bent down and gently lifted Kristen in his arms. "No sense in waking her," he said quietly.

"Thanks." She motioned toward the hallway. "First room on the right."

Once they had settled the still-sleeping Kristen in her bed, Dillon followed Adrienne back into the living room. He glanced at his watch. "I didn't realize it was so late. Next time I guess I should rent only one movie."

Next time.

Adrienne didn't dare dwell on the words for fear she was making too much out of nothing. Instead, she busied herself with picking up the throw pillows, while Dillon ejected the video and snapped it into its plastic case.

As if by mutual consent, they both started toward the front door. The cool evening air was brisk and fresh, and it seemed as if thousands of stars lit up the heavens. Adrienne couldn't resist the lure of the gorgeous night, so she followed Dillon outside and walked him to his car.

"How beautiful, she said, her eyes heavenward.

"Yes... beautiful," he agreed, but the tone of his voice indicated he wasn't talking about stars.

Adrienne glanced at him and caught her breath. He was staring at her. Even in the dim light, there was no mistaking the raw need reflected in his eyes. She shivered with her own responding need, and for long moments she couldn't look away, reluctant to break whatever spell had been cast.

"Thanks for bringing the food and videos," she finally said, wondering at the sudden breathless quality in her voice.

Still holding her gaze, Dillon opened the car door and tossed in the videos. Then, without really knowing how it happened, she was suddenly caught up in his arms, arms that were firm and gentle, that made her feel warm and cherished, yet desired and special in the possessive way he held her.

"You're more than welcome," he whispered before he bent his head and kissed her.

When his lips touched hers, she felt as if her feet had left the ground and she was on a flight to join the stars. With a throaty growl that sent frissons of desire dancing in her stomach, he took the kiss deeper, demanding as well as giving.

Adrienne wrapped her arms around his neck, and suddenly felt as if she was soaring through the galaxy. With his hard length pressed intimately against hers and a myriad of pulsating sensations vibrating through her, time and space meant nothing, and Dillon's hot mouth and even hotter body meant everything.

When he ended the kiss, he still held her close. "I've been wanting to do that since the first day I saw you."

Adrienne felt her heart begin to melt. The pull of attraction between them hadn't been a figment of her imagination after all.

"And now that I have," he continued, "I'm not sure it was such a good idea."

As his last words sank in, Adrienne stiffened. She tried to pull away, but he wouldn't release her.

"I think you're misunderstanding," he whispered, gathering her even more tightly against him. "I'm not sure kissing you was such a good idea, because now that I have, I find I want more than just kisses."

Before she had time to reply, he gave her one last, searing kiss, released her and slid into his car. Adrienne was still standing on the edge of the driveway when the taillights of his car disappeared around the corner.

THE TASTE OF ADRIENNE and the feel of her, warm and pliant, pressed against him, was all Dillon thought about on the drive home. But it wasn't simply a case of needing a physical release. A cold shower would help take care of that problem.

No, he thought. His interest in Adrienne went deeper than just the physical pull. Other men might be content with a relationship based on mutual sexual attraction, but for him, there had to be more to it. And until now, until he'd met Adrienne, he'd never been able to define what that "more" was.

Dillon pulled into his reserved parking space and shut off the car. For several minutes he sat there, staring at nothing in particular. Adrienne seemed to possess a curious combination of inner strength, vulnerability and ingenuousness that appealed to something deep inside him. With her, Dillon knew, a man would never have to wonder or worry about loyalty or trust.

He groaned, then stepped out of the car and locked it. The only trouble, he thought, was that if he ever allowed himself to start a relationship with her, he had a sneaking feeling he would never want it to be over.

Why now, of all times? Why couldn't she have come along before he'd taken on the mess at the club...or later? Dammit, he had his hands full, and it would take all of his energies to save Twin Oaks. Even then he might still fail. And worse than that, what if he had to terminate her job? How could he enter a relationship knowing he might have to fire her?

ADRIENNE PUSHED the wheelchair quietly into her daughter's room, so it would be on hand when she woke up the next morning. As she turned to leave, she heard Kristen's sleepy voice call out.

"Mom?"

"I thought you were asleep." Adrienne knelt beside the bed and smoothed Kristen's hair away from her face.

"I was...kinda."

Adrienne smiled. "Kinda, as in playing possum?"

"Aw, Mom."

Even in the dim light shining through from the hallway, she could see Kristen's face turn pink, and she smiled. "It was pretty nice of Dillon to bring over the hamburgers and videos, huh?"

Kristen shrugged. "Yeah, I guess so." She paused, then rolled onto her back and looked up at Adrienne. "You like him, don't you?"

Adrienne nodded. "Of course I do."

Kristen shook her head. "I mean *really* like him."

This time Adrienne nodded more slowly. "Yes, I guess I do."

"Do you still like Dad?"

"Oh, Kristen. It's not the same. You know your dad and I...well, we—we decided a long time ago that we'd both be happier living apart."

"Do you think you might change your mind?"

Adrienne sighed, then shook her head. "No, hon. I don't think so."

Back in her own bedroom, Adrienne undressed, slipped on her gown and slid in between the cool sheets. She thought about her conversation with Kristen. Had she said the right things? Despite all the times she and her daughter had talked about the break up of the marriage, Kristen still seemed to be harboring secret hopes that just weren't possible.

Adrienne punched her pillow and tried to get into a more comfortable position. Why did life have to be so damned complicated? She'd dated men before. Not that many, but a few. So why did Kristen seem so concerned about Dillon? Was she that obvious about how she felt about him?

Thoughts of Dillon conjured up the kiss they'd shared, and Adrienne grew restless with the memory. A couple of men she'd dated after her divorce had kissed her, but their kisses hadn't stirred up anything but feelings of friendship. And neither man had left her restless and yearning for more.

Several minutes passed before Adrienne decided that sleep was impossible. Throwing back the sheet, she sat up and grabbed her robe. Maybe a cup of hot chocolate would help, she thought, heading for the kitchen.

Just as the microwave beeper signaled that the cup of instant cocoa was heated, Adrienne heard a car door slam, followed a few seconds later by the sound of a key in the front door.

"Hot chocolate?" she asked when her uncle strolled into the room.

Louie nodded. "Didn't expect you to still be up."

Adrienne handed him the cup, then turned and spooned more cocoa into another mug, adding milk. She shrugged as she popped it into the microwave. "It hasn't been that long since Dillon left."

Louie pulled out a kitchen chair and seated himself. "How did Kristen like the movies?"

Again, Adrienne shrugged. "She fell asleep halfway through the second one."

For several seconds there was nothing but the whir of the microwave filling the silence, and Adrienne wondered if she should come out and ask her uncle about his part in Dillon's showing up, or let it pass.

When the microwave beeped, she removed the steaming cup and walked over to the table. Her uncle glanced up, and it was then she noticed the lipstick on his cheek.

"I still haven't figured out why Dillon showed up tonight," she said, seating herself across from him. Ignoring the urge to grill her uncle about his outing and the lipstick, she instead gave him a sly look. "You wouldn't have any ideas on that, would you?"

Louie smiled sheepishly, looking as guilty as a kid caught with his hand in a cookie jar.

"Uncle Louie, you didn't?"

His eyes widened with false innocence. "Didn't what?"

"You did!" she groaned. "You set me up again."

"Now, hon. Don't jump to—"

"How could you? After all the times I've asked you not to. Don't you understand? It's embarrassing...especially with Dillon. He's my boss!"

Louie took a hasty drink of the chocolate, then gave a huge yawn that Adrienne knew was fake. "Could we discuss this tomorrow, hon? I'm pretty bushed."

Without waiting for her to reply, he shoved his chair back and hurried out of the room, leaving Adrienne alone with her thoughts.

Her uncle meant no harm, she told herself. And Dillon wasn't the sort of man who could be easily manipulated unless he wanted to be. The more she thought about the evening, the more she realized just how much attention he'd paid to Kristen. With the exception of their kiss, everything—the movies, the hamburgers, the teasing—was geared to please a child, not the child's mother.

"Of course," she whispered, as understanding dawned on her. Dillon had been there when Jack had called to cancel his weekend outing. Was it possible that he had tried, in his own way, to make up for Jack's insensitivity? And if he had, why would he do such a thing?

A warm glow started near her heart and spread throughout her insides. The extra attention he'd paid Kristen, the gentleness and understanding he'd shown, was something she couldn't easily dismiss.

But neither could she dismiss their parting kiss. That part of the evening certainly hadn't been for Kristen.

If she was right—if he was the type of man who would give up his evening to somehow make up for the disappointment he knew Kristen had experienced, Adrienne could easily fall in love with Dillon Reynolds.

CHAPTER EIGHT

WHEN ADRIENNE ENTERED the club on Tuesday morning, the first person she saw was Eva.

"Guess what?" The waitress blurted, grinning from ear to ear.

Smiling, Adrienne answered, "What?" She'd noticed that Eva had seemed preoccupied and depressed for several days. It was a relief to see her in a happier mood.

Eva leaned over, and in her low, throaty voice, whispered, "I got a raise."

Adrienne's smile faltered. "A raise? When...how?"

"Mr. Franklin just told me." Eva beamed. "Isn't that great?"

Adrienne nodded, managing to hang on to the facsimile of a smile. For a few more minutes, she listened to Eva talk about her sick husband, then she excused herself and hurried toward the stairs.

When she reached the second floor and peered into Franklin's office, she saw that he was talking on the phone. She hesitated only a moment before she marched inside and shut the door behind her.

He glanced up and frowned, but motioned for her to be seated. Within minutes, he hung up the receiver.

"You look like you're about to explode. What's wrong?"

"I know it's really none of my business, but I just ran into Eva. She said you gave her a raise."

Franklin shifted uneasily in his chair and glanced down at some papers. "Just a small one," he said.

Adrienne drew in a deep, frustrated breath. "Does Dillon know? Did he approve it?" When Franklin shook his head, Adrienne groaned. "I know you weren't at the management meeting, but he must have talked to you afterward about what he told everyone."

Franklin looked away. "I know what he said, but Eva's husband has to have surgery, and he won't be able to go back to work for at least six weeks afterward. It was either give her a raise or see her start looking for another job. There are special circumstances that warrant special considerations. Besides, we need to keep our good employees."

Something in his tone put Adrienne on the alert. A feeling of dread washed over her. "Is Eva the only one?"

Again Franklin lowered his gaze to his desktop. "Not exactly."

"What do you mean?"

"Mick got an offer from a club in New Orleans, so I made a counteroffer to keep him."

Adrienne gripped the arms of her chair. "What kind of counteroffer?"

Franklin shrugged. "Fifty percent of the pro-shop profits."

Adrienne's fingers tightened even more. She didn't believe for one minute that Mick had received an offer from New Orleans or any other club, for that matter. Knowing the crafty golf pro, she figured he had sized up the situation between Dillon and Franklin and had grabbed at the opportunity to carve out more of the so-called pie for himself.

Adrienne wanted to shake Franklin, to tell him that Mick had played him for a fool. But one look at his pale face and she realized Franklin already knew he'd been manipulated.

"I'd appreciate it if you wouldn't tell Dillon just yet," he said. "At least not until I have a chance to talk with him."

Adrienne sighed. She didn't like being put in the middle—again—but she didn't relish being the one to break the news to Dillon, either. She finally shook her head and rose to her feet. "I won't," she said. "But you'd better tell him soon, before Mick Starky or someone else does."

"No one knows about this but you, and Mick won't say anything. He gave me his word."

On her way back to her own office, Adrienne wondered how Dillon would react. He wasn't going to like this latest development one bit. She'd seen how hard he'd worked over the past two weeks, and knew the kind of hours he was putting in to save Twin Oaks. As sure as the sun rose in the east and set in the west, she knew he wouldn't put up with any moves made behind his back. She figured that the cocky golf pro might find that he had manipulated himself right out of a job.

And Franklin? Adrienne could only hope that this latest catastrophe wouldn't drive a larger wedge between father and son.

WITH UNSEEING EYES, Franklin stared into space after Adrienne left and concentrated on trying to breathe. He'd just taken a pill, so the tightness in his chest should have eased up by now. Maybe he needed to take another one.

He grimaced, wondering just how upset Dillon was going to be with him. He shouldn't have interfered. He'd promised Dillon he wouldn't. So why had he?

For the same reason you won't give in and retire like the doctors suggested. Because you're an old, stubborn fool.

Just the thought of retiring caused the pain in his chest to sharpen. He broke out in a cold sweat. Reaching into his coat pocket, he retrieved a small plastic bottle and uncapped it. He shook out another pill and placed it into his mouth.

Unlike many of his contemporaries, he dreaded the thought of never coming in to the office again. He liked to feel needed, to feel important. Twin Oaks was the one thing in his life that he had halfway succeeded at ... until lately. Lord knows, he'd been a a poor husband and a failure as a father. His life was his work.

The pill seemed to be taking effect and the pressure in his chest eased up somewhat. Franklin shoved back his chair and stood up carefully. Maybe if he went home and took a nap for a couple of hours, he'd feel even better. He glanced at his watch. Myrna would be heading out for the beauty shop for her weekly appointment. If he went home now and slept for an hour or so, she wouldn't know and wouldn't worry.

Rest. That's all he needed. Just a little rest and he would be fine.

FOR THE NEXT HOUR, Adrienne stayed in her office and occupied herself with returning phone messages left by people wanting to book various functions.

In between calls, she worried—about Dillon, and about Franklin's latest bombshell. There wasn't a heck of a lot she could do about Franklin, but his son was another matter, one she would have to deal with.

When all the calls had been made and she was left with no more excuses for staying holed up in her office, she took a deep breath and headed toward the door. Just the thought of facing Dillon after Friday night set her heart racing.

Falling for the boss was the oldest taboo there was in the business world, and probably one of the dumbest things she'd ever done.

After worrying for two days, she'd finally concluded that just because she'd fallen for the man didn't mean she had to act like a fool. After all, she was a grown woman, well able to control her wayward emotions. And her falling for him didn't necessarily mean he returned the feelings. Oh, he desired her, she was sure of that. But she doubted very seriously if his feelings went any deeper.

Adrienne straightened her shoulders and opened her door—and suddenly found herself almost nose to nose with the devil himself. She yelped in surprise.

"Sorry," he said, reaching out to steady her. "I didn't mean to startle you."

Adrienne swallowed, then cleared her throat. "I—I was just on my way down to the dining room."

Dillon didn't step back nor did he release his hold on her arm. For a moment Adrienne wondered where all her hard-won logic had disappeared to. And for a moment she feared, yet hoped, that he would close the small distance that separated them.

He released her suddenly, as if she were charged with an electrical current.

"If you've got a few minutes, I'd like to talk to you. In fact..." he glanced at his watch "...why don't we talk over lunch?"

When they reached the bottom of the stairs, Adrienne turned left, intending to go into the dining room. Dillon grabbed her arm. "I'd rather go somewhere else." He urged her to the right toward the double front doors. "Somewhere a little more private," he added, "where we won't be disturbed or overheard."

Alone...together...private.

Adrienne swallowed the sudden lump in her throat and followed him to his car. The sun was shining brightly and the chilly morning had warmed considerably. Adrienne drew in a breath of the clean, pine-scented air.

Just a business luncheon, that's all he'd meant. She'd be silly to think anything else. He probably wanted to review the list of staff members he planned to lay off. She slid into his car and fastened her seat belt. It was totally ridiculous to think he might want anything else...like an intimate lunch with just the two of them.

Too nervous to do anything but watch the passing scenery, Adrienne didn't ask where they were going. Several blocks later, he totally surprised her by pulling into the parking lot of a well-known catering shop.

"Be right back," he said.

When he returned to the car a few minutes later, he was carrying a basket. "Lunch," he offered as an explanation. "One of the members told me this place is great and that I might want to try and steal their chef."

He laughed. "Don't look so horrified. I was just kidding. Our cooks are doing fine for now. Besides, we can't afford to hire a chef until after that bank note is paid."

Did "we" include her? she wondered, glancing out the window. Or was he simply using the word loosely, meaning the club?

Adrienne grew uneasy just thinking about the logic of the situation. If they couldn't afford to hire a chef, how could they afford to keep on an assistant food and beverage manager? And if it came down to choosing between her and Joe Blount, she knew she didn't stand a chance. Joe had all the credentials and the seniority.

It wouldn't matter that she'd worked her butt off the past few years or that she did a better job than Joe.

When the car stopped, Adrienne looked around. The place Dillon had picked for their impromptu picnic was a quiet, secluded roadside park bordering a small lake, a place she was achingly familiar with. She opened the car door and stepped out into the warmth of the sun.

Dillon slid out of the car and, for a moment, watched her walk slowly to the edge of the water. The filmy, flower-patterned skirt she wore fluttered in the gentle breeze, giving him teasing glimpses of her long legs.

He'd told himself they needed privacy, away from wagging tongues and curious ears. He didn't want an audience for what he planned to talk about, and she needed to be prepared for what was coming.

But as he looked at her now, discussing his father's health and his continuous interference was the last thing he wanted to do. For a fleeting moment, he wondered if subconsciously he'd just sought an excuse to have her all to himself.

You're playing a dangerous game, Dillon, old man.

He forced his gaze away and reached inside the car for the picnic basket. *Business,* he reminded himself. *Keep your mind on business.*

"I'd forgotten how beautiful and peaceful it is here," Adrienne said, still staring out across the lake, which was surrounded by thick woods.

Ducks swam in the lake, and an occasional splash from a white perch stirred up the water. The sounds of nature were all around, and as always, she found it hard to believe that such a serene paradise existed just miles from the teeming city of Houston.

Dillon approached, carrying the basket. "You've been to this particular spot before then."

She nodded. "Years ago, when we first moved into Twin Oaks and Kristen was small. I used to bring her to feed the ducks. She loved chasing them...."

Dillon saw the look of despair that shadowed her face. In that brief moment, he felt her suffering, felt how painful it must be knowing that the same little girl who once chased ducks would never be able to walk or run again. And how much more painful, knowing the reason why.

He set the basket on a wooden picnic table and walked over to her. He had the overwhelming urge to reach out and pull her close, to somehow try and comfort her. Instead, he crossed his arms against his chest. Touching her was too dangerous. He'd learned that on Saturday night.

"When I was a kid, I used to sneak off and come here every chance I'd get," he said. "Kept a fishing pole hidden over near that old bald cypress tree." He pointed across the water. "Then one day, Dad followed me." He shrugged. "From then on, it was off limits."

Adrienne tilted her head to look at him. "Why? Too dangerous by yourself?"

Dillon chuckled. "Nope. All those times I sneaked off, I was supposed to be working. Dad was always giving me odd jobs to do around the club."

His story was rewarded with a sweet smile. "Like today?" she teased.

Dillon frowned. Then it dawned on him what she meant. "I wish it was as simple as that," he said.

Her smile faded. "Why are we here? You said you wanted to talk about something."

He nodded. "I do, but let's talk while we eat. I'm starving."

They both returned to the picnic table. He motioned for her to be seated. When he opened the basket and pulled out a bottle of wine that the caterer had furnished, he suddenly remembered her aversion to alcohol and he groaned.

"What's wrong?"

He held out the bottle. "Sorry. I forgot you don't drink."

She gave him a curious look. "I don't drink often," she said. "But I'd hardly classify an occasional glass of wine as drinking."

"I just thought that since...I mean, you did say you don't keep liquor in your home." Dillon busied himself pouring the wine and hoped she'd accept his explanation without probing deeper as to why he would even mention it. He handed her a glass.

She took a sip, her gaze never leaving his face. "I don't keep it in my home because of Kristen. Part of my ex-husband's problem is... alcoholism. He was never abusive, but..." She shrugged. "He did get sullen and short on patience when he drank. Kristen learned to associate drinking with her father's bad moods."

Dillon couldn't help himself. He reached out and covered her hand with his. "You don't have to explain," he said. "It's really none of my business."

For several seconds she continued to stare at him. "Why did you come by Saturday night?"

Her question caught him completely off guard. No matter how hard he'd tried to convince himself that his visit had been strictly for Kristen's sake, it was the same question he'd asked himself during the long restless night he'd spent after leaving her house.

Dillon started to pull back his hand, but Adrienne turned hers up and quickly locked her fingers with his. She squeezed.

"It was because of Kristen, wasn't it?"

Such trust was glowing in her dark eyes that he couldn't have told her a lie even if he'd wanted to. He nodded. "Partly."

She gave him a puzzled smile.

"I called that day to speak to you and Kristen answered. She told me she'd been grounded and I guessed the reason why." Dillon ran his forefinger along her jawline, as if he was caressing a piece of fine silk. "I just figured you both could use a little diversion."

Adrienne closed her eyes, and for a moment allowed herself the luxury of enjoying Dillon's touch, as well as the satisfaction of knowing that she hadn't misjudged his motives. When she opened her eyes, he was but a breath away, and her pulse began to race.

"Ah, Adrienne," he whispered. "Kristen was only part of the reason. You were the other part. Feel what you do to me." He placed her hand over his heart. It was pounding almost as hard as her own. "Each time I get near you, I can't seem to think straight."

Adrienne shifted their hands to her own thudding heart and was pleased when his eyes clouded with desire. "Neither can I," she whispered.

As she held his hand between the soft, upper swells of her breasts, a jolt of sizzling heat shot through Dillon. He slowly slid his hand over her breasts and pulled her closer.

Her lips tasted of sweet wine and desire. The feel of her soft, full breasts crushed against his chest made him groan, and a hunger began to grow deep within him, a hunger that he knew wouldn't be satisfied with just kisses.

He slid his hand down and then up again, beneath the delicate cotton sweater she wore. At the first touch of her satiny skin, he took the kiss deeper, plunging his tongue into the honeyed depths of her mouth.

The throaty sound she made was a cross between a groan of desire and one of frustration, and she returned the kiss like a starving woman feasting on a luxurious meal.

Her hands kneaded his sinewy back, then slid up to his neck, urging him on, begging for more. Dillon pulled away only enough to slide his hand back to her breasts. Through the sheer lace of her bra, they felt full and ripe, and he flicked his thumb back and forth over her pebble-hard nipples, wanting nothing more than to replace his thumb with his mouth. Just the thought of suckling her made his already hard manhood throb insistently.

When Adrienne suddenly jerked free, it took Dillon a second to realize why. Still holding her close, he glanced over his shoulder. Another car had pulled up alongside his, and it was the sound of the door slamming that had alerted her to the intrusion. A short, stocky man was heading their way, a casting rod in one hand and a tackle box in the other.

Since his back was toward the man, Dillon knew that their embrace looked as innocent as a simple kiss. He eased Adrienne away. Her lips were kiss-swollen and her face was flushed—whether from embarrassment or passion, he wasn't quite sure.

"It's okay," he whispered. "He didn't see anything."

The color in her cheeks darkened, but she remained silent as she scooted away from him and picked up her wineglass.

"Hey, folks." As the older man approached their table, he raised his fishing rod and saluted with a grin. "Nice day for a picnic," he said, walking slowly past them. "Supposed to rain tomorrow, so thought I'd get in a little fishing."

Dillon acknowledged the friendly man's greeting with a nod, but remained seated.

He watched until the old fellow disappeared around a stand of trees. When he turned back to Adrienne, she had removed a small checkered tablecloth from the basket and was spreading it out on the table.

Busywork.

Dillon sighed, knowing she must be feeling embarrassed. When she reached inside the basket again, he stilled her hand with his own. "I'm sorry. I got a little carried away. Next time I'll make sure we won't be disturbed."

Next time?

Adrienne gave him what she knew was probably a poor attempt at a smile and he released her hand.

After Dillon had unpacked the basket, she tried to concentrate on what he was saying. Between bites of fried chicken, potato salad and baked beans, he told her about his plans for the following day.

"Even though the layoffs are a start, I'm afraid they won't be enough. The annual member-guest tournament is coming up next month, and I'm hoping that will help, too. Pro-shop sales are always high during the tournament, and according to Mick, we've already got more golf teams signed up than ever before."

Adrienne almost choked on the last bite of chicken she'd taken. No wonder Mick had given his word to Franklin to keep quiet! Another thought struck her. What if Mick had been telling the truth about a job in New Orleans. What if it was true? What if he had already accepted the offer without telling anyone? And what if he'd decided to play his present position for every dime he could get, planning to make off with the extra cash from the tournament sales as soon as it was over? Of course, she had no proof; this was strictly speculation. And even if she could prove her suspicions, she'd promised Franklin she wouldn't tell Dillon.

Adrienne took a sip of wine to wash down the chicken and the sour taste that thinking about Mick had left in her mouth. Once again, Franklin had put her in an untenable position.

"One thing still worries me," Dillon continued. "My father won't let go. He's still trying to pull strings behind my back."

Adrienne swallowed hard, careful to keep her eyes directed anywhere but at Dillon.

"But what worries me even more is that I'm almost positive there's something wrong with him, that he's sick."

At that, Adrienne shot him an anxious glance. "I was beginning to wonder if I was the only one who had noticed."

"Oh, I noticed all right. But when I try to talk with him, he changes the subject or just ignores me."

Adrienne sighed. "I know. He does the same thing to me." She reached for a napkin and blotted her mouth. "What about your mother? Have you talked with her? Maybe she knows something."

Dillon shook his head. "She would be the last person he would tell if he's ill. He's always tried to shield her from the more unpleasant realities of life." Dillon began to put the lids back on the containers of uneaten food. "That's why when she called and literally begged me to come home, I knew things had to be pretty bad."

He began to pack the leftovers back into the basket. "I made an appointment with Dad's doctor for this afternoon," he said. "Hopefully, I can get some answers."

During the drive back to the club, Adrienne was torn between trying to cope with the sizzling tension between her and Dillon, and worrying about Franklin and the club.

Each time Dillon looked at her, she could feel the air almost crackle with desire, could feel a hunger deep within herself crying out, demanding to be satisfied. And each time she looked at him, she knew he could see that same desire mirrored in her own eyes.

Hoping she could ignore the traitorous feelings and maintain some kind of control, Adrienne gazed out the window and tried to think of something else. Impossible, she decided, almost groaning out loud when she thought of having to work side by side with him through the rest of the afternoon. It wouldn't take the staff long to pick up on the tension between them. Even now they were probably speculating on where he had taken her and why.

Adrienne suddenly frowned, remembering the promise she'd made to Franklin. She chanced a look at Dillon. How would he react if he found out she'd known all along about Mick's deal with Franklin? She shivered, knowing the answer.

THAT EVENING, as Dillon hurried toward the conference room, he glanced at his watch. Ten after six, dammit! His first council meeting and he was late, thanks to the afternoon traffic. Still, it couldn't be helped. And he was glad that he'd had the chance to talk with his father's doctor.

Later, he thought. He'd have to think about what the doctor had said later, after the council meeting.

Dillon entered the conference room and closed the door behind him. The president of the twelve-member council, Mitchell Kelly, stopped talking and grinned.

"Ah, Dillon. Come on in."

Everyone seated at the table turned to stare.

Mitchell waved his hand toward the empty chair near the end of the table. "I think by now you've met everyone, haven't you?"

Dillon nodded and slipped into the chair. He glanced down. On the table in front of him was a binder with his name on the front.

"Now where were we?" Mitchell asked, more to himself than to anyone there. "Oh, yes. We were just reviewing the minutes from our last meeting."

Dillon opened the binder to the minutes. For the next fifteen minutes he listened as the council went over and finally approved them. Then each committee chairperson reviewed minutes of any committee meetings held during the previous month.

Finally they got around to the finance-committee report, something Dillon was particularly interested in.

When Ted Jamison began to speak, Dillon studied him, trying to analyze just what it was that made him distrust the middle-aged man. With his dark blond hair sprinkled with just a hint of gray and his snappy clothes, which Dillon recognized immediately were custom designed, he looked like what he was—a successful banker. No wonder the council had elected him finance-committee chairperson.

But something about him was too smooth, too calculating, Dillon thought. No matter how hard he tried, he simply didn't like or trust the man.

"If you'll look in your binders, you will find the list of our long-term goals." Ted Jamison waited until each council member had the list in hand. "As you can see, we're well on schedule with the improvements and purchases."

Dillon scanned the extensive list and sucked in his breath. No wonder the club was going bankrupt and had cash-flow problems! Each piece of equipment, from expensive tractors to walk-in freezers, was being replaced systematically.

Jamison continued, "As you can see, the next items we intend to purchase are fifteen new golf carts. Now, if there are no further questions—"

"I have a question," Dillon said. "Actually, it's more of a statement." He could tell Jamison didn't like being interrupted, but he didn't give a damn. "After reviewing the financial statements of this club, there's no way we can afford fifteen new golf carts . . . or anything else that's listed. At least, not for a while."

"Of course we can," Jamison blustered. "Besides, this list was approved by the council over a year ago. It's a done deed and we will proceed on schedule."

Dillon stood, turning his full attention to Jamison. "Not unless this council is ready for Twin Oaks to go bankrupt and end up being foreclosed on by your bank."

A murmur of surprise rippled throughout the room. Everyone started talking at the same time, and Mitchell Kelly pounded his gavel, trying to bring order out of the sudden chaos.

When the noise finally died down, Mitchell gave Dillon a measured look. "I think you and I need to have a talk before this goes any further. And until we do, I'm tabling the long-term goals."

"Now just a minute!" Jamison stood abruptly. "My committee approved that list." He glared at Dillon. "And no upstart should be allowed to come in and make wild speculations . . . or accusations."

Mitchell Kelly took a deep breath. "Nevertheless, I'm tabling the list for now, Ted. Franklin still owns the club and he brought Dillon in to run it. I have to trust that Franklin knew what he was doing."

Dillon figured that if Jamison was smart, he'd back off. His father was loved and respected by every person in the room, and there was no way Jamison could dispute Mitchell's logic without casting aspersions on Franklin.

With a sour look of disapproval, Jamison sat down. But Dillon figured they hadn't heard the last from him . . . not yet. It was plain that Jamison had ulterior motives for what he'd been doing . . . but what were those motives?

CHAPTER NINE

SIPPING WHAT HE GUESSED was at least his fourth cup of coffee, Dillon sat on his small patio and watched pale pink hues spread across the eastern skyline, heralding the dawn of another day.

Surgery is the best solution, but your father refuses to even discuss it. If he doesn't at least slow down, he's going to get into some serious trouble.

The doctor had been frank with him. "I've known your family for a long time," he had said. "Franklin can be very stubborn, but I think he will listen to you. I have to tell you, I'm really worried...."

The words still haunted Dillon, as they had during the long tortuous night. But what the hell could he do?

After the council meeting, it had been well past ten o'clock before he'd been able to check out of the hotel and move his sparse belongings into the condo he'd finally found time to rent two days earlier. Even with the furniture he'd had delivered from storage, the place looked pretty empty, but it was worth it for the privacy and the view, he decided.

He'd spent the remainder of the night tossing and turning, thinking about the problems at Twin Oaks, about the council meeting . . . but most of all, about his father. Somehow he had to come up with a way to force his dad to slow down.

With a flick of the wrist, Dillon threw the remaining dregs in his cup onto a nearby bush and stood. He could try talking to his father. "Sure you could," he grumbled. Hell, they couldn't even discuss the weather without disagreeing. And lately his father's moodiness seemed to be worse than ever.

Dillon slid open the glass doors and headed for the bathroom. There was only one thing he *could* do and he didn't like the thought of it. And neither would his father. Nor would Adrienne, he thought, staring into the mirror above the bathroom sink and rubbing his whiskered jaw.

Two hours later, freshly shaved, showered and dressed, Dillon unlocked the front doors of the club and entered. He punched in the code to shut off the burglar alarm and headed for the kitchen. Within minutes after he'd unlocked the back door, the kitchen staff began arriving.

As Dillon listened to the *thunk* of the time clock being punched and the good-natured banter among the employees, he felt as if the weight of the world was balancing on his shoulders.

On top of everything else, after today, almost one-third of the serving staff would be jobless.

That the council had readily agreed with his decision last night to cut the staff should have lessened his burden.

It didn't.

And reminding himself what he'd told Adrienne, that for the sake of all, a few had to be sacrificed, didn't make it any easier.

Dillon glanced at his watch and took a deep breath. The sooner he got started, the sooner he could get it over with.

"Mr. Reynolds?"

Dillon turned, to find Eva coming toward him at her usual brisk pace. She stopped. With her hands planted firmly on her hips, she tilted her head up to one side and gave him the once-over. "What happened to you? You look like hell."

In spite of his mood, Dillon felt a grin tug at his lips. The Swedish woman with her gravelly voice was often too blunt and outspoken, but she had a heart of gold and worked like a demon. The members adored her and so did he.

"Rough night," he answered. "Couldn't sleep."

At that, she raised her eyebrows and pursed her lips. "Sounds to me like you need a good woman to warm your bed. I'd volunteer, but you're a little young for me. Besides—" she gave him a teasing wink and laughed "—my old man wouldn't like it."

The tug at his lips turned into a full-blown smile. Most of the staff was still a little standoffish when they were around him, but not Eva. "Other than deflating my ego, was there anything else you needed?"

She grinned. "Oh, yah. I wondered if your father is coming in today."

Dillon shrugged. "As far as I know."

"Do you know when?"

"Probably around ten, as usual. Why? Is there something I can help you with?"

Eva hesitated a moment, as if trying to decide whether to say more. "When I talked with him day before yesterday about my raise, I forgot to ask when it would start. Since this is the last day of this pay period, I wondered if it starts tomorrow."

Raise.

A sinking feeling of despair and anger washed through him. Years of being a manager had taught him to cover his emotions well, and with an effort that bordered on physical pain, Dillon was able to answer Eva in an almost normal voice. "I'm not sure about that. I'll check with him and let you know."

Seemingly satisfied for the moment, she nodded, then hurried back toward her station.

Dillon walked slowly toward the office, remembering how painstakingly he had gone over the new policies with his father. He should have known better, should have realized his father couldn't resist a hard-luck story.

Was Eva the only one he'd given a raise to? Dillon could feel a burning in his gut and he knew it had nothing to do with the quantity of coffee he'd consumed during the night. His father had to be stopped, for his own and for the club's sake, or everything Dillon was trying to do would be for nothing.

ADRIENNE WISHED she was anywhere but sitting across from Dillon in the small cramped office. With the dismissal of each employee on the list, her heart grew heavier. And from the looks of Dillon, she suspected he felt the same, only doubly so.

It was obvious that he'd had a rough night. The grapevine had it that he'd butted heads with Ted Jamison at the council meeting. But the defeated slump of his shoulders now was the result of a morning filled with telling people they no longer had a job.

There was something else eating at him, too, she sensed. Something he wouldn't or couldn't come to grips with, that had nothing to do with her, the council or the layoffs. But what?

When the waitress he'd just dismissed stood abruptly and hurried out of the room, Adrienne could tell that the young woman was near tears, and she felt like crying herself. She turned back to Dillon and saw the same pain reflected in his eyes.

"Does she have a family?" he asked. "Someone who can help her out for a while?"

"I'm not sure," Adrienne answered.

"Do you think you could find out?"

Adrienne nodded. "Of course," she answered, wishing she could say or do something to take that bleak look off his face.

"Damn, I hate this. If only I didn't have to..." Dillon sighed and shook his head. "How many more?" he asked, his voice low and rough.

"Only two."

"Thank God." He glanced at his watch. "It's past eleven. Has my father come in yet?"

Suddenly it hit her. Whatever else was eating at Dillon had to do with Franklin. Adrienne slowly shook her head. "The last time I checked, Joanne said she hadn't seen him. Speaking of your father, were you able to talk with his doctor yesterday?"

Dillon nodded. "As I suspected, Dad has a heart condition. The signs are all there—the sweating, the paleness, the irritability. The doctor said he had suggested surgery." Dillon grimaced, then gave a humorless laugh that made Adrienne wince. "My father thinks he's indestructible."

"What about medication? I've seen him take pills. Won't that help?"

Dillon gave a defeated shrug. "I guess...if he would only slow down."

"Maybe if you talked with him. If his doctor feels he should have surgery, you need to..." Her voice trailed off and a heaviness settled beneath her breasts. Need to what? she asked silently. Force him to have surgery? Force him to slow down?

Adrienne sighed. No one knew better than she did that you couldn't force someone to do something they didn't want to, even if it was for their own good. How many times had she begged Jack to stop drinking?

"I'm sorry," she said softly. "It's really none of my business. I—I just care what happens to him."

Dillon shrugged. "There's nothing to be sorry about, and believe me, you didn't say anything that I haven't already thought about. I am going to try and talk with him about it, but he hasn't showed up yet."

"Maybe he's on the golf course."

"Hmm, maybe," Dillon said, and reached for the phone. He punched out a number. "Mick, did my father tee off this morning?" After a short silence, Dillon mumbled a frustrated curse, depressed the button and punched out another number. "Joanne? I want to know the minute my father shows up." He started to hang up the phone, then hesitated. "Joanne, are you still there? I also need the council minutes from the past two years, when you get a chance. Please."

Replacing the receiver, Dillon closed his eyes, reached up and rubbed the back of his neck. Adrienne wanted to go to him and massage his stiff muscles, to somehow help ease the tremendous strain he was under. If only there was *something* she could do.

She was still watching him when he opened his eyes and looked directly at her.

"Thanks... for everything," he said softly.

"You're welcome," she whispered, wondering if it was possible to actually feel it if he reached through space and caressed her with a look. Surely, things like that didn't happen in real life.

He cleared his throat. "I guess you'd better go find the next one on the list. Let's just get this over with."

Adrienne slowly got to her feet. At the door, she hesitated but didn't turn around. "If you're concerned about your father, you could call your mother. She might know where he is." She chanced a quick glance, but he kept his eyes trained on the paper before him.

"No. She'd just worry if he wasn't there."

Two HOURS LATER, Adrienne seated herself at a small table in the dining room.

"You eating by yourself?"

She nodded and attempted a smile when she glanced up at Eva.

The waitress held out a pitcher. "Iced tea?"

"Yes, please."

Picking up a glass, Eva filled it, then stuck a wedge of lemon on the rim. "The buffet is good today," she said. "The corn-and-clam chowder is delicious, and make sure you try the chicken."

"Thanks, Eva. I will." As the waitress bustled off to seat a group of members standing in the doorway, Adrienne glanced across to the other side of the busy dining room, toward the door to the Governor's Room.

When the last person on the layoff list had been dealt with, Dillon had asked her to set up an emergency lunch meeting between the executive council and himself. An hour had passed since Mitchell Kelly, the current president, three other council members and Dillon had entered the small, private dining room. Once they'd been served, she'd heard Dillon give Eva firm instructions that they weren't to be disturbed. Then he'd closed the doors.

Wondering what was going on, Adrienne sighed and slid out of her chair. She headed for the buffet line, helped herself to a bowl of chowder, then returned to her table.

She had just finished her meal and was eyeing the lavish pastries artfully displayed on the buffet table when she noticed Franklin, his face rigid and flushed, hurrying toward the Governor's Room. Within seconds, the council members, looking harried and flustered, filed out, leaving Dillon and Franklin behind.

Out of the corner of her eye, Adrienne saw Mitchell Kelly making a beeline toward her. Alarms went off in her head. Something was wrong.

"I have to leave, so could you please go to the Governor's Room right away? All hell is about to break loose, and I don't want those two left alone right now. I suggested—and Dillon agreed—that it might make things easier if a third party was present." Before she had time to question him, Mitchell turned on his heel and strode away.

Adrienne hurried toward the private dining room. The closer she got, the louder the muffled voices sounded. She rapped on the door, then opened it and entered.

Father and son were glaring at each other like two bulls. Franklin looked pale, and Dillon looked dangerous and determined. She quickly closed the door behind her. "Dillon? Franklin? What's going on here?"

Still scowling at his son, Franklin waved a hand toward Dillon. "Don't ask me, ask him. He seems to have all the god damn answers."

His bitter tone stunned Adrienne. She'd never known Franklin to raise his voice.

"Dillon?" She cautiously approached him. Laying her hand on his taut arm, she asked, "What's wrong?"

He continued to glower at his father. She could tell from the way his jaw was set and his hands kept clenching that he was having a hard time fighting for control. For a moment she wasn't sure he was going to answer her or even acknowledge her presence.

"Whatever the problem is," she said softly, evenly, "I'm sure it can be worked out. But not here." She squeezed his arm, willing him to at least look at her. "There are too many ears listening in the dining room. Couldn't we at least go upstairs to the office?"

After another tense moment, she felt the bunched-up muscles in his arm slowly relax. He took a deep breath, then sighed. "You're right." He glanced up at his father. "Well?"

Franklin still looked as puffed up as an old bullfrog, but he finally gave a curt nod, whirled around and stomped out of the room.

Adrienne was well aware that every eye in the dining room was watching as they passed through. Not a word was spoken as they all marched up the stairs. On her way into Franklin's office, she gave Joanne strict instructions that they weren't to be disturbed unless there was a dire emergency.

Adrienne closed the door firmly behind her. Franklin lowered himself stiffly into his chair, refusing to look at either Dillon or her. Two chairs faced Franklin's desk. Dillon threw himself down on one and Adrienne eased into the other.

She glanced warily from one man to the other and waited. Silent seconds stretched into uneasy minutes. Neither seemed willing to make the first move, and she felt like throttling both of them.

She finally glared at Dillon, willing him to say something. He turned toward her. For a moment he allowed her to see the pain reflected in his eyes. Then he turned away, and she detected a hint of a challenge in the way he stared at Franklin.

"Did you give Eva a raise?" The tone of his too soft, raspy voice was worse than if he'd yelled. Adrienne shivered.

Franklin looked up and thrust out his chin belligerently. "What if I did?"

"What else have you done behind my back?" Dillon snapped.

"Behind *your* back—!" Franklin shot up out of his chair. "You're one to talk, going to see my doctor, calling in the council and telling them God knows what. Well, let me tell you something, buddy boy. I'm not senile yet, and I still own this club. Council or no council, I can do anything I damn well please."

Dillon didn't budge, and in that same low voice that Adrienne found frightening, he said, "We had an agreement—an agreement that if I came back, I would run things as I see fit. You violated that agreement. Either you honor it now or I walk. And this time, I won't be back."

Adrienne couldn't believe what she was hearing. How could Dillon be so...so rigid? And to his own father, his own flesh and blood?

For interminable seconds, Franklin stood there, staring at Dillon. His face grew paler by the moment, and his eyes were a battlefield of emotion. When he finally spoke, his voice was one of defeat. "Okay... okay!" He slumped back into his chair. "You win. You win."

Adrienne felt as if she'd just seen a war-torn general surrender in humiliating defeat.

Franklin leaned forward, resting his elbows on his desk. He covered his face with his hands. "What do you want me to do?"

Drawing her eyes from Franklin, she swung her gaze to Dillon. Even before he answered, she sensed what was coming.

Dillon kept his eyes trained on his father. "Dad, please understand. I didn't want to do this—I still don't. But you've left me no choice." Several tense seconds passed, seconds in which Dillon had to keep telling himself that he was doing what he had to do.

If he doesn't at least slow down, he's going to get into some serious trouble.

It's for his own good, he reminded himself. Dillon sighed wearily. "I've already spoken to the council," he said. "And I want you to retire."

A painful knot lodged in Adrienne's throat. Her eyes stung as she tried to hold back tears. *No!* she wanted to cry out. *Your father loves this place. It's part of him. It's his life.*

Franklin slowly lowered his hands and stared bleakly at Dillon. "When?" he whispered.

"As of today," Dillon answered, his own voice a strained whisper.

Unable to fight back the tears any longer, Adrienne stood up, and without a word to either man, walked out of the office, closing the door firmly behind her.

Through a blur of pain, she saw Joanne's questioning look, but she ignored it and headed straight for the ladies' room. Once inside, she locked the door, then crumpled against it, shaking with silent sobs. All she could think about was how Franklin had given her a chance and hired her when no one else would, how he and Myrna had made her and Kristen part of their family, how Twin Oaks wouldn't be the same without Franklin there.

And Dillon. What a fool she had been to think he was different! How could he humiliate his own father like that? And how could she have fallen in love—again— with a man who would turn on his own flesh and blood, hurt his own family?

Adrienne finally pushed herself away from the door. She couldn't stay holed up in the bathroom the rest of the day. There was work to be done. Besides, thinking about what had happened and brooding about it wouldn't change things.

Just before quitting time, Dillon cornered her in the kitchen. "We need to talk," he said.

Adrienne carefully avoided eye contact. "Can it wait until tomorrow?" Pretending to be preoccupied, she continued scanning the banquet sheet for a function scheduled later that evening. "I have to pick Kristen up from therapy."

"I—I need to explain—"

"Mr. Reynolds."

Dillon turned abruptly toward the approaching waitress. "What?" he snapped. "Can't you see I'm busy?"

"Sorry. There's a phone call for you on line one, and a prospective member waiting for you in the office. Also, Joanne said to tell you she left the council-meeting minutes on your desk."

Dillon swore beneath his breath. "Okay, okay. Sorry I was so abrupt. I'll be right there."

Adrienne could feel his eyes willing her to look at him. She cursed her hand for shaking as she tacked the banquet sheet back onto the bulletin board. Dillon turned on his heel and strode out of the room.

Calling herself a coward, Adrienne made a hasty exit in turn, breathing a sigh of relief only when she was safe in her car.

ASPIRIN. If she didn't get some aspirin soon, and if Kristen didn't stop her incessant chatter, Adrienne thought she might start screaming. Her head felt as if someone was pounding on it with a sledgehammer, and all the way home, Kristen had talked nonstop about the coming weekend, wondering and worrying about where her father was going to take her.

The minute she stepped inside the house, Adrienne headed for the bathroom.

"Kristen, have you got homework?" she called out while she searched the medicine cabinet for some aspirin. She'd put it on yesterday's grocery list for her uncle to buy, she was certain.

Kristen wheeled up to the door and groaned. "Do I have to do it now? I'm hungry."

No aspirin. Adrienne slammed the cabinet door. Ignoring Kristen's whining, she asked, "Did Uncle Louie say where he was going?"

Kristen shook her head. "All he said was that he'd left a casserole in the refrigerator and he wouldn't be in till late. Can we eat now?"

"In a minute," she answered absently. "Go start on your homework." Maybe he'd left the aspirin in the kitchen.

Ignoring another groan from her daughter, Adrienne headed down the hallway. After searching several cabinets, she finally spied the bottle of tablets sitting on the window ledge above the kitchen sink. She shook out two and was washing them down with a glass of water when the phone rang. She winced at the loud sound, then snatched up the receiver.

"Hello," she snapped, unable to quell the irritation she felt.

"Did I catch you at a bad time?"

"Oh . . . Franklin. Ah, no, no you didn't." Adrienne pulled the phone cord across the kitchen and sank into a chair at the table. "How—how are you?" Immediately, she kicked herself for asking such a stupid question. How did she expect him to be?

"Tired," he answered. "I've had better days, to say the least."

"Franklin . . . I'm sorry. I didn't—"

"Dillon only did what he had to do. I called because I didn't get a chance to talk with you before I left. I don't want you holding this against him. I knew it was coming. I guess I just didn't want to face it. And hell, who knows? Maybe it's for the best. I still own the majority of stock, and now I can just kick back and enjoy life a little. Let someone else worry for a change." He paused, and with a chuckle that Adrienne could tell was forced, he said, "Myrna thinks it's great. She's already making all kinds of plans."

"That's wonderful," Adrienne said, trying to inject some enthusiasm into her voice. "I—I just want you to know how much I appreciate everything you've done for me . . . and Kristen. If I can do anything . . . anything at all." Adrienne felt her throat grow tight and she swallowed. "Just call," she finished on a whisper.

"I'll be fine. You take care of Kristen and don't be such a workaholic."

"I won't," she promised. When she heard the click on the other end, Adrienne slowly hung up the phone.

Later, with Kristen fed and the dishes washed, Adrienne reached up and rubbed her temple. The aspirin had only dulled her headache. A long soak in a hot tub of water might make her feel better, she decided.

As she walked down the short hallway, she stopped at Kristen's door and peeked inside. Kristen had fallen asleep with a history book lying open beside her on the bed.

Adrienne tiptoed over to the bed, and for a moment, stared down at her daughter. Even in her sleep, she looked tired, the telltale exhaustion of her physical therapy evident in her pinched features, in tightness around her lips.

Adrienne bent down and removed the history book. She pulled the blanket over Kristen and placed a light kiss on her forehead. Turning off the bedside lamp, she tiptoed out of the room, careful to leave the door slightly ajar in case Kristen needed her during the night.

When she turned toward her own bedroom, she heard the faint but distinct sound of a knock at the front door. She closed her eyes briefly, thinking with longing of the hot bath she'd hoped to take.

With a sigh, she pivoted and retraced her steps to the living room. It was probably Uncle Louie, she decided. He'd more than likely forgotten his keys again. As a precaution, she stopped at the window and peeked out. She drew in a swift breath of disbelief.

Of all people, why was Dillon at her front door at this time of night? She didn't want to see him, didn't want him here. Not yet. Not until she could wade through the confusing mix of emotions she was experiencing. Squaring her shoulders, she strode to the door and jerked it open. "What do you want?" she asked with chilly politeness.

"I need to talk to you."

"About what?"

"I'd rather do it inside."

When he'd come in, Adrienne shut the door and turned her back to it. She leaned against it and crossed her arms against her breasts. "Well?"

Dillon reached up and rubbed his neck. "I—I want to explain about this afternoon, about my father," he said, his voice sounding even more weary than he looked.

"What's to explain?" she retorted. "Just because you banned him from his own club, the club that he built from the ground up." She laughed, a short, sarcastic sound. "Why, I can't imagine what you'd have to explain. Who cares if you humiliated the man—your own flesh and blood, I might add. And who cares that he's not well? Certainly not you, his only son."

"Is that what you really think of me?" Dillon's hoarse voice was filled with pain, and he smiled sadly. "I know how it looked, and even though I don't necessarily like the things my father does..." His lips tightened into an angry, determined line. "I do love him," he said. "My mother, too. I care about both of them. I *had* to force him to retire, for his own sake...for his health. It was the only way."

His explanation had the same effect on her anger as a pin popping a balloon.

"I—I..." She drew a deep, ragged breath, remembering that he'd wanted to explain and had tried to, earlier at the club. "Dillon, I'm sorry. I didn't realize... I had no right to—"

He shook his head. "Don't," he said. He reached out and gently pulled her into his arms. "Don't apologize. You needed to blow off steam."

She felt his warm, moist lips brush against her forehead, her cheek, her neck. Then, with a tenderness that made her ache, she felt his mouth cover hers with just enough pressure to make her yearn for more.

Reveling in his scent—of maleness and the spicy cologne he preferred—Adrienne breathed deeply, clinging to his broad shoulders. She returned the kiss with a fervor that she hadn't realized she possessed.

He reached down and pulled her hips firmly against his. He was hard and ready, and when he thrust against her—once, twice, a third time—a shaft of longing shot through her, making her moan with need.

Dillon's tongue slid across her lips, seeking entrance to the secrets beyond. Even as she readily opened her mouth, giving him access, Adrienne shoved her fingers through his thick hair, cupping the back of his head and luxuriating in the rich, full texture. Her own tongue met his in a fierce, heated duel of passion, until finally, with a gasp born of desire and frustration, Dillon pulled away.

"Oh, God," he whispered. "You feel so good." He tasted her again, then nuzzled her cheek. "Too good," he growled near her ear. "We have to stop. Much more of this and I won't be held responsible for the consequences. Besides," he said gravely, "we still need to talk."

Feeling deliciously vulnerable and a little dazed, Adrienne pulled her head back and stared up at him. "Don't look at me like that," he begged.

She turned her head to the side and laid it against his shoulder. She could still feel the physical evidence of his desire pressed against her hip, and she could feel the heavy thudding of his heart beneath her hand splayed across his chest. A thrill of feminine conquest ran through her just knowing she had that kind of power, that kind of an effect on him.

But he was right, she unwillingly admitted, her mind slowly beginning to clear. They had to stop...this time. Kristen was asleep just down the hallway and Uncle Louie could come home at any minute.

But there would be a next time, she vowed, a time for just the two of them without the chance of an interruption. There had to be, she thought desperately. She'd been too close to discovering that certain something that had always eluded her. She'd been right on the brink. She was sure of it.

A little embarrassed at her lascivious thoughts, especially in light of Dillon's restraint, she forced herself to step away from him. He'd said they needed to talk, and even though talking was the last thing she wanted to do with Dillon Reynolds at this moment, she figured she didn't have much choice in the matter.

"How about some coffee?" she offered, her voice sounding strangled even to her own ears.

Dillon sighed, hooked his thumbs in his pants pockets and nodded. "Sounds safe enough."

CHAPTER TEN

SEVERAL MINUTES LATER, they sat across from each other at the kitchen table nursing cups of coffee. Dillon took a sip, then cleared his throat. "Do you remember the first day I got here?"

"How could I forget?" she answered, rolling her eyes toward the ceiling in a playful, teasing way that made him smile.

"Bad, huh?"

"Let's just say that wasn't one of my better days."

Dillon's smile faltered. "I—I thought you and my father were, er, involved, you know?"

Adrienne sighed, remembering how angry his insinuations had made her. "I suspected as much, but..." She shook her head. "I never could figure out why you would think such a thing, and to tell you the truth, I felt pretty insulted that you would make that kind of judgment, considering you didn't even know me."

Dillon shrugged, looking a bit sheepish. "I had my reasons. Anyway, it didn't take me long to find out I was wrong," he hastened to assure her. "And I guess that's why I was so rough on you that first day and then later, after dinner that night."

Reasons? What reasons? she wondered. "Why are you telling me this now?" she asked, still confused.

Dillon reached across and covered her hand. "To let you know I understand about you being upset today, that from experience, I know things aren't always as they seem."

Adrienne nodded and gave him a sympathetic look. "Your father called me earlier, and if it's any comfort, he told me you had no choice, that you only did what you had to do."

A look of relief passed over Dillon's face. Adrienne turned her hand and clasped his. "He also told me that I shouldn't hold it against you," she added softly, giving his fingers a little squeeze. "And I don't."

Dillon's steady gaze held her captive. His thumb rubbed back and forth over her fingers. "For a while there," he said, his voice taking on a more intimate sound, "I was beginning to wonder. Last night and to-day were hell. I figured the only way he would slow down was if he was forced to."

He grimaced. "I didn't plan on handling things quite the way they happened, but—" he shrugged "—I think it was for the best. When I learned that he'd given Eva a raise in spite of what we'd discussed, well, there's just no way the two of us could continue working together and still save Twin Oaks. It didn't work before, so I don't know why I thought it would work this time. After I graduated from college, he wanted me to manage the club. And I tried...for two years I tried, but..." Dillon fell silent, and from the way he shifted uncomfortably in his chair, Adrienne got the distinct feeling that he'd said more than he'd intended to.

Outside, a car door slammed and he gave Adrienne a questioning look. "Were you expecting someone?"

"It's probably Uncle Louie," she said, reluctantly pulling her hand free. But as she waited, expecting her uncle to walk in at any moment, she wished for once that he'd stayed out just a little later than usual.

At the sound of someone knocking on the front door, Dillon started to rise, but Adrienne waved him back as she stood. "I'm sure it's just Uncle Louie. He probably forgot his keys again."

Before she could turn away, Dillon reached out and grabbed her arm. "Are we okay now?"

Adrienne smiled at him shyly. "We're okay now," she answered.

In the living room, she stopped at the window, pulled back the curtain and peeked outside. Standing on the front porch were a man and a woman. The man had the woman wrapped in an embrace and he was kissing her as if they were the only two people in the world.

Adrienne froze in stunned surprise. "Uncle Louie?" she whispered.

"Is it Louie?"

Adrienne jumped at the sound of Dillon's voice and dropped the curtain as if it was suddenly charged with an electrical current. Managing a curt nod in answer, she told herself she hadn't *really* been spying on her uncle. So why did it feel as if she'd just stuck her head into a hot oven?

Dillon gave her a puzzled look. "Aren't you going to let him in?"

She shifted her eyes toward the front door, then back to Dillon. "Ah, sure...in a minute. He, ah, has a friend he's saying good-night to."

Dillon's eyes began to twinkle and his lips twitched into a smile. "A woman friend?" he asked teasingly.

"Yes, of course a woman," she replied stiffly, suspecting he was more amused at her embarrassment than at the idea of her elderly uncle having a lady friend.

A sharp rap finally sounded again, and Dillon was still chuckling when Adrienne unlocked the door.

"Sorry, darlin'," Louie said as he stepped past her. "Forgot my keys."

Taking her time closing the door, Adrienne glanced casually toward the automobile parked on the curb, just in time to see the car door slam shut. The late-model car looked vaguely familiar, but she couldn't place where she'd seen it before. Since it had tinted windows, it was impossible to see inside, even with the streetlight hovering directly over it. Finally telling herself that it was really none of her business who her uncle saw socially, she pulled the front door firmly shut.

When Louie spied Dillon, a grin split his face, a grin that Adrienne decided looked suspiciously like one of relief. *Probably thinks I won't ask any questions with Dillon here,* she figured.

"Hey, Dillon!" Louie slapped him on the back and shook his hand. "I wondered whose car was in the driveway. Good to see you again."

"Uncle Louie, who was that woman?"

For a second, her uncle's smile faltered, but then it widened again. "Just a friend, hon. Just a friend. Is there any coffee made?"

Adrienne nodded. "We were in the kitchen, but—"

"Great. I could use a cup." He turned abruptly to Dillon. "I'm sure glad you're here."

Adrienne was left with no choice but to trail after the two men toward the kitchen. Later, when Dillon left, she would talk to Louie and insist he tell her more about this new friend. It wouldn't be prying, she assured herself. Just genuine concern. After all, Louie was at a vulnerable age, an age where an unscrupulous woman could easily take advantage of him.

"I heard some gossip tonight that you might be interested in." Louie continued talking once they were in the kitchen. He paused to pour himself a cup of coffee, then joined them at the table. "One of your members, a banker named Ted Jamison, dropped in at the Stomping Grounds tonight—"

Adrienne raised her eyebrows. "Ted Jamison was at the Southern Stomping Grounds?" Somehow she couldn't picture the pompous banker lowering himself to step foot in a common lounge. She shot her uncle a shrewd glance. "How do *you* know he was there?" she asked pointedly. "You saw him?"

"Well...yes." He nodded, looking decidedly uncomfortable. "Heard they had a great band playing tonight, so I stopped by for a few minutes... Like I was saying, Jamison came in." Louie turned back to Dillon. "Man, talk about sloshed to the gills! Anyway, he was spouting off and bragging how he was fixin' to make a killing on a real-estate deal he had going. We're talking megabucks here."

Dillon frowned. "What makes you think I'd be interested in Jamison's real-estate deal?"

"Well, it's no secret that Twin Oaks is in trouble. Even if I hadn't already known from listening to Adrienne, all anyone could talk about tonight were the layoffs. They were giving a blow-by-blow description...."

At mention of the layoffs, Dillon felt as if a vise had suddenly squeezed his insides. He gazed starkly at Adrienne, who was listening intently to her uncle. Dillon could just imagine what the people he'd laid off today were saying about him.

A sick feeling stirred in his stomach. What if he had to let Adrienne go? Would she understand or would she hate him? And how could he survive if she never wanted to see him again?

Adrienne smiled at something Louie said, and Dillon remembered how sweet her lips had tasted, how womanly she'd felt pressed against him, all soft and giving.

He lowered his gaze to his empty cup. Maybe further cuts wouldn't be necessary. He still had his ace in the hole. If the weather held, the upcoming member-guest golf tournament should bring in enough to tide them over.

"...some land that your father owns."

The older man's words jolted Dillon to the core. "Say that again," he demanded.

Louie's eyes widened and Adrienne gave him a puzzled look.

"Sorry," Dillon apologized quickly. "Guess my brain's on overload and I'm having a hard time following you."

"Jamison was at the Stomping Grounds to meet some hotshot attorney," Louie repeated. "Guess he didn't realize that a lot of club employees hang out there. Anyway, I heard them talking about this piece of prime property, and they mentioned your father's name. Well, I put two and two together, and it seems that this property is the only tract of land around here large enough to fit the needs of Pro-Chem."

Dillon's brow furrowed in concentration. "Pro-Chem? The international chemical company?"

Louie nodded. "Yeah. They've gotten so big that they're having trouble getting rid of all the chemical waste produced by their plants. It's been all over the news lately that they're looking to build a waste-processing plant, but with all the environmental stuff going on—saving the wetlands and such—none of the other states they've tried so far will agree to let them do it."

"But Uncle Louie, if none of the other states would allow it, why would we?"

"My guess is that Jamison has some key politicians in his hip pocket. For the right price, they could be persuaded to go along with him."

"No way!" she scoffed. "Once the public finds out, they won't stand for it."

"They won't if they're aware of what's going on," Dillon put in. "But we all know that certain issues are railroaded through before anyone realizes what's happening. It's just hard for me to believe Jamison would be so damned devious. Besides, the only other property my father has now, at least that I'm aware of, is some land in back of the golf course."

Dillon remembered well the day his father had decided to purchase the land that the Twin Oaks community was built on. He'd hocked everything he could get his hands on to purchase it. The club with its pools, tennis courts, driving range, and eighteen-hole golf course were only part of the parcel. Most of the rest had been subdivided for houses and apartments.

Dillon took a swift breath and flinched, as if someone had punched him in the gut. All of it had been financed together as one property. All of it except what his father had sold off, including the final, undeveloped portion that Pro-Chem was interested in, was mortgaged together. And the whole property was now being used as collateral for the loan from Ted Jamison's bank. If they couldn't pay it off, Jamison had a perfect right to foreclose.

"That bastard!" he hissed, unable to contain his fury.

"Dillon?" Adrienne touched his arm. "What is it? What's wrong?"

"The property that Jamison was bragging about is tied up with the club. The bastard knew my father would never sell the land if he found out what it would be used for."

Motivation. Dillon had wondered about Jamison's motivation, and now he had a damn good idea what it was. "He knew there was a good possibility my father wouldn't be able to come up with the loan money. He's just sitting back and waiting to cash in. Pro-Chem will probably pay a fortune for that land. The son-of-a-bitch knew what he was doing when he railroaded his so-called long-term goals through council."

"But you *will* be able to make the payments," Adrienne insisted vehemently. "I know you will."

Dillon forced a smile, touched by her loyalty and her naiveté. He might be many things, but he wasn't so sure he was a miracle worker. To Louie, he said, "If you hear anything else, be sure and let me know. Meanwhile, I've got some checking around I want to do."

"Sure thing," Louie replied.

"More coffee, Uncle Louie?"

The other man shook his head and yawned. "Thanks," he said. "But it's way past my bedtime." He shoved his chair back and stood.

"See ya next time, Dillon." Louie bent and brushed a hasty kiss on his niece's cheek. "Good night, hon."

Adrienne watched her uncle walk out of the kitchen.

"I wonder who that woman was."

Dillon looked up, suddenly realizing that Adrienne was speaking to him.

"I just hope she's not some fortune hunter, out to get her hands on his money. If she is, she's in for a surprise. I don't think he's got that much."

"Aren't you overreacting? Louie is a grown man, well capable of taking care of himself."

"Well, of course he's a grown man," she answered. "But I don't want some woman thinking that—"

"Lighten up, Adrienne," he said. "I believe there *are* more important things in this world than worrying about your uncle's love life."

The stricken look on her face made him want to bite his tongue. "I'm sorry," he said. "The bombshell Louie laid on me tonight has me in a tailspin, but that's no excuse to behave like a jerk. I don't want to hurt you...ever. And I had no right to take my frustrations out on you."

He lifted her hands to his lips and brushed a kiss on each of them. "It's just that I care about you, and it upsets me to see you do this to yourself. I know you love your uncle, but you can't protect everyone in the world from being hurt. Louie's happiness is no more your responsibility than Kristen's relationship with her father."

Adrienne didn't want to respond to the feathery touch of his lips, the sincerity in his voice, or the fact that he'd admitted he cared about her. But there was no way she could prevent her hands from trembling when she felt Dillon's soft lips brush her knuckles.

What he'd said had hurt, but he was right. She did want to protect Louie and Kristen.

"Adrienne, talk to me. Don't shut me out."

"Is it so wrong to want to protect the people you love? Isn't that what you did today, with your father?"

"That's not quite the same thing. Yes, to a certain degree, I was able to manipulate circumstances to force him to retire, but if he still refuses to take care of himself, I'll worry but I won't feel it's somehow my fault."

It is the same thing, Adrienne thought, but saying so would be fighting a losing battle. Dillon was just too self-sufficient and strong willed to admit it. Doing so would be tantamount to admitting he cared too much, and caring too much smacked too much of being like his father. But now was not the time to argue the point. Dillon had enough on his mind.

If only there was some way she could erase that tortured look on his face. "I know you're worried about the club," she said, her words soft and cautious. "And I'm not completely dismissing what my uncle told you. But I know how gossip and rumors fly around here. Most of it's the product of some employee's fertile imagination."

Dillon shook his head. "Not this time. Call it gut instinct or whatever, but there are too many coincidences to ignore. For one thing, Jamison has sat on the council for the past two years, plenty of time to influence the finances. I need to do a little research, but I'd be willing to bet that Pro-Chem started its search for a Texas site just about the time Jamison decided to run for council at Twin Oaks."

"Even if that's true, there is an alternative. If worse comes to worst, call a general-membership meeting and tell the members what's going on. I can't help but feel that if they knew, they'd come up with the money you need."

Again Dillon shook his head. "I can't do that, at least not yet. Without facts or proof, I'd look like a fool. Besides, that would be as good as admitting that my family can't handle the management, that we failed." *Failed again,* he added silently. Dillon could well remember those lean, humiliating days of his youth. He cleared his throat. "I suspect that's why my father hasn't gone to the membership yet, either."

"I disagree. I don't think it's a question of failure or success. Most of the club's members live in the surrounding community, which your father developed. Not only would this waste-processing plant be a potential health risk, but having something like that in the neighborhood would devalue their property as well. I think it's only fair that they know what might end up in their own backyard."

Dillon closed his eyes for a moment. She was right. The members needed to know what they were up against.

"Tell you what," he said, looking at her thoughtfully. "Let me do some checking around first. If what Louie says is true, I promise I'll call a general-membership meeting and inform the stockholders of what's happening."

Adrienne heard what he said and what he didn't say. He'd inform them, but his pride wouldn't let him ask for money. She gave a nervous laugh. "Maybe you won't need money from them. Surely with the payroll money you save from the layoffs, you'll be able to cover the loan."

Hoping he sounded more convincing than he felt, he answered, "You bet. And with the member-guest tournament coming up in a few weeks, along with a little creative bookkeeping, maybe it will be enough."

Adrienne grew very still, reminding Dillon of a small rabbit cornered by a fox. "Ah...Dillon. About the tournament."

Dillon stared into her dark eyes, and something told him he wasn't going to like what she was about to say.

"Did Franklin talk to you about the deal he made with Mick Starky?"

"Deal? What deal?"

Adrienne lowered her gaze, but not before he saw her pained expression. "Maybe you should ask your father about it," she whispered.

"Adrienne, the whole idea behind making Dad retire was that he wouldn't have to worry about this stuff. Come on. Just spit it out."

"Mick Starky threatened to quit. He said he had an offer from a club in New Orleans. With the tournament coming up, I guess Franklin panicked. He offered Mick fifty percent of the pro shop's profits if he would agree to stay."

The silence seemed to stretch out for an eternity. The sound of a distant siren could be heard outside, and somewhere down the block a dog barked. When Adrienne finally ventured a cautious look at Dillon, her uneasiness grew. His eyes were as cold as green ice and his jaw looked as if it was carved from granite.

"That son of a bitch!"

Adrienne flinched. "I know you were counting on that tournament," she whispered, but from the look on Dillon's face, she didn't think he was listening.

"Well, that tears it!" he snapped. "Now I don't have a choice."

"Choice?" she questioned.

He grimaced, then sighed deeply. "I had hoped to get by without further cuts," he said.

Adrienne's heartbeat slowed to a dull thud. "Further cuts," she whispered.

Dillon didn't reply, but continued to stare at her with a peculiar expression on his face, one that seemed both sad and pained. Finally, he shook his head and stood. "Stop worrying." He walked around the table and pulled her to her feet. "It's late. You're tired and so am I. Let's just call it a night, and start again tomorrow." His lips stretched into a semblance of a smile. "You know what they say—things always look better in the morning after a good night's sleep."

He could see the questions in her eyes, questions he didn't dare—couldn't—answer. Not now. Dillon drew her into his arms, bent his head and, intent on banishing every thought from her mind except what they felt for each other, kissed her as if he was a starving man and she was the last morsel of bread on earth. She was everything that had been missing in his lonely life, and he couldn't bear the thought of losing her.

But if he lost Twin Oaks, there was more than a good possibility he'd lose Adrienne, he realized, tightening his arms around her. Like it or not, he wouldn't have a choice...wouldn't give her a choice. She deserved better than having another man in her life who was a failure.

CHAPTER ELEVEN

WHEN THE PHONE BUZZED on Thursday afternoon, Adrienne eyed it as if it was a rattlesnake. *It never fails,* she thought. Just when she was ready to leave for the day, she got a call that delayed her.

Dillon had come in for a couple of hours that morning but then he'd left, mumbling something about an appointment. With him gone most of the day, and being short of staff, she'd had about all she could take.

When the phone buzzed again, Adrienne sighed deeply and picked up the receiver. "Yes, Joanne."

"Line two. It's your regular Thursday-afternoon caller. Sorry."

Jack.

Adrienne's fingers tightened on the receiver. With everything so hectic, she'd completely forgotten about the upcoming weekend.

For a minute she was tempted to ignore the call and tell Joanne to take a message. But what good would delaying it do? Adrienne drew a steadying breath. "I'd say thanks, but you'd know I was lying."

"Sorry again," Joanne offered.

Adrienne leaned forward and punched the line two button. "Yes, Jack."

"Oh, great! I'm glad I caught you before you left."

Sure, she thought sarcastically. *Before I left and you had to call me at home and risk talking to Kristen.*

"Will you give Kristen a message for me?"

Adrienne stiffened but kept silent.

"I—I won't be able to see her this weekend," he continued. "We're snowed under with work here at the office. I just don't see how I can get away. I know what you said about not calling you," he rushed on. "But if you'd just tell her for me this one last time, I'd really appreciate it, and I promise I won't call you again."

Until the next time, she thought. It was evident Jack hadn't paid the slightest attention to her warning, that he didn't believe she'd actually meant what she'd said. *Had* she?

"Stop being the go-between. Your ex-husband's a grown man. Let him handle his own problems. And let Kristen learn to deal directly with her father instead of blaming you...." Dillon's words gave her strength. Slowly, a peace she hadn't known for a long time seeped through her, and one by one, she felt the heavy chains of responsibility that had ruled her for the past seven years begin to fall away.

"Adrienne? Will you tell her for me?" Jack persisted.

Feeling strangely detached and immune to the pathetic tone in his voice, she finally answered him. "Sorry, Jack. I can't do it. Like I told you the last time, if you don't want to see your daughter, *you'll* have to tell her."

"But—"

Adrienne gently replaced the receiver, cutting off the rest of Jack's argument.

Later, in her living room, Adrienne kicked off her shoes. "Yum," she said, entering the kitchen. "What is that wonderful smell? I'm starved."

Louie and Kristen were seated at the table, their heads close together as they concentrated on a recipe book lying open between them.

Kristen looked up first. "Chicken Parisienne."

"Served with rice and green beans," Louie chimed in.

"And peach cobbler and ice cream for dessert," Kristen added, licking her lips.

"Ahem." Louie cocked his head toward Kristen and frowned.

Kristen shot her uncle a disgusted look. "I know, I know. Only if I eat the green beans."

Adrienne smothered a chuckle. There were very few healthy foods that Kristen didn't like, but green beans rated top of the list. She'd heard Louie tell her daughter time and again that if he could learn to eat yogurt, she could certainly learn to tolerate a few green beans.

Halfway through the meal, Adrienne glanced across the table at her daughter.

"Did your father call this afternoon?" The question had been nagging her ever since she'd spoken with him.

Kristen looked up, her blue eyes bright and hopeful. "Not yet," she answered.

Adrienne felt an ache at the back of her throat and swallowed. *Please, Jack. For once in your life, do the right thing,* she prayed silently.

ON FRIDAY AFTERNOON, Jack pulled into Adrienne's driveway. When he'd switched off the engine, he stared at the front of the house for several minutes, willing himself to get out of the car and walk the short distance to the front door. After he'd spoken to Adrienne, he'd lost count of the number of times he'd picked up the telephone to call Kristen and cancel their weekend. A couple of times he'd actually dialed the number, but had hung up before it had time to ring.

"Damn," he whispered, mentally calling himself every name for a coward he could think of. At that moment, a movement in the window caught his attention.

Kristen.

She was staring out at him, probably wondering why he hadn't emerged from the car yet, he figured. Before he had time to react, the curtain fell, and within seconds, the front door opened.

With a smile as bright as sunshine lighting up her face, Kristen wheeled herself down the short ramp. In her lap was a small overnight bag.

As Jack reached for the car door handle and shoved it open, he summoned up an answering smile, but inside, his stomach knotted.

"I was afraid you weren't coming," Kristen said, staring up at him.

Her searching look made him want to crawl into a hole somewhere, and Jack felt a pang of guilt stab his chest.

"But when you didn't call, I knew you would though." She grinned. "And I'm glad you did."

She was glad he'd come. She was *glad*. Suddenly, Jack forgot about the wheelchair, forgot about his guilt and remorse. It didn't matter what he'd done. His daughter loved him . . . she was glad he'd come!

Now, for the first time, what Ray and the rest of the group had been trying to tell him for months made sense. There was absolutely nothing he could do about the past. The past was done. All he had control over was now, this minute. And at this moment in time, the shining, trusting look of love on his daughter's face made him feel ten feet tall. If she could forgive him, then he sure as hell should be able to forgive himself.

FOR A SUNDAY AFTERNOON, the club was unusually busy. Adrienne glanced around the ballroom one last time to make sure that everything was set up for the championship-tennis-tournament-awards party. The tournament had been going on since Friday, and more members than ever before had signed up for the annual event.

Satisfied that the tennis people would have nothing to complain about, she glanced at her watch. Four o'clock, and Joe still hadn't showed up to relieve her. Should she leave or should she wait for him? Of course, the staff could always call her at home if they needed to.

And as each minute passed, she was hard pressed to stifle the apprehension that had been building all afternoon. She'd feel better once Kristen was safely home.

Jack had told her he'd return Kristen at four-thirty, and Adrienne wanted to be there, since Louie wouldn't get home until later from his dinner with his "friend."

Adrienne frowned and glanced around. Louie had successfully sidestepped every attempt she'd made—some subtle and some not so subtle—to find out more about his lady friend. She kept reminding herself of what Dillon had said about her uncle being a grown man, but she still wondered why he was being so secretive.

She walked over to Eva, who was putting final touches to the buffet table. "I'm going to leave now, Eva. Joe should be here any minute, but if there's a problem before he comes in, call me at home."

"Yah, I will," Eva said over her shoulder.

At six o'clock, Adrienne stood in her kitchen, stirring a simmering pot of spaghetti sauce. A car door slammed outside and she paused, the wooden spoon poised in midair. She'd lost count of how many times she'd hurried to the window during the past hour.

But peeking out the window at every sound would not make Jack and Kristen arrive any sooner, she told herself firmly and resumed stirring the spaghetti.

A few minutes later she heard the scrape of a key, then the sound of the front door opening.

"Mom?"

Adrienne let out a sigh of relief and called out, "In here, honey." Lifting the spoon from the sauce, she rapped it sharply against the rim of the pot, laid it on the counter and headed for the living room.

Kristen's eyes were bright and lively and her lap was loaded with plastic bags and paper sacks as she wheeled into the middle of the room. Behind her, Jack had his arms equally full. Her daughter looked so happy that Adrienne didn't have the heart to scold him for bringing her home late. "My goodness, what's all this?"

Kristen grinned. "We went all the way into Houston to the Galleria. Wait till you see the neat clothes Dad bought me."

Adrienne shot Jack a questioning look. She knew his finances weren't in much better shape than her own, and she wondered how he could afford to splurge.

Jack shrugged. "The wonders of plastic money," he said by way of explanation.

There was something different about him, Adrienne thought. He looked better, somehow more at peace, than he had in months. She forced herself to smile, then turned back to Kristen. "From the number of packages you've got there, it might take all night for you to show me everything."

Kristen giggled. "I can't wait to call Katie."

"Where do you want these?" Jack asked.

"Oops. Sorry, Dad. Follow me."

A few minutes later, Jack returned. "She's on the phone with..." He hesitated, his brow knitted in concentration.

"Probably Katie," Adrienne supplied.

"Yeah," he nodded. "That's the one. Got any coffee?"

It took Adrienne a minute to realize that he didn't intend to leave right away. Always before, when he'd dropped Kristen off after one of their rare weekends together, he'd been in a hurry, barely taking the time to say goodbye.

"No, not brewed," she answered hesitantly, wondering why he wanted to hang around this time. "But I guess I can make some."

While Adrienne prepared the coffee, Jack recounted everything that he and Kristen had done over the weekend.

Something about him *was* different, she realized. But she couldn't quite decide what. Several times she even thought she detected a note of pride in the way he talked about how independent and self-sufficient Kristen had become.

Why the sudden change? she wondered, pouring steaming coffee into the two cups on the counter.

"Kristen tells me your new boss has come around a couple of times."

Careful to keep her expression neutral, Adrienne nodded and handed him his cup. She sat down at the table opposite him and spooned sugar into her coffee.

"I believe she said his name is Dillon?"

Again Adrienne nodded, but remained silent.

Jack glanced down at his cup and stared at it for several seconds. Then he lifted his gaze to Adrienne, and she sensed a challenge in the way he was staring at her. "Have you known him long?"

"He's Franklin's son," she answered, beginning to resent his not so subtle interrogation. "Franklin is retiring and Dillon is taking his place."

A worried frown deepened the lines in Jack's forehead, and he took a sip of the coffee. "Kristen sure seems taken with the guy," he said, lowering his cup back to the saucer. "That's all she talked about—Dillon this, Dillon that. Are you sure this guy's okay to be around her?"

"There is absolutely nothing wrong with Dillon Reynolds," she said, a bit more sharply than she'd intended. It rankled that Jack, of all people, would question her judgment.

A sheepish expression crossed his face. "Sorry," he mumbled. "Guess I was out of line. I didn't mean to insinuate anything. I've already told Kristen that I'll pick her up next Friday night. That is, if it's okay with you," he added, replacing his cup in the saucer. "I think we need to spend more time together than I've been able to in the past."

"Mom?"

Both Jack and Adrienne swiveled around as Kristen entered the kitchen.

"What happened to the squeak?" Adrienne asked, surprised she hadn't heard the telltale creaking of the noisy wheelchair that always heralded Kristen's entry.

Kristen beamed at Jack. "Dad fixed it for me. He said the axle bolt was loose." She turned back to Adrienne. "A call beeped in while I was talking to Katie. It's the club, I think."

Adrienne gave Jack an apologetic look as she stood. He waved his hand. "Go ahead." He shoved back his chair. "It's time I was heading home anyway. Kristen will lock up after me."

Adrienne nodded and walked over to the counter and picked up the extension.

"What do you mean, he never showed up?" she asked a few seconds later. "Did he call in?"

"No ma'am" came Eva's curt answer. "I tried to phone him, but no one answered, and we got a big problem. That new member, Mr. Cones, is drunk and refuses to leave so we can close up. I called Mr. Reynolds—the young one—but didn't get an answer, so I called his father's house, thinking he might be there. Some lady answered and said they had all gone to the hospital."

"Hospital," Adrienne repeated, and leaned against the counter for support. Her heart began to race. "Why? What happened?"

"She said they were having a dinner party, and Mr. Franklin started having chest pains and passed out."

"What hospital, Eva?" she demanded. "Did she tell you which one?"

"Twin Oaks Plaza. What about Mr. Cones?"

"Oh, God. I don't know." Adrienne couldn't think. Had Franklin had a heart attack? Was he still alive? "Just handle it the best you can," she finally said.

"Threaten to call the police if you have to. And lock up," she tacked on belatedly.

Adrienne hung up the phone and jerked open the cabinet drawer where she kept telephone directories. Her hands shook so badly she could hardly turn the pages. When she finally located the hospital, she grabbed the receiver and punched out the number.

The switchboard answered on the third ring, and after interminable minutes dragged by, she was finally connected to a nursing station.

"Mr. Dillon Reynolds, please."

Several more agonizing moments passed before she learned that Franklin had been transferred from the hospital by helicopter to the Medical Center in Houston.

A STEADY RAIN BEAT against the cloudy windowpane, and lights blinked in the distance. Dillon stared bleakly out of the hospital window into the black, dismal night. He kept telling himself that none of this was his fault, that what he'd told his father the night before hadn't been the reason for the heart attack. But no matter how hard he tried to convince himself, guilt sliced at his insides like a thousand slivers of glass.

He glanced over his shoulder to reassure himself that his mother was okay. She was lying on a sofa, eyes glazed, staring but unseeing.

Dillon turned back to the window. For a while, he'd wondered if he might lose them both. She'd held up admirably, even when they'd learned his father was going to be airlifted to the Medical Center. It was when the orderlies had taken Franklin away that she'd unraveled at the seams, sobbing hysterically.

The attending doctor had quickly ordered her a sedative, but for a while Dillon had wondered if even that would calm her. She'd sobbed the entire time it had taken them to drive to the medical center. Once there, he'd persuaded her to lie down, and the medicine had at last lulled her into a silence.

He shoved his fingers through his hair and squeezed his eyes shut. But the image of his father sitting at the head of the table, clutching his chest and gasping for air, wouldn't go away.

He opened his eyes and drew in a deep breath. How long would they have to wait? How long before they knew something?

Across the room, a door opened, and Dillon turned to see who had entered.

Adrienne. Her dark eyes were a well of sympathy and understanding, conveying to him just how much she cared. She walked over to his mother, knelt down and picked up her hands gently in her own. He couldn't hear her low, murmured words but could tell from the look on his mother's face that they were comforting.

Dillon felt his chest tighten with emotion, an emotion so strong that he had to look away, lest Adrienne see it. He turned back to the window.

He loved her.

The realization slammed into his gut like an iron fist, and for long seconds, he couldn't seem to draw a breath.

"Dillon."

The whispered sound of his name on her lips melted his insides. But it was the tentative touch of her soft, warm hand on his arm that finally broke loose the confusion and torment that had plagued him since he had first realized his father might die. He turned to her, and with a groan of despair that came from the depths of his soul, pulled her into his arms.

Adrienne felt shudder after shudder rack the proud, stubborn man in her arms, and her throat ached with the tears he refused to shed, even as they ran freely down her own cheeks.

"It's okay," she soothed, rubbing her hands up and down his back and wishing she could somehow take away his pain. "It's okay," she whispered again as his arms tightened convulsively around her.

She knew almost instantly when his storm of emotion began to subside. Slowly, she felt the tense muscles in his shoulders relax. Then, with one last shuddering sigh, he released her and stepped back. He reached for her hands. "I'm glad you came," he said, his voice low and raspy. "I . . . I—"

Adrienne pulled one hand free and placed a finger on his lips, shaking her head. "I'm here for as long as you need me."

She was still holding his hand when the doctor came in an hour later. "He needs surgery," the green-garbed, middle-aged man said bluntly. "He's got three blocked arteries."

"What are his chances?" Dillon demanded.

The doctor met Dillon's penetrating gaze without blinking. "I have to tell you the surgery might not work. There's a fifty-fifty chance. But without surgery..." He shook his head. "I don't think we have a choice."

Dillon shifted his gaze to his mother, but Adrienne could tell from her frightened, withdrawn look that Myrna was past making decisions.

Adrienne squeezed his hand, hoping to convey the support that his mother wasn't capable of giving. After a brief glance her way, a glance that was both agonizing and grateful, Dillon turned back to the doctor and nodded. "Do it."

Once the doctor had left and the proper papers were signed, time seemed to drag by. And with each passing minute, Adrienne grew more apprehensive. After an hour of watching Dillon pace back and forth, until she was sure he would wear a permanent path in the carpet, she'd gone in search of coffee, hoping he would stop at least long enough to drink it.

During the second hour, a nurse came in to inform them that everything was going as expected, and Dillon settled next to Adrienne on the hard sofa. He pulled her close and slung his arm around her shoulder.

And they waited.

At some point, Dillon laid his head back and closed his eyes, but Adrienne knew by the granite set of his jaw and the thin line of his lips that he wasn't sleeping. And all the while, Myrna lay on the sofa opposite them, un-moving.

Adrienne leveled her gaze on the doorway, willing the doctor to come through it. What was taking so long? she wondered for the hundredth time. Had something gone wrong?

It was four o'clock in the morning when the doctor finally burst through the door. Dillon was off the sofa in a flash.

He rushed over to his mother, slid his arm beneath her shoulders and gently helped the fragile-looking woman to a sitting position. Keeping his arm protectively around her, he looked up at the doctor. "Well?" he demanded, his voice a fearful rasp.

Adrienne eased over toward the sofa, and Dillon reached up and grabbed hold of her hand.

As the older man walked over to stand in front of them, the look on his face was neither encouraging nor discouraging. "The surgery was successful, and he's holding his own," he said bluntly. "But he's not out of danger yet. We've transferred him to the intensive care unit."

He knelt in front of Myrna and took both her hands in his. "When they get him settled, you can see him briefly," he said softly. And for the first time since Adrienne had arrived, she saw a sparkle of hope light up Myrna's faded eyes.

The doctor patted her hand , then stood. He slid his penetrating gaze to Dillon. "Another forty-eight hours should tell us if he will stabilize."

As DILLON SLOWLY AWAKENED, he squinted against the glare of sunlight shining through the hospital window. The past forty-eight hours had dragged by, their passing marked only by the changing shifts of the hospital staff, the brief visits they were permitted every so often to see Franklin and the gallons of hot, bitter coffee they consumed.

He turned his head slightly to glare at the clock on the wall and was surprised to realize that he'd been asleep for more than two hours. Next he sought out the sofa across from him, and felt a moment of relief that his mother had finally succumbed to sleep.

Adrienne stirred in his arms, and Dillon gently shifted to accommodate her movement. His arms ached from holding her, but it was the sweetest ache he'd ever experienced. God, she was beautiful, he thought, allowing his gaze to linger over each flawless feature of her face. But in his mind, he wasn't seeing the outward, superficial beauty. More important was the beauty within her, a beauty of the spirit, which in his estimation was far more rare and precious than anything he'd experienced.

Dillon nuzzled the top of her head with his chin, loving the feel of her silky hair against his rough, unshaven jaw. She again stirred in his arms and snuggled closer as if she belonged there. And she did, he thought fiercely. In the past weeks she'd become such an integral part of his life that he couldn't imagine a day passing without her in it.

There was a commotion at the door, and Dillon craned his neck to see who had entered. At the sight of the doctor, he stiffened, both hope and fear crushing his chest until he wasn't sure he could breathe. He gently nudged Adrienne awake, then stood.

The doctor gave them a tired but encouraging smile, and Dillon felt his lungs expand and his heart lift with jubilation.

"A week to ten days in the hospital and he should be able to go home. They're moving him to a private room now."

A sob of joy came from behind him and Dillon turned to see Adrienne holding his mother, both of them laughing while tears of relief streamed down their faces.

CHAPTER TWELVE

SATURDAY EVENING, Adrienne stared into the dresser mirror. Leaning forward, she dotted the dark circles beneath her eyes with a foam-tipped applicator, willing the cream concealer to live up to its advertisement and hide the results of her exhaustion. Joe Blount had finally called in to say he'd had to go out of town on an emergency. His sister had been in an automobile accident, and he hadn't returned to work until today.

Muted male laughter mixed with girlish giggles drifted through her closed bedroom door.

Be careful what you wish for or you may get it. The old saying popped into her head, and she grimaced.

At least twice in the past week she'd come home, tired and frazzled, to find Jack camped in her living room. Between the hectic hours she had spent at the club all week and worrying about Franklin's recovery, Jack's presence underfoot was just one more aggravation. Thank goodness he was taking Kristen back to his apartment for the night.

Suddenly Adrienne smiled. The only bright spot during the whole week was her date with Dillon tonight. Franklin was being released from the hospital the following day, and Dillon had insisted that the news called for a celebration.

Dinner and dancing. Adrienne sighed. How long had it been since she'd gone out for an evening of pure enjoyment? Too long, she decided, adding extra strokes of mascara to her eyelashes.

She replaced the mascara brush in its tube, laid it on the dresser, then stepped back. Critically eyeing her image, she turned first to the left, then the right. The soft knit dress she'd chosen was one of her favorites. The periwinkle color suited her. She smoothed her hands down the sides of the fitted bodice, the cummerbund waist and the full, sweeping skirt. The dress was simple yet had just the right touch of elegance, she thought with satisfaction.

There was a soft knock on her bedroom door, then it opened and Kristen wheeled into the room. "Dad and I are leaving," she announced.

Adrienne turned to face her daughter and gave her an approving look. Decked out in one of her new blouses and a new pair of jeans, and with her hair softly curled, she looked radiant.

Kristen eyed her mother suspiciously, then suddenly frowned. "I thought you were off tonight."

"I am," Adrienne answered.

Christian waved a hand at her. "Then why are you all dressed up?"

"I'm going out for dinner."

"By yourself?"

Adrienne slowly shook her head. "No. I'm going with Dillon."

Her daughter's eyes widened in surprise. "On a date?" she blurted out.

"Well . . . yes."

Kristen stared at her, and Adrienne could see confusion battling in her eyes. She knew by the not-so-subtle hints her daughter had been dropping over the past week that Kristen hoped that she and Jack might become interested in each other again.

Adrienne closed the short distance between them and knelt beside Kristen's chair. "You do like Dillon, don't you?"

Kristen hesitated, giving Adrienne a suspicious look. "Well . . . yeah," she finally answered. "He's cool."

"Well, I like him, too. A lot," she added with emphasis.

"But what about Dad?"

Adrienne gazed steadily at her daughter, willing her to understand. "We've been over this before, honey. I still care about him," she said gently, reaching out to smooth back a strand of Kristen's blond hair. "But only as a friend and only because he's your father."

Kristen's eyes flared with defiance. She jerked away from Adrienne's touch. "You don't care about him!" she cried. "If you had, you wouldn't have divorced him in the first place. You—"

"Kristen, that's enough!" Jack's voice sliced through the air.

Adrienne looked up and met his bleak gaze. She knew he'd overheard. His eyes conveyed more than words ever could: disappointment, guilt, remorse. And finally, reluctant acceptance.

Kristen glared at her father. "But, Dad—"

He held up his hand, cutting her off. "It's time to leave," he said briskly. Then he smiled. But it was a parody, a sad little grimace. "And I think it's past time you and I had a talk. Give your mom a kiss and let her finish dressing."

Listening to the silence of the house a few minutes later, Adrienne couldn't believe how hard it was to let go. For a moment, she'd wanted to shield Kristen—and Jack—from the pain of the ugly truth. But it wasn't her choice any longer. Her heart ached at the thought of all of Kristen's illusions being shattered by what Jack would tell her.

And Jack himself... Was he strong enough to do what had to be done without falling to pieces, without drowning himself in a bottle again?

ADRIENNE GLANCED at Dillon, thinking again how handsome he looked in his navy suit and crisp blue shirt. She sighed and turned her gaze out the side window as his car sped along the interstate.

The elegant restaurant he had chosen was everything he had claimed it would be and more. They'd been given an intimate table for two, complete with candles and champagne. The food had been excellent, as was the service from the tuxedo-clad waiter. But all she could think about was Kristen.

"You've been pretty quiet all evening. Is something wrong?"

Dillon's low voice was like a caress and Adrienne gave herself a mental shake. There was absolutely nothing she could do about Kristen and Jack, and spoiling her night out with Dillon with her morose brooding was unfair to him and to herself.

"I'm fine," she answered, forcing a smile. "It's just been a long week."

"It has been a long week," he agreed. "And after tonight—after that dessert you talked me into—I might not live to see another one."

"What?" She sputtered, laughing. "If I remember correctly, you were the one who insisted we couldn't leave without trying the chocolate mousse."

Dillon shrugged. "There's only one thing left to do."

As he reached over and picked up her hand, Adrienne tilted her head and eyed him suspiciously, afraid to ask what he had in mind.

With his eyes ahead on the highway, he lifted her hand to his lips. His warm breath whispered across her skin just before she felt his lips touch each of her knuckles, sending shivers of awareness rippling through her. "We'll have to find some way to work off those extra calories," he said, his voice low and suggestive.

Adrienne found it hard to draw a deep breath. Sudden images flitted through her mind, of Dillon and herself lying in bed, skin against skin . . .

"Dancing," he said emphatically, giving her hand a playful squeeze before releasing it. "Some good old, down-home dancing is just what the doctor ordered, don't you think?"

Adrienne squirmed. Her cheeks felt as if they were on fire, but she managed to reply, "I'm not much of a dancer, but if you don't mind having sore toes tomorrow, I'm game."

"There's one thing I should do on the way, if you don't mind—swing by the club and check on that wedding reception scheduled for tonight."

"Sure," she replied, smothering a sigh of disappointment. For just one night, she had hoped that they could forget all about Twin Oaks.

Once at the club, Adrienne waited in the dining room while Joe accompanied Dillon to the ballroom. She glanced around the busy restaurant, noting with satisfaction that her suggestion of a lobster night had been well received. Almost every table was filled.

Several minutes passed, then out of the corner of her eye, she noticed Dillon returning, and she watched as council members, including the president, surrounded him. From the angry looks on their faces and the stiff way Dillon was holding himself, it was clear something was going on.

Aware that Adrienne was waiting for him, Dillon shook his head. "You can't blackball Jamison," he told the group. "If you kick him out of the club without a good reason, he can sue us."

"I think selling us out to Pro-Chem is a damn good reason," Mitchell Kelly growled.

Dillon shook his head again. Striving for patience, he kept his voice low and reasonable. "He hasn't done anything *yet*. And he won't be able to if we pay off the loan. Just be patient and give me time. Now, if you'll excuse me, I have someone waiting for me."

Dillon shook Mitchell's hand, then turned and headed toward Adrienne.

"Let's get out of here," he said when he reached her.

Adrienne fell in step with him, lengthening her stride to keep up. "What was that all about?"

Dillon paused at the front entry and held the door open for her. They had parked beneath the front portico, and he remained silent until they were both seated in the car.

She turned to face him. "Well?"

He switched on the engine and jerked the gear lever into Drive. "Just the usual complaints," he replied briskly. "Nothing to worry about."

Adrienne sighed, knowing that as far as Dillon was concerned, the subject was closed. She turned her gaze to the road ahead and wondered how she could have fallen in love with such a stubborn man.

Several minutes later, when he turned the car down a street she was unfamiliar with, she frowned. "Where are we going?"

Dillon glanced her way, and she was relieved to see that he looked less tense than he had earlier. "I believe dancing was the next item on the agenda, and I hear the

Stomping Grounds has a band guaranteed to make you tap your feet.''

THE SOUTHERN STOMPING Grounds wasn't the sleazy beer joint Adrienne had imagined it to be. They had been inside for only five minutes and already there was no way she could keep her foot from tapping to the lively beat of the country-and-western band.

After several moments of searching, they had found an empty bar stool. Sitting with her back to the bar and her heels hooked on the rung, she sipped her soft drink and watched as laughing couples whirled around the dance floor to the raucous music. With his warm body pressed tightly against her side and his arm slung around her shoulder, Dillon was wedged between her and the man seated on the next stool.

A familiar face suddenly whirled by and Adrienne drew in a sharp breath. "Uncle Louie!" she exclaimed, her eyes straining to follow him as he disappeared in the sea of people.

Dillon leaned over. "Did you say something?" he shouted, his voice barely audible above the deafening music.

Adrienne turned her head and motioned toward the dance floor. "I just saw Uncle Louie," she said loudly.

Dillon shook his head, indicating that he couldn't hear her.

Adrienne raised her voice until she was almost yelling. "I said that I just saw—" the song ended and the music stopped abruptly "—Uncle Louie." The sound of her voice carried throughout the suddenly quiet room. Adrienne cringed, but Dillon laughed right along with the people surrounding them.

Then the crowd directly in front of them parted. "Did I hear someone call me?"

Dillon nudged her gently. "Loosen up. It *was* funny."

Adrienne felt as if her cheeks were on fire, but a smile twitched at her lips, and the laughter she'd been straining against finally bubbled to the surface.

Louie grinned at her and slapped Dillon on his back. "Hey, good to see you again." The band started up another lively tune, and Louie, his eyes twinkling with mischief, turned his attention to Adrienne. "Come on, darlin', let's show 'em how it's done."

"But—" Before she could protest, he had her out on the floor, whirling and stomping to the beat as the crowd moved like a giant wave to the music. There was no escaping and no stopping, so she hung on for dear life.

Adrienne was astounded by her uncle's expertise and his agility. While she huffed and puffed, trying to keep up with him, he was grinning and laughing, having the time of his life. When the song ended, the musicians announced they were taking a short break. Louie leaned down and kissed Adrienne's cheek. "You did real good, darlin'. Real good," he repeated with a satisfied grunt. "But then, I always knew you could."

While they made their way through the milling crowd, Adrienne searched for Dillon in the dimly lit, smoke-filled room. When she finally located him, he was standing near a table, a drink in one hand and his other hand clasping the elbow of a dark-haired woman. His head was tilted toward her, and even from across the room, Adrienne could hear his husky laughter. She tried unsuccessfully to smother the flash of jealousy that streaked through her as her uncle led her toward them.

As Adrienne and Louie stopped at the table, the lights came on and the dark-haired woman turned toward them with a smile. With one hand still at the small of Adrienne's back, Louie cleared his throat and motioned toward her. "I believe you know Carol," he said softly, dropping his hand and moving closer. He placed his arm around her waist, raised his chin and, in an almost defiant voice, said, "Carol is the friend I've been telling you about."

A picture of Carol's car flashed through Adrienne's mind. No wonder it had looked so familiar; she'd seen it parked beside her own in the employees' parking section several times.

Dillon pulled out a chair, then tugged at Adrienne's arm. "Let's sit." He motioned for the other couple to join them, but Louie shook his head.

"The band's coming back in a minute. Save us a couple of chairs, though."

Dillon nodded. When Louie pulled Carol toward the dance floor, he slid an empty chair close to Adrienne and sat down. "Well? What's the problem?"

Wishing she could ignore the entire situation, Adrienne watched her uncle take Carol in his arms as they waited for the band to play. But with Dillon, she knew it was useless to play dumb. She also knew that she was overreacting. "I . . . why—"

"Just spit it out, sweetheart."

She faced him, almost nose to nose. "He's old enough to be her father," she blurted.

"So?" Dillon challenged. "What of it?"

Adrienne couldn't answer, nor could she bear the challenging look in Dillon's eyes. She lowered her gaze to the scarred tabletop.

She had no answer, no reason or excuse for feeling like she did except . . . *jealousy.* She was also being selfish, she decided. Louie and Kristen were the only family she had, and she'd held on to both of them, like a spoiled child unwilling to share her favorite toy.

The band tuned up for its next set and Adrienne glanced over at her uncle. Despite his age, he really seemed to grab at what life offered with every ounce of gusto he possessed. Just what *did* it matter if Carol was almost half his age?

It didn't, in fact. As Dillon had so pointedly reminded her, her uncle was a grown man. And Carol, Adrienne admitted grudgingly, was a nice woman. If the two of them enjoyed each other's company, then who was she to question her uncle's actions?

Adrienne turned to Dillon, and on impulse, leaned over and kissed him. His eyes widened with surprise. "Thanks," she whispered. "You're right. It really doesn't matter."

Dillon rewarded her with an understanding smile. "Be back in a minute," he mouthed above the music.

Wondering what he was up to, Adrienne watched him make his way through the crowded tables toward the band stage. The music stopped and the band leader bent down. When she saw Dillon slip something into the man's hand, she grew even more curious. Then Dillon turned and walked toward her. His gaze held hers across the short distance, transmitting an unmistakable message. He had a predatory, smoldering look about him, and Adrienne shivered in anticipation.

He stopped in front of her, his eyes burning with a jade flame of desire. When he held out his hand, Adrienne knew that he was asking for more than just a dance, that the dance was just a prelude of things to come.

The choice was hers. She could either take what he was offering, knowing there would be no declarations of undying love and forever, or she could spend the rest of her life wondering how it might have been.

The minute she placed her hand in his, the strains of *Unchained Melody,* an old, familiar love ballad, filled the room.

The words of the song and the message they conveyed hummed through her. On the edge of the dance floor, Dillon's arms closed around her, and she felt as if she'd suddenly stepped into the outer stratosphere where nothing existed but the two of them, moving in unison.

As the powerful words vibrated between them, Dillon wrapped her more tightly against him, his hard, solid thighs pressing against her intimately. When his broad, unyielding chest rubbed sensuously against her breasts, a spark of heat ignited deep inside her and began to spread.

His hot breath caressed her cheek, and he pulled her arms up around his neck, until nothing but the thin layers of their clothing separated them.

As they swayed to the music, the slow heat that had been building burst into an aching need. And that illusive something that she had always wondered about, had always been denied, seemed to hover around the outer edges of her feminine core, teasing her, taunting her.

When the last strains of the music died, Dillon slid his hands up to her shoulders and he pulled away just enough so that she was looking up at him. "Come home with me."

Adrienne couldn't have denied the longing and need she heard in his quiet, raspy request no more than she could deny the hunger and craving she felt. He was in her blood, in her soul, branded in her heart and mind forever. And she wanted him.

THE RIDE TO Dillon's condo was a blur for Adrienne. Concentration on anything but the man sitting next to her was impossible. The very air around them seemed charged with an urgency that negated everything but the necessity to complete what had been started on the dance floor.

The moment they stepped inside his living room, Dillon reached for her, dragging her into his arms. When his lips covered hers in a searing kiss of desire, Adrienne groaned, wanting more than just kisses, and the fire within her exploded into an all-consuming, raging inferno.

Dillon suddenly pulled away, gasping like a man who had just run a marathon. Adrienne tugged at his suit coat, and he shrugged out of it, letting it fall to the carpet. When she reached for his tie, he stilled her hands with his own, bringing her fingers to his lips and kissing each one. Then slowly, ever so gently, he backed toward a short hallway, pulling her along with him.

For a brief moment, he left her standing in the doorway of what she assumed was his bedroom, while he switched on a bedside lamp. The soft glow illuminated the starkness of the room, which held only a king-size bed, a lamp stand and a dresser.

Dillon loosened his tie and walked toward her. "Since the first day I met you, I wondered how you'd feel in my arms." He slid the tie from around his neck and dropped it. Pulling his shirt free of his pants, he unbuttoned the sleeves.

"I wondered a few things myself," she said boldly. Reaching out, she began to work on his shirt buttons, her fingers clumsy with impatience.

Dillon gave a little jerk each time her hands came in contact with his bare chest. A generous sprinkling of dark hair ran from below his neck down to the waistband of his trousers, disappearing beneath. When he shrugged off his shirt, she wanted to bury her face against that hair-roughened chest and kiss him there.

He reached behind her and she heard the almost-silent rasp of her zipper. Then, ever so slowly, he inched the dress down her arms and over her hips until she stood before him in only her half-slip and lacy bra. They finished undressing each other in silence, until they stood facing the other one, marveling at the differences between man and woman, so unique yet so perfectly created for each other.

''You're more beautiful than I imagined,'' he whispered, taking in with a searing gaze the firm fullness of her breasts, her narrow waist and the flare of her hips.

Adrienne had never thought of herself as beautiful. She was too tall, her breasts weren't quite as firm as they used to be and she still had faint but visible stretch marks running along her hips from her pregnancy. But at that moment, with Dillon's gaze sweeping over her, his eyes burning with desire, she felt beautiful.

She let her own gaze drift downward and her breath caught in her throat. She'd known that he was handsome, tall and rugged-looking with a lean and muscular build. But even in her most vivid of daydreams, she had never imagined that he could look so...so overwhelmingly virile, so all-male, with his broad, hair-covered chest, his flat stomach and his long, powerful thighs.

As if compelled by some unknown force, she reached out and touched him. She felt Dillon quiver and then a strangled sound erupted from his throat.

"Careful, sweetheart," he growled. "Or this will all be over before it starts."

Adrienne jerked her hand back, and with a strained chuckle, Dillon pulled her to the bed and eased them both down until they were lying side by side facing each other, bare skin against bare skin, hair roughened legs tangling with silky smooth ones.

He slid one arm beneath her shoulders, pulling her closer, and began kissing her, his mouth demanding yet gentle, kissing first her lips, then the tender part of her neck below her ears. All the while, his free hand caressed her—along her back, her shoulder, then down her side.

He cupped the fullness of her breast as if weighing a precious jewel, his thumb rubbing back and forth over the ever-hardening nipple.

"Oh," she gasped, loving what he was doing, loving him and wishing he would never stop the exquisite torture. She could feel the smooth hardness of Dillon's back beneath her fingers, and she kneaded his taut muscles with an urgency she didn't understand. His hips surged against hers, and she drew in a sharp breath as the evidence of his desire pressed hard and hot against the apex of her thighs, as if seeking the warmth and shelter that only she could give.

Then, suddenly, she felt his tongue flick against her aching, pebble-hard nipple. Once. Twice. And then again, just before he took it into his hot, hungry mouth. He was gently pulling and sucking, causing her most secret place to contract each shattering time, and she couldn't hold back the strangled moan that seemed to come from deep within. Nor could she still her quivering legs.

"Yes, oh yes," she cried, moving restlessly, wanting, needing even more. She was teetering on the edge. She could feel a pressure building in her core, like nothing she'd ever experienced before. She felt hot, wet and empty. So empty. She ached to be filled. God, it had been so long. "Please. Dillon, please," she begged. "Now!"

Dillon released her breast and rolled her onto her back. "Hold on, baby. Just hold on," he growled. For several seconds, he fumbled in the drawer of the bedside table.

Responsible.

The word flashed through her mind even as she moved restlessly against the bed. She would always be able to rely on Dillon to take responsibility for his actions.

Then he was back, poised above her, his weight resting on his elbows and thighs, almost but not quite touching her. She could feel the heat radiating from him, could smell the scent of male desire as he took her mouth in a searing kiss, his tongue plunging within, filling her with its slick roughness and tangling with hers in a duel of battle and conquest.

She arched her hips, seeking him, needing him. At the same time Dillon lowered himself on top of her, sliding within her slowly, ever so slowly, until he was sheathed deep inside.

For what seemed an eternity, he didn't move and she couldn't. He felt so good buried deep within her, filling and soothing the aching, empty void.

"Ah, Adrienne."

Her name was a whispered benediction on his lips, a groan of deep contentment. She reveled in the delicious sensation of being completely covered by him, his muscled hardness, gently, protectively shielding her with his strength.

"You feel too good. So warm, so tight. I want to wait... Oh, God," he groaned. "But I don't think I can."

With his searing gaze locked with hers, Dillon moved, withdrew, then buried himself again. At first slowly, with a rhythm as old as time, then more urgently.

The quickening within her grew with each stroke, building to a throbbing crescendo. This was what she'd been missing, she realized. She'd never come this far before. Then she couldn't think. All she could do was hold onto Dillon as he brought her to the brink of the universe, then took her over the edge.

She cried out and Dillon sank inside her one last time, burying himself deep within her quivering thighs. He stiffened with his own need, shuddered, and then the cosmos shattered into a million pulsing stars.

REALITY RETURNED SLOWLY, like an unwelcome visitor, and Dillon breathed deeply of the intoxicating scent of spent passion, savoring it like the last drop of an exotic perfume.

With Adrienne's warm, soft body curled against him, he lay staring at the dappled, early morning sunlight on the bedroom ceiling. Her deep, even breathing told him that she had finally drifted off to sleep.

Even now, after making love twice more, he could feel himself grow hard just thinking about her.

Tonight shouldn't have happened, he thought. It would have been a hell of a lot less painful to have wondered what he would miss than to *know* what he might never have again. Dillon felt his chest grow heavy and his throat tighten with an emotion he didn't want to feel.

God, he loved her. Wanted to spend the rest of his life with her. But how could he even think such thoughts when his life was so uncertain? If he couldn't save Twin Oaks, he'd be out of a job... and so would she.

CHAPTER THIRTEEN

ADRIENNE UNFOLDED the wheelchair and held it steady until Kristen had swung herself from the car seat and settled comfortably. From inside the car, she retrieved the well-worn school bag and handed it to her daughter.

She leaned down and hugged Kristen. "Have a good day, hon. Uncle Louie will pick you up this afternoon."

"Okay," Kristen mumbled, shrugging away.

Frowning, Adrienne watched her daughter wheel down the sidewalk toward the front doors of the school. Other kids lined the sidewalk in small groups, mingling, laughing and talking. Kristen looked neither right nor left, but continued on a straight path toward the building.

After a moment, Adrienne slammed the car door, walked around to the driver's side and slid inside. Ever since Jack had dropped Kristen off late Sunday night, the girl had been unusually quiet and withdrawn. Monday evening she had hardly touched her dinner, and when Adrienne had approached the subject of her weekend, Kristen had sidestepped the issue by claiming she had loads of homework she had to get done. Then she'd disappeared into her bedroom.

Adrienne sighed as she watched the school doors close behind her daughter. She shifted the car into drive, glanced in the rearview mirror and pulled out onto the street. Maybe she should call Jack and ask him what had happened when he and Kristen had talked. Maybe if she understood just exactly what he'd said to Kristen . . .

You're doing it again.

Adrienne tightened her grip on the steering wheel. She'd promised herself that she wouldn't interfere, that she'd let them work out their own problems. Yet here she was, at the first sign of trouble, ready to barge in and take over. Reminding herself that whatever had transpired between Jack and Kristen had to be resolved by them alone didn't ease her anxiety in the least.

SEATED AT HIS FATHER'S desk, Dillon stared at the figures on the spread sheet. "Damn!" he muttered. No matter how he plugged in the numbers, the results were the same. There was too much money going out and not enough coming in. At this rate, there was no way he could meet the loan payment.

Even if he used his own savings and the profits from the sale of his Florida beach house, he was still short. The two long days he'd spent going from bank to bank, trying to borrow the money, had proved fruitless. With Twin Oaks being used for collateral for the loan from Jamison, not one lousy bank was willing to take a chance on him or Twin Oaks. He had nothing but debts to back up a loan.

He had to make more cuts. *What about Adrienne?* After Friday night how could he possibly tell her he had to fire her? She'd never believe he hadn't known all along he would have to cut her job. But he hadn't, dammit.

Was saving Twin Oaks worth the cost, losing the only woman he'd ever truly cared about, the only woman he'd ever truly loved?

What's more important? Saving a few at the expense of all, or saving all at the expense of a few?

As his own words came back to haunt him, Dillon swore again. When he'd spoken those arrogant words to Adrienne, he hadn't been in love with her.

He shoved back from the desk and stared up at the ceiling. He wanted to smash something, to shout, to rail against the fates for giving him a piece of heaven, then snatching it away.

He sighed and closed his eyes, willing himself to think logically, with his head and not with his breaking heart.

Reality.

He had to concentrate on reality. And reality was the five-hundred-plus club members and their families, the golf pro, the tennis pro and their staffs, the kitchen employees, the greens employees and the dining room staff. So many people depending on him. But most of all, he thought of his mother and father. The rest of their retired lives depended on his ability to pay off the loan.

He looked at the figures again. It was possible that if he cut one more person from each department, the money saved from those salaries, along with his savings and the sale of the beach house, would almost be enough to pay the remainder of the debt. And if the weather held for the member-guest tournament... On and on and on, he thought. Too many variables. Too many things that could go haywire at the last minute.

But dammit, he had to try. He had no choice.

And what about Adrienne?

Dillon swore again. After today, he'd have to forget her, because it was a sure bet she'd want to forget she had ever met him.

LATER THAT AFTERNOON, Adrienne stood at the copy machine in the reception area and watched as it spit out the copies of the work schedule for the upcoming week.

She gazed over at the closed door of the manager's office. Dillon had finally moved in, but it was still hard getting used to thinking of Franklin's office as now belonging to him.

Dillon.

Adrienne felt her cheeks grow warm and she shifted her gaze back to the copy machine.

Saturday night had been wonderful. More than wonderful, she thought, remembering how time and time again, Dillon had shown her another side of the art of making love. Each time had ended in a climax more devastating and earth shattering than the last, leaving them both drained and in awe of the powerful chemistry between them.

But that had been Saturday. Monday he'd been out of the office all day. He'd called in and talked to her, but he'd sounded preoccupied.

And today? Adrienne grimaced. She'd seen him and talked with him, but it was as if Saturday night had never happened, as if the romantic, passionate man he'd been had only existed in her imagination. Today he seemed even more remote, more distant.

The manager's door opened abruptly. Adrienne glanced up and was shocked to see how haggard Dillon was.

"I need to talk to you."

His rough voice didn't sound any better than he looked, and Adrienne's stomach suddenly felt queasy. She nodded, quickly gathered the schedule copies and then walked toward him.

Dillon closed the door, the firm click sounding ominous in the too quiet room. He motioned for her to be seated. Once he was behind the desk, he seemed to take an inordinate amount of time shuffling a stack of papers and files before he finally spoke.

"There's no easy way to say this except to come right out with it."

Adrienne's sense of uneasiness grew. Her hands felt wet and clammy, and she placed the stack of schedules on the floor by her chair. She rubbed her palms against her skirt. "Has—has something happened? Your father—"

Dillon quickly shook his head. "Dad's fine."

His clipped answer did little to ease her sense of foreboding. She clenched her hands tightly. "Please. You're making me nervous."

Dillon dropped his gaze to the top of his desk. "I'm sorry." He took a deep breath. "I have to cut more jobs. I never dreamed it would come to this, but what I've done so far just isn't enough."

The last was spoken harshly, as if he loathed himself, and Adrienne's instinct was to comfort him, to somehow reassure him that everything would be okay. But a tiny fear deep within began to take root and she kept quiet.

"You have to believe me. I have no choice. My decision has absolutely nothing to do with your abilities to handle your job. I've made some inquiries, and if you're interested, there are a couple of possibilities you might want to check out. I care about you..."

His voice trailed away, and the fear began to spread, leaving Adrienne cold and numb.

Dillon pulled a folder from the stack on the desk, and from where she was seated, she recognized it as an employee file.

"All I can give you is two weeks severance pay..."

The rest of his words were lost to Adrienne as she fought to come to grips with what he was saying.

Somewhere beneath the haze of disbelief, the thought finally surfaced that she was being let go, laid off. Then, like wave after wave relentlessly pounding against a shoreline, a more devastating realization crashed around her, hitting her with a force so powerful that she almost doubled from the agonizing pain of it.

Saturday night.

Had he known Saturday night? Icy fingers of numbness crawled through her veins, freezing out everything but that one awareness. She lifted her chin and stared at him in disbelief. "You used me!" Her accusation hit its mark and Dillon paled.

"No—"

"How long have you known?"

His face was a mask of misery, but Adrienne was beyond feeling anything except the sting of his betrayal.

"I swear, I didn't know until this morning."

"I don't believe you," she said, her voice barely a whisper.

Dillon's head snapped up. His eyes burned with an intensity so strong that Adrienne cringed. "You have to believe me. This has nothing to do with Saturday night." His voice rose ominously. "Dammit, I care about you. I..." He slammed his fist down on the desk. "But this is business. That was—"

"Business!" Blind, red-hot anger, like a sudden, blazing inferno, sprang up within her. She gripped the sides of the chair. "You knew this was going to happen, yet you said nothing. But worse, you played me along, like some naive, blind fool, and let me think that I was... That you—"

"No!" he roared. "It wasn't like that! Haven't you heard a word I've said? Don't you understand? I didn't know, and now I don't have a choice." He snatched up a piece of paper and shook it at her. "This is a list of job openings, possibilities of other management positions. Good possibilities—"

Adrienne sprang from the chair, snatched the list from him and ripped it in half, then ripped it again. With an effort born of fury, she hurled the torn paper at him, the pieces fluttering around him like wounded butterflies.

"You can take your list and stuff it," she shouted. Then she whirled around, and with a vicious twist of the doorknob, flung the door open. With one last look at him, a look that contained every bit of contempt she could muster, she slammed the door behind her.

Ignoring Joanne's wide-eyed, shocked stare, Adrienne stormed down the hallway to her office, snatched up her purse and almost ran for the stairway.

Fueled by Dillon's betrayal and her own indignation, her temper continued to rage during the short drive home. Everything she'd worked for during the past six years, everything she'd accomplished, was gone, destroyed by the one person she had finally allowed herself to love.

Adrienne hit the steering wheel with the heel of her hand. "Damn him!" she cried out.

When she pulled into the driveway, she switched off the engine and sat staring straight ahead, her fingers wrapped around the steering wheel in a death grip.

Finally willing herself to calm down, she took deep, gulping breaths. Slowly, ever so slowly, she felt her anger drain away until at last it sputtered and died, leaving the cold ashes of Dillon's betrayal.

Empty.

God, she felt so empty...except for the dull pain building beneath her breasts. Adrienne bit her lip, determined to keep it at bay.

Noises surfaced around her. A group of children laughed and played on the sidewalk next door. Her neighbor was trimming a row of hedges. Her world was falling apart, yet everything seemed so...so normal.

She had to get inside the house. As in the eye of a hurricane, the lull before the storm, she knew that at any moment the full force of her humiliation was going to hit. And when it did, she had to be where it was safe, where there would be no witnesses to her shame.

On legs that felt like leadened weights, Adrienne made it to the house and through the front door. She could hear voices in the kitchen. The smell of cooking wafted around her, making her nauseous. Her uncle and Kristen were preparing dinner.

God, don't let them see me like this, she thought. As quietly as possible, she hurried down the hallway, until she finally reached the safety of her bedroom. She cautiously closed the door behind her and turned the lock.

Too bright, too cheery. The room was a mockery of the sorrow she felt inside. As if in a dream where everything switched into slow motion, Adrienne walked to the window and snapped the blinds closed. Better, she thought. Dark, just like the empty space where her heart used to be.

Slipping her shoes off, she made her way to the bed. She jerked back the covers, slid in between them and pulled them up to her chin.

So cold. She shivered and burrowed deeper, wondering if she would ever feel warm again.

For long moments she lay there, feeling nothing except a building, aching pressure. Her eyes blurred. With the back of her fist, she dashed away the salty tears that trickled down her cheeks. She would not cry, she swore. She had to get through this, had to be strong. She'd been through worse and she'd survived. And she'd survive this.

A great, heaving shudder rippled through her, and from somewhere within the room came a soft, keening sound. When she realized it was coming from herself, she clamped her teeth together until her jaw ached, trying to stem the awful noise. But instead of subsiding, the sound broke into huge, racking sobs.

"Oh, God," she cried. How had everything gone so wrong, gotten so confusing? Minutes passed, an eternity of despair. Someone was shouting. It took a moment for her to realize that the pounding she heard was coming from her bedroom door.

"Adrienne! Let me in!" Her uncle was shouting. She could hear the concern in his voice.

Can't let him see me like this, she thought. "I—I'm okay," she called out, her voice catching in between sobs.

"Then let me in."

"No...please...just leave me alone." She groaned and rammed a fist against her mouth as if that would stop the horrible sobs that kept pouring out of her.

She held her breath, and when several moments passed and she heard nothing further, she let out a shuddering sigh. Then suddenly, the door opened.

Adrienne stared through a blur in disbelief as her uncle marched in. In the six months that he'd lived with them, she'd never seen him lose his temper, utter an angry word, or look so...so furious.

He shook his finger at her. "Young woman, I realize that this is your house and I'm living here on borrowed time, but dammit, we're family. If you hurt, I hurt. If Kristen hurts, we both hurt. Now I want to know what the hell is going on."

Adrienne glared at him. "I locked that door!"

Louie gave her a level look and held up his other hand. Between his forefinger and thumb was an ordinary hairpin. "Next time you want to keep me out, try a dead bolt. And I'm not leaving until you tell me what's got you in such an all-fired uproar."

For long moments, Adrienne couldn't speak. All she could do was stare at him. He was her father's brother, and although there was little physical resemblance, a long-forgotten childhood memory suddenly surfaced, the memory of her father demanding to know how her knees and elbows had gotten so skinned up. She hadn't wanted to tell him, but he'd kept at her until she did. When he'd found out that the school bully had been picking on her and had shoved her down when she'd tried to fight back, he'd been furious. Then he'd hugged her and told her that it was one of his jobs as her father to protect her, to be there when she needed him.

For a long time, she'd had no one to be there for her, no one to depend on except herself. And through it all— her parents' deaths, her teenage pregnancy, Jack's alcoholism, the hours she'd sat by Kristen's bedside, praying that her little girl would live, and Jack's final desertion—through it all she'd been strong, had needed no one...until now.

"Oh, Uncle Louie," she cried.

Within the space of a heartbeat, he was beside her, his arms wrapped around her. "It's okay, darlin'," he crooned. "I'm here." He patted her awkwardly on the back while she sobbed against his shoulder. "Let it all out. That's right, just let it go."

"He—he...I lost my job," she sobbed. "And he knew, dammit. He—he knew it was going to happen. Saturday night, I—I thought he cared about me, but he didn't." She shook her head and clutched at her uncle's back. "He couldn't— Oh, God, how could I have been such a blind, stupid fool?"

"Now, now, darlin'. You're nobody's fool," Louie said, his voice gruff with emotion. "And it's not the end of the world."

He pulled back and smoothed her hair away from her face. His faded blue eyes narrowed, and when he spoke, his voice was strong with conviction. "You're the strongest, most capable young woman I've ever had the good fortune to meet. Your father, rest his soul, would have been so proud of you." He gently squeezed her shoulders. "You have absolutely nothing to be ashamed of, do you hear?" When she didn't answer, he gave her a little shake. "Well, are you listening?"

Adrienne sniffed inelegantly and nodded.

"Now, that's better. Your old uncle has been around and seen some things in his day and time, and believe me, when I say we'll get through this, we will...together," he emphasized.

Adrienne groaned. "You don't understand. Without the extra income, I won't be able to keep Kristen in her school and I won't be able to finish my degree. I depended on that money."

The door bumped against the wall, and Adrienne's gaze flew to the doorway. Oh, no, she thought. Kristen shouldn't see her like this.

"Mom?"

Adrienne pulled back from Louie, sniffed and quickly scrubbed at her wet face.

Kristen rolled farther into the room. "Mom, it's okay. I—I don't like that snooty private school anyway, not since Susan left. Katie goes to public school, and she says it's great." She suddenly looked sheepish and shrugged. "At least as great as school can be."

Louie chuckled and winked at Kristen. He turned back to Adrienne. "There, that's one of your problems solved." He cleared his throat and tried to look more serious. "Now, about college. Appears to me that this might turn out to be a blessing in disguise. Instead of going part-time, now you can go full out."

"Yeah, Mom," Kristen piped in. "If you go full-time, you could probably finish in a couple of semesters."

Adrienne looked at her daughter, then at her uncle. "And how are we suppose to eat? How am I supposed to pay tuition?"

Louie patted her on the arm. "You just let me worry about that for a change. I've got a little put back, and we won't starve."

Adrienne shook her head. "Oh, no. I couldn't let you do that."

"And why not?" he asked indignantly.

"I—I..." She shook her head again. "I just couldn't."

Louie gathered her hands in his. "Listen to me," he said softly. "I've roamed all over this earth like some kind of Gypsy, never setting down roots anywhere, always moving on to the next horizon. Don't get me wrong. There's not much I regret about the way I've lived my life, but..." He stared hard into her eyes. "Living like that... well, no one ever needed me, and a body sometimes craves to feel needed. I came here hoping that maybe it wasn't too late, that maybe I could help in some way. And since I don't have any young'uns of my own, the least you can do is let an old man pretend and dream a little."

Adrienne didn't think she had any tears left to cry, but she felt her eyes fill until fat, wet teardrops spilled down her cheeks. And through them, she smiled.

Reaching out, she wrapped her arms around her uncle, giving him a hug.

"You're not old," she whispered. "And you're the best." She pulled back and kissed him on his cheek. "I love you."

"Me, too," Kristen added, rolling her wheelchair closer so she too could kiss him.

Louie gave a suspicious sniff and cleared his throat. "Well, now." He cleared his throat again. "Since we've got all that settled, I've got a ground-meat casserole warming in the oven that will make your mouth water."

Kristen raised her eyebrows in an exaggerated grimace. "That's just his fancy name for meat loaf and potatoes."

Adrienne's shaky smile grew wider. "Sounds good to me. Why don't you two go dish it out, and as soon as I wash my face, I'll be right there."

"Go on, squirt, and mind your momma." Louie gave Kristen a pat on the shoulder. "Set the table for me."

With a shrug of her shoulders and one last, worried look at her mom, Kristen wheeled herself out of the bedroom.

Louie waited a moment until Kristen disappeared. He turned to Adrienne. "About Dillon."

Adrienne felt her stomach knot up.

"I know, I know." He held up his hand. "All I want to say is that you need to give it some time. Don't get me wrong—I'm not defending what he did—but maybe he...well, all I know is that he's a good man. And whether you believe it now or not, I still think he cares about you."

Before she could protest, her uncle turned and strolled out of the room.

In the bathroom, Adrienne stared at her reflection in the mirror. Her uncle's words kept reverberating in her head. *Give it some time.* Ignoring the thoughts, she frowned. Her hair had come loose and hung in matted tangles, making her look like a wild woman. Her eyes were red and puffy, and mascara streaked her cheeks. She twisted the spigot and cold water poured out of the faucet full force.

He's a good man. So what? she thought. Cupping her hands, she splashed the cool liquid against her face, then grabbed a hand towel. There were lots of so-called "good men" in the world.

He cares about you. "Humph," she snorted. If Dillon cared about her, as her uncle seemed to think he did, he certainly had a strange way of showing it. She blotted her face dry, then picked up her hairbrush.

No, this time her uncle was way off base. Besides, she had no one to blame but herself for being so stupid and naive. And that's what she'd been, she thought, wincing with each painful stroke of the brush. Yeah, he cared all right. Just long enough to get what he wanted—her knowledge and expertise about the club and its employees, and her body, willing and eager, in his bed.

Well, what did you expect? A confession of undying love?

Adrienne glared at her reflection and carefully laid the hairbrush on the sink counter. That was exactly what she'd expected came the painful answer. Blinking rapidly against another bout of tears, she turned away from the mirror. Who needed Dillon Reynolds or his snooty country club anyway? she asked herself bitterly.

But as she entered the dining room, a tiny voice of truth whispered that *she* needed Dillon and that she really did care about Twin Oaks. Plastering on a too-bright smile, she gritted her teeth, determined to ignore the voice.

DILLON SAT ALONE on a bar stool in the club's main lounge. Except for the bartender and a group of people seated at a table in the corner, the bar was almost empty. Strains of music filtered over the sounds of clinking glasses, occasional laughter and chatter coming from the restaurant across the foyer.

Dillon had never felt so alone in his whole life. And he was breaking his own cardinal rule. Some club managers saw nothing wrong with having a couple of drinks in the evening and socializing with the members. But Dillon had never done so.

He glared at the half-full glass, then downed the rest of the liquor in one swallow. Catching the bartender's attention, he motioned for a refill—his third, but who the hell was counting?

LATE THE FOLLOWING afternoon, Dillon walked up to Adrienne's front door. He reached inside his breast suit pocket and pulled out an envelope. Holding it by the corner with one hand, he tapped it against his palm and drew in a deep breath for courage. Adrienne had stormed out of his office the day before without taking her severance pay or the letter of recommendation he'd written for her.

After a moment, he straightened his shoulders and finally knocked on the door. Only a day had gone by since he'd seen her, but it felt like an eternity. Several moments passed and no one answered. When he reached up to knock again, the door suddenly swung open.

"What are you doing here?" Kristen glared up at him nastily, as if he were a bug she wanted to squash. He hadn't counted on seeing her.

"You made my mom cry."

Her accusation stung. A disturbing picture of Adrienne in tears flashed through his mind, making the self-loathing he already felt even worse. He had no idea what to say to Kristen.

He cleared his throat. "May I come in?"

"Why?"

Dillon held up the envelope. "I have something for your mom."   Face to face with Kristen's blatant hostility, he suddenly wished he'd mailed the damned check instead of bringing it by himself.

He cleared his throat again and felt a slow heat crawl up his neck. Who was he kidding? He'd grabbed at the excuse to see her again.

"Is your mother home?"

Kristen gave him a look cold enough to freeze ice cubes, wheeled her chair around and, without a word, left him standing in the doorway. Feeling more uncomfortable with each passing second, Dillon stepped inside the living room and closed the door behind him.

The television was on, turned to a sitcom that Dillon knew was popular with teenagers. From the direction of the kitchen came a faint whistling, accompanied by the sound of rattling dishes. Probably Louie, he thought.

It seemed an eternity before Adrienne finally appeared in the doorway. The sight of her was a shock and his heartbeat faltered. Her hair was pulled up in a lopsided ponytail. Without make-up, and dressed in faded jeans, a sweatshirt and tennis shoes that had seen better days, she looked like a bedraggled teenager.

She lifted her chin and frowned, reminding him of the way Kristen had looked at him earlier.

"You wanted to see me?"

Dillon nodded, suddenly feeling foolish and tongue-tied. At that moment, he not only wanted to continue feasting his hungry eyes on her, he wanted to hold her, to feel her pressed close to him again.

He took a step toward her, but stopped abruptly at the sudden appearance of Louie and Kristen.

Louie nodded gravely. "Dillon," he said, acknowledging his presence but not offering his usual enthusiastic greeting. Kristen refused to even look at him.

Louie turned to Adrienne. "Kristen and I are going for a walk before it gets dark. We'll be back in about thirty minutes."

Coming here had been a mistake, Dillon realized as he watched Louie and Kristen leave. Instead of feeling better and more at peace, as he'd foolishly hoped, he felt ten times worse than before.

"What do you want?"

Adrienne's unemotional tone cut him to the quick. What he wanted was to somehow take away the cold, hard look in her dark eyes.

Instead, he held out the envelope. "I brought you this."

Adrienne eyed it as if anything he offered was suspect. But after a moment, she finally took it.

"It—it's your severance pay... and a letter of recommendation."

Adrienne had already figured out what was in the envelope. It was more out of some morbid sense of curiosity than anything else that she ripped it open and pulled out its contents. After a cursory glance at the check, she stuffed it into her jeans pocket, then quickly scanned the letter.

The glowing words of praise jumped out at her, each one adding to the mounting pain that seeing Dillon again had caused. Her insides quivered and she was tempted to wad up the paper and throw it across the room. But she'd acted childish enough the day before in his office, she figured, and she wasn't about to let him see just how deeply he'd hurt her.

She carefully refolded the paper and laid it on a nearby table.

"I'm sorry I can't give you any more than two weeks pay," he said. "God knows, you deserve more." He lowered his gaze to the floor. "Maybe later I can add another two weeks... after I pay off the loan...."

"What's the matter?" she lashed out. "Afraid I might cause problems?"

Dillon jerked up his head and stared at her. Every bit of color in his face seemed to fade, leaving his skin ashen.

"I don't need a payoff," she quickly retorted. "And I don't need you. I can get along just fine without you and Twin Oaks."

"Oh, Adrienne..." He shook his head and there was a wealth of hurt and longing in his eyes. "Is that what you really think of me—that I'm trying to pay you off?"

His question hung between them and his words swirled about her, penetrating the wall of defenses she'd built around her heart. Once before, the day he'd forced his father to retire, Dillon had asked her the same thing. And just as she'd known then that he wasn't guilty of what she'd accused him of, she knew now, deep down, that he hadn't meant the offer to be a payoff.

Answering him truthfully would tear away the last shred of pride she had left, however, so she did the only thing she knew to do. She ignored the question.

"Look," she replied stiffly. "You've done what you came to do, so please, just leave."

"I'll leave...in a minute," he said. "But first I think you should know something—something I should have told you Saturday night."

At the mention of their night of lovemaking, Adrienne suddenly felt weak in the knees. She bit her lower lip to keep it from trembling.

"I love you," he whispered.

She threw up her hand as if to ward off a physical blow and backed away. "No!" she cried. "Don't say that! Not now."

Dillon set his jaw. "Why not? It's true, whether you choose to believe it or not. And I want to make sure you completely understand how I feel."

"Oh, I understand all right." She lifted her chin and stared him straight in the eyes. "I understand that you've got a twisted idea of what love is. I'm not sure you even know the meaning of the word. You don't profess to love someone just to soften the blow you know you will be dealing her. Love isn't something you can switch off during business hours and switch on afterward. Sometimes you have to make allowances. Sometimes there's just no way you can separate emotions into neat little compartments."

"Ha! Now you sound like my father. And that kind of thinking is exactly why Twin Oaks is in the shape it is now."

Adrienne shook her head. "Just what did he do to you that's made you so bitter?"

Dillon stared at her, his eyes suddenly glacial. "That's in the past. It has nothing to do with now."

Adrienne shook her head. "I think it does. I think you still haven't let go of it, whatever it was. Even the slightest hint that you might be like your father makes you just that much more determined to be the opposite."

"That's ridiculous. And besides, it's none of your concern what happens between my father and me." Dillon strode quickly to the front door. With his hand on the knob, he glared at her over his shoulder. "I've told you how I feel. If and when you're ready to talk about it reasonably, you know where you can find me." With that, he jerked the door open and slammed it behind him.

"Don't hold your breath," Adrienne whispered to the empty room.

CHAPTER FOURTEEN

ON A CLEAR APRIL MORNING, Dillon pulled his car into
his parents' driveway and switched off the engine. He
reached up and rubbed his neck and let out a weary
sigh. He'd never realized just how much responsibility
Adrienne had shouldered until he'd let her go, until he'd
actually witnessed just how little work Joe Blount did.
The past weeks without her had been hell...in more
ways than one.

He missed her—missed seeing her smiling face each
morning, missed talking to her, kissing her, holding her,
teasing her. And he missed Kristen and Louie.

Dillon groaned and shoved open the car door. He
climbed the steps of his parents' home and punched the
doorbell. When his mother had called, insisting that he
come over for lunch, he'd jumped at the chance to get
away from the club for a few minutes. Since his parents
had returned from the trip they'd taken, he'd felt guilty
that he hadn't taken time to visit them. The door swung
open.

"It's about time. Two o'clock is too late to be eating
lunch."

Dillon eyed his mother, noticing her tan was a shade
darker and that she looked rested. The worry lines that

had marked her face the past weeks since his father's surgery seemed smoother, less pronounced. He smiled, glad his parents had finally taken time to visit their relatives in Florida.

"Sorry I'm late," he said, following her back to the cheery, oversize kitchen. "One of the members cornered me as I was heading out the door."

"Humph! Don't give me those excuses," she said in her usual no-nonsense way. "I've heard them all before." She motioned for him to be seated in the bay-window breakfast nook, which was already set.

Dillon glanced at the two place mats. "Where's Dad?"

"He ate about an hour ago. Said he had an errand to run." She paused, her eyes narrowed. "And you can get that look off your face," she said. "He *did* have something to do and he's *not* avoiding you. You're the one who's late."

Dillon jerked his head up, surprised at the scolding tone of her voice.

"Here." She set a plate of chicken salad in front of him. "Eat your lunch, and then you and I are going to have a heart-to-heart that's been long overdue. And I mean eat every bite. You've lost weight," she said accusingly.

Dillon stared at her, wondering just what he was in for. He finally shook his head and picked up his fork. There was no use doing anything but what she told him. He'd learned a long time ago that she wouldn't talk about whatever was on her mind until she was good and ready. Dillon felt a smile tug at his lips. His mother never changed.

Twenty minutes later, she whisked away his empty plate, poured them each a cup of coffee and sat down again opposite him. Leaning forward, she rested her arms on the table. Her fingers tapped out a nervous code against the oak tabletop. "First of all, you know I usually mind my own business. I've tried never to interfere in your life or with the decisions you've made."

Dillon silently acknowledged the truth of her words.

"Seven years ago, when you left here, you almost broke my heart. Not because you left—parents expect their children to make their own way in this world. But what I couldn't understand, didn't understand until recently, was the way you left and the reason you left."

"Mom, I don't—"

"No!" She shook her finger at him. "For once in your life, you're going to listen."

Dillon clamped his mouth shut, but he felt as if the lunch he'd just eaten had suddenly turned sour.

"Your father and I did a lot of talking while we were driving to Florida, more talking than we've done in years. And you know what I found out?" Without giving him time to answer, she rushed on. "All this time, I've blamed him for being too hard on you, being too set in his ways to give you a chance seven years ago. Do you realize I almost divorced him because of you?"

The sick feeling in Dillon's stomach grew worse.

"And all that time," she continued, "all those years of blaming him, resenting him . . . it was your fault, not his."

She nodded her head vigorously. "Yes, your fault. Contrary to what you believed, in all our married life, your father has never, *never,* been unfaithful to me. You thought he was having an affair, didn't you?"

Dillon neither denied nor confirmed what she'd asked.

"Humph! He was no more having an affair with that poor woman than I'm the Queen of Sheba. And you . . ." Her voice rose a decibel. "You didn't have the decency, respect or maturity to see past the nose on your face. Oh, I know what you heard, but you interpreted it wrong."

Dillon glared at his mother. "I don't want to hurt you, Mom, but he was seen with her and they weren't exactly shaking hands, if you know what I mean."

"Yes." She nodded vigorously. "She hugged him and kissed him."

Dillon felt his temper heat even higher.

"Out of gratitude," she practically shouted. "He'd just handed her the money that the members had collected to help her with her husband's hospital bills. I should know. I was sitting in the room with them."

WHEN THE PHONE RANG, Adrienne jumped. She looked up from the term paper she'd been slaving over for most of the afternoon. Shoving her chair back from the dining room table, she hurried to the extension in the kitchen. "Hello."

"Hey, it's Jack."

Adrienne slumped against the cabinet. Why did she think, every time the phone rang, that it would be Dillon? It was over.

"Adrienne?"

"Yes, Jack, I'm here."

"Is Kristen home yet?"

Adrienne sighed. "No. Today is her therapy day, remember?"

"Oh, geez. I keep forgetting. I got off early and thought I'd pick her up for dinner. I mean, if it's okay with you."

Adrienne hesitated. "I'm sure she'd love that, but she's usually pretty tired after her therapy sessions. Then there's homework...."

"Damn. Guess I just wasn't thinking."

Adrienne couldn't help but smile. What a difference a few weeks could make, she thought. She never had found out specifically what Jack had told Kristen the night they'd had their talk, but from what she had gathered from the little Kristen had said, her daughter hadn't made it easy on him.

The important thing, she'd decided, was that both Jack and Kristen had survived. And now Jack couldn't seem to see enough of his sassy-mouthed daughter.

"How about I pick her up from therapy for you?" Jack asked, interrupting her thoughts. "From what Kristen's told me, I know you've got finals coming up."

She hesitated, then finally agreed. "I could use the extra time to finish up this paper I've been working on."

Several moments of silence passed, and Adrienne began to wonder if Jack had something else on his mind besides Kristen. When she heard him take a deep breath, she grew even more curious.

"I think it's great that you've gone back to school full-time." The words were said in a rush, as if he was afraid she might interrupt. "I don't have a whole lot of extra—money, that is—but if I can help..."

Adrienne was surprised at his offer and touched. "I really do appreciate the offer, Jack," she said. "But so far I'm managing okay." *Thanks to Uncle Louie and unemployment benefits,* she added silently.

"Well, if you change your mind, just let me know. And no strings attached," he added, as if he'd read her mind. He paused for several seconds. "I feel I at least owe you that much," he finally said. "That and a whole lot more."

"You don't—"

"Yes, I do," he insisted. "It's because of you that Kristen is such a wonderful girl, so smart, so great, so... If it weren't for you doing what you did—you know, insisting that I talk to her and all—I might never have known my own daughter. For that, I'll always be grateful."

A few minutes later, when Adrienne hung up the phone, she felt the sudden sting of tears. It seemed that everything was working out better than she'd ever expected. Her uncle had decided to stay on permanently

in Houston and was out looking for a condominium to
buy. Jack seemed to have finally come to terms with his
guilt over what had happened to Kristen.

And Kristen . . .

Adrienne wiped away the tear that escaped down her
cheek. Kristen finally had her father back. And since
she'd transferred to the nearby public school, her whole
attitude about school was different. Each morning as
she dropped her off, Adrienne had noticed that instead
of heading straight for the classroom as she had before, Kristen now lingered outside, joining the other
laughing students.

It seemed that everyone was adjusting well and that
everything was just wonderful. Yeah, she thought. Just
wonderful. A sob caught in her throat and she swallowed hard. If she was doing so great, then why did she
feel so empty and depressed? And why was she so damn
lonely?

Adrienne grabbed a paper towel, jerked it loose from
the roll and blew her nose. *Enough,* she decided,
straightening her shoulders and marching back to the
dining room. She simply wouldn't think about what
might have been. After all, she had her whole future in
front of her, everything to look forward to. And once
she had her degree, she could take her pick of job op-
portunities.

Several minutes later there was a knock at the front
door, and Adrienne groaned. At this rate, she'd never
finish. When she opened the door, she couldn't help
smiling, however.

"Franklin! What a nice surprise. Come in," she said, motioning for him to enter. "You look great." He had lost weight and looked healthier than she'd seen him look in months.

"What brings you over to my neck of the woods?"

"Figured that was the only way I'd ever get to see you again." Franklin scowled good-naturedly. "Myrna and I have about given up on you coming to see us."

Adrienne shrugged self-consciously, but didn't know what to say. How could she tell her old friend that seeing him and Myrna was too poignant a reminder of their son and of everything she had lost?

"Got a cup of coffee for an old man?"

Adrienne laughed and shook her head. "You're far from over the hill yet, and of course I've got coffee. Come into the kitchen while I fix us some."

While the coffee dripped, Adrienne seated herself opposite Franklin at the table. "So, tell me what you've been up to lately."

Franklin grinned. "Myrna and I had a great time in Florida. I even laid out on the beach like all the other tourists and got a tan."

Adrienne chuckled. "That's wonderful!"

Franklin's grin faded. "Yes, it was. I'm just sorry I didn't take more time off years ago when Dillon was a boy. I missed out on a lot of his growing-up years by always being too busy. I didn't realize until lately just how much both he and Myrna resented all the hours I spent working. At the time, I thought I was building something, doing it for my family. I guess I had my priorities all screwed up. This trip taught me a lot. Money isn't everything. Being there for your wife and son when they need you means more than a fancy house and the things that money can buy."

Adrienne frowned. "Speaking of money. The bank note is due soon, isn't it?"

Franklin nodded. "In two weeks, unfortunately."

"Will he make it?" Adrienne asked softly, hesitantly.

"He might have made it if his house in Florida had sold," Franklin answered. He stared down at his steaming cup. "But with the economy like it is..." He glanced up, and there was pain in his eyes. "Dammit, he's tried so hard and there's nothing I can do but sit back and watch. Did you know that he's barely taking enough salary to live on? Not only did he let you go, he let Joe Blount go, too. He's been staying there day and night, trying to do everything himself. He's refused my help and I don't dare interfere, not after...well, there's just nothing I can do."

Adrienne reached over, placing her hand on his arm. "What happened between you two? Why does he...why is he—"

"So hostile," Franklin finished for her.

Adrienne closed her eyes briefly. She waved her hand. "No...never mind. It's really none of my business."

Franklin gave her a pointed look. "I think it is considering you're in love with him." He paused. "You are, aren't you?"

Unable to answer, Adrienne stared at the tabletop.

"Just as I thought," he said after a moment. "And I suspect those feelings are returned."

Adrienne swept her hair away from her face impatiently. "He—he said he loved me, but..." She swallowed against the ache in the back of her throat and fought down the familiar feeling of despair and hopelessness. "I just don't understand him," she whispered. Then she raised her gaze to Franklin. "Why won't he ask for help? If he went to the members and explained the situation, I'm sure they would come up with the money. If the members knew what was happening..."

Franklin shook his head. "He won't," he said bluntly. "Not even if it means losing the club. With him, it's a matter of pride." He leaned back his head, drew in a deep breath and then released it in a sigh of frustration. "And I can understand that. It all goes back a long way. When he was a kid, I tried my hand at a couple of different ventures and almost went bankrupt before I could sell out. At Twin Oaks I wanted to be successful without asking for help. Dillon is a lot like me even though... Well, I wasn't much of a father."

"Humph!" Adrienne snorted. "Lots of kids have parents who have to work hard. They don't end up hating everything their parents stand for—"

She gasped as she realized what she had said. "Oh, Franklin, I'm sorry. I had no right to say such a thing."

Franklin patted her hand. "Don't be," he said. "I've known for a long time how my son feels about me. And yes, there's more to it. Dillon came to work for me fresh out of college," he said. "God, that boy was so full of energy and ideas, he made me tired just watching him. But even then I was pretty set in my ways, and he was headstrong, wanting to change everything, determined to be better at everything than me. And God help me, I was just as determined to show him that I could finally succeed at something.

"Anyway, after a couple of years of butting heads at every turn, he finally got so fed up with me that, in a fit of temper, he quit. To keep him from leaving, I promised him full control over personnel without my interference and a block of stock in the club." Franklin paused to take a thoughtful sip of his coffee, then set the cup back in the saucer.

"It all came to a head one day when he fired the woman in charge of food and beverage for mismanagement. When she came to me and told me, I gave her back the job. The minute Dillon found out, he came straight to my office and confronted me about it."

Franklin sighed. "Anyway, to make a long story short, he got it into his head that the reason I hired her back was because I was having an affair with her. Damned gossip." Franklin made a sound of disgust. "When he accused me right out of having an affair, I denied it...but he didn't believe me. He was so damned hotheaded and angry, he was ready to believe the worst."

"Why did you give her the job back?" Adrienne asked softly.

Franklin sighed. "She was the sister of an old school friend. Her husband was dying of cancer and she was trying to cope with hospital bills and three teenagers."

"Did you tell him that?"

Franklin shook his head. "He didn't give me the chance. He just stormed out, and by the time I got home, he'd packed up and left. I didn't know at the time and didn't find out until it was too late that he'd already lined her up with another job, one that paid pretty well but didn't have quite so much responsibility. We didn't hear from him for almost a year, except for a letter now and then addressed to his mother. And when he did call, he'd only speak to Myrna. It's just been in the last couple of years that he finally began to talk to me again."

A LONG TIME AFTER Franklin had left, Adrienne sat at the dining room table staring into space, her term paper forgotten.

She'd known from the beginning that Dillon could be single-minded and stubborn. And yes, he'd been hurt and angry. But what she couldn't understand, what didn't make sense, was how a man so conscientious of his responsibilities could sit back and do nothing when an option, a viable option, was staring him in the face.

Adrienne closed her eyes and shook her head. Pride. Damned, misplaced, male pride. Somewhere along the line, he'd gotten pride mixed up with common sense. He was so bent on proving he didn't need anyone's help that he'd been blinded . . .

Pride. And not only Dillon's. Wasn't that exactly what she was guilty of, too? Wasn't that exactly the reason she'd been content to wallow in self-pity for over a month, refusing to take the first step, waiting for Dillon to come begging, crawling back?

Adrienne felt a rush of heat climb up her neck and she squirmed in her chair. When Jack had walked out on her, she'd been hurt badly, her pride crushed. When she'd finally picked up the pieces and carved out a life for herself and Kristen, she'd done so with a vengeance.

She'd elected herself responsible for everyone she came in contact with. By being responsible, she could be in control. And if she was in control, then no one could hurt her again . . . no one until Dillon.

She'd accused him of having a twisted idea of love, of not knowing the meaning of the word. But did she? Like Dillon, hadn't she gotten caught up in pride, too? And like him, wasn't she still caught up in the past, unable to let go?

There was nothing wrong with healthy pride, she concluded. It was the other kind—the self-destructive, selfish kind—that made people bitter, ruined lives and destroyed love.

Love.

Adrienne slowly stood. Even if it was too late to salvage her relationship with Dillon, maybe it wasn't too late to help him save Twin Oaks. Surely there were times when there was nothing wrong with interfering in someone else's life, especially if it was done for the right reasons, if it was done out of love. If neither he nor Franklin could put aside their pride long enough to ask for help, she would do it for them.

LATER THAT EVENING, the minute Adrienne heard Carol's car pull into the driveway, she rushed to the front door. Stepping out onto the porch, she waved to get her uncle's attention.

"Uncle Louie," she called out. "Would you ask Carol to come inside for a minute?"

Once they were seated around the kitchen table, she began. "I have an idea that I want your opinion on, an idea that I think might save the club."

Louie slid a wary glance toward Carol, as if to say, "I told you so."

Noticing the look, Adrienne rushed on. "I know, I know, it's none of my business anymore. I don't work for Twin Oaks, but I..."

Louie smiled kindly and reached over and took Adrienne's hand. "But you love Dillon," he finished for her.

Adrienne fought to hold back the sudden tears that sprang into her eyes. "I—I care what happens to Twin Oaks...and yes, I love him."

"After everything that's happened, I don't think he would appreciate your interference."

Carol scowled at Louie and jabbed him in the ribs with her elbow. "Leave her alone and let her talk." She turned to Adrienne. "Men! A lot they know. Go ahead, hon. Don't mind him. What's your idea?"

Adrienne smiled at Carol, grateful for the other woman's understanding. "I want to get the word out about what's going on, about what Ted Jamison is trying to do and about the chemical-waste processing plant Pro-Chem intends to build. But first we have to find out exactly how much money is still needed. I know Dillon already has most of it, but it's not enough. I figure if the stockholders know, they'll come up with the rest he needs."

"That's no problem," Carol declared. "Joanne can get the total easily enough from the accountant. And as far as getting the word out, we'll just use the good old Twin Oaks grapevine."

Adrienne grinned. "I was hoping you'd say that. Let's see. Today is Friday. The club is closed on Monday, so how about if all the 'grapes' meet here Monday evening?"

Louie and Carol burst out laughing.

Adrienne chuckled and continued. "By Monday, Joanne should have the info we need. And if my guess is right, a couple of days is all it will take for the employees to spread the word."

DILLON STARED at the calendar, wishing he could hold back time. Three days left, he thought. Three lousy days and it would all be over.

He cursed and turned his attention back to the figures on the printout sheets spread across his desk. He'd had the accountant rerun them twice, but they still told the same story.

He'd lost. First Adrienne, and now Twin Oaks.

All of his planning, all of his scheming, all the long, hard hours of working day and night . . . all the long, lonely days and nights without Adrienne in his life . . . and for what?

All for nothing, he decided wearily. All for some idiotic sense of misplaced pride.

Dillon closed his eyes, recalling the visit he'd had with his mother the week before, a visit in which he'd finally learned the truth about the kind of man his father really was.

He cursed again. God, what a fool he'd been all these years. And the only excuse he had was stupidity and ignorance. When he thought about all the self-righteous bunk he had spouted off to Adrienne, about misunderstandings and jumping to conclusions, he wanted to go crawl into a hole somewhere.

And when he thought about how cruel he'd been, how unfairly he'd treated his father for years, he wanted to hang his head in shame.

Dillon stared at the phone. There was one last ace he could play. He could go to the stockholders, tell them everything. Adrienne had said they had a right to know, and once they did, he was sure they would come up with the extra money.

Before he could change his mind, he picked up the phone and punched out Joanne's extension. "Would you see if you can get Mitchell Kelly on the phone for me?"

A few minutes later, Joanne called back. "He's on line two."

"Thanks." Dillon punched the button. "Mitchell—"

"Ah, Dillon. I'm glad you called. I was going to phone you first thing this morning, but I had a minor emergency here at my office. The executive council and I need to meet with you about a matter that's been brought to our attention—today for lunch, if possible."

"Lunch is fine. I have something I need to talk with you about, too."

Three hours later, closeted in the largest of the private dining rooms, Dillon faced the executive council. He felt wired, ready to explode, wondering what Kelly and the rest of them wanted to talk to him about.

Mitchell Kelly cleared his throat to get everyone's attention. "I've called this meeting today to discuss an issue that all of us have known about but no one wanted to face." He turned his gaze to Dillon. "First of all, let me say up front that no one blames our new manager for Twin Oaks's money problems. Quite the contrary. Everyone I've talked to has nothing but praise for Dillon and the excellent job he's done. We have only ourselves to blame for letting Jamison pull the wool over our eyes, so to speak. We all assumed—wrongfully—that since he was a banker, he was the logical choice for finance-committee chairperson. We also wrongfully assumed that his long-term proposal was affordable. No one ever bothered to question him or his motives."

Dillon nodded curtly even as he felt an uncomfortable heat creep up his neck. He had learned from the council minutes that ever since Jamison had been elected, he'd methodically proposed project after project that had drained the club's reserves, forcing his father to ask for a loan. And the council, ignorant of Jamison's scheming, had gone along with the banker.

He'd also learned over the past weeks that filling his father's shoes was an almost impossible task. His father was a much-loved, much-respected man and Dillon, while not totally comfortable with his laid-back management tactics, had come to realize that love and respect were equally important.

Dillon swallowed hard. Mitchell Kelly's words meant more than he or the others would ever know.

Mitchell squared his shoulders. "Now, for the business at hand. Over the past few days, I've received so many phone calls and had so many conversations with stockholders that my ear is sore."

"Me, too!" another director said, and a chorus of agreement echoed throughout the room.

"Somehow the word has gotten out about our little problem," Mitchell continued. He pulled an envelope from the briefcase propped against the leg of his chair. "In this envelope, I have checks and cash totalling well over a hundred thousand dollars."

A murmur of astonishment arose from the other council members. Mitchell rapped against the table for order.

"And I might add that the money came not only from stockholders, but from employees as well."

Another murmur rippled through the room, and when everyone finally quieted again, Mitchell turned to Dillon. "If my figures are correct, that should cover the rest of what you need to pay off that damned bank note. Am I right?"

For several shocked moments, Dillon couldn't move, and he couldn't have uttered a word if his life depended on it. How? When? Who? The questions raced through his mind. When he finally could speak, his words came out hoarse and choked with emotion. He nodded his head. "A hundred thousand will more than cover the debt."

Mitchell grinned. "Now that we've got that settled and out of the way, what was it that *you* wanted to talk about, Dillon?"

All Dillon could do was shake his head. "Someone has already beat me to it. I was going to suggest an emergency stockholders' meeting and..." He felt his face grow warm. "I was going to throw myself on their mercy and beg for the money if I had to."

A burst of laughter traveled around the table and, unable to help himself, Dillon joined in.

Mitchell rapped again for order.

Dillon stood. "I appreciate this." He gestured toward the envelope. "But if I had asked for the money myself, it would have been with the understanding that somehow I would have paid it back. I still intend to do that."

Mitchell motioned for Dillon to be seated. "I'm sure we all appreciate your good intentions, but since there's cash as well as checks and no one kept a record, I don't think that's possible. Besides, not one person who contributed said a word about being paid back." He cleared his throat. "Now that that's settled, there's a couple of more things we need to discuss before we leave."

He sent Dillon a serious look. "There's one I'm afraid you won't have any say-so about. Sorry, but it's unanimous that if Ted Jamison doesn't resign his membership by the end of the month, the council will take action to revoke it. And we don't give a damn if he sues. That's why we carry insurance."

When Dillon opened his mouth to protest, Mitchell shook his head and held up his hand. "I know you don't approve. You made that clear a few weeks back. But believe me, by the time the members in this club get through giving him the cold shoulder, he'll resign without a protest. And now the last thing."

Dillon noticed that Mitchell suddenly looked uncomfortable.

"After the fact, we realized why you forced Franklin to retire," he finally said. "And everyone knows you had no choice. But now, well . . ." He directed his gaze at Dillon. "The thing is, we all miss him being around. Of course, it's up to you," he hastened to add. "And we'll back you one hundred percent, whatever you decide. But a lot of the members would like to see him hanging around again. Not necessarily as the owner, or running the place. Not working, but as one of us—a member coming to Twin Oaks to have a good time.''

An hour later after a relaxing lunch, Dillon headed for his office with the envelope firmly in his grasp. As soon as the accountant could verify the amount, he intended to take it straight to the bank. He couldn't wait to see the look on Jamison's face when he handed over a check for the full amount owed.

Dillon felt his grin spreading into a full-blown smile. For the first time since he'd come home to Twin Oaks, he felt like he belonged, really belonged. With the loan paid off and all the cost-effective changes he'd made, the club would soon be in the black.

And then what?

Dillon suddenly frowned. The elation he'd felt faded, and in its place, settled a deep emptiness. By the time he reached his office, the emptiness was an ache of need, of longing.

Adrienne.

Without her, was any of it worth it?

CHAPTER FIFTEEN

DILLON PACED back and forth, waiting for his father to show up. He stopped, glanced at his watch, then continued to pace. When he had finally worked up enough nerve to call his father, he'd asked him to come to his condo, knowing that there they wouldn't be disturbed.

Dillon glanced around, satisfied that the place looked presentable. When the doorbell finally did buzz, he felt as if his stomach had just flipped upside down. He couldn't remember the last time he'd been so nervous.

He opened the door and the two men stood facing each other. Dillon noticed his father looked fit and healthy and more relaxed than he'd seen him since he'd returned to Twin Oaks. He finally motioned for his father to come in.

"Nice place," Franklin said, looking around with approval.

"Thanks. Want something to drink?"

"Got any orange juice?"

Dillon nodded. "Have a seat and I'll get you a glass."

When he tried to pour the juice and it sloshed over onto the floor, Dillon cursed beneath his breath. He grabbed a kitchen towel and mopped up the mess, then threw the towel into the sink. When he'd placed the carton of juice inside the refrigerator, he grabbed a beer for himself.

"Here you go." Dillon walked over to his father and handed him the glass.

Seating himself in a overstuffed chair opposite the sofa, Dillon popped the top on the beer and took a long drink. As the cool liquid slid down his dry throat, he tried to remember the apology speech he'd mentally rehearsed for two days, but none of his carefully thought out words came to mind.

The silence in the room stretched out endlessly. How to begin? he wondered, his hands gripping the beer can like a vice.

Just spit it out and get it over with.

He cleared his throat and finally looked up. "The loan has been paid, but then you knew it would be, didn't you?"

Franklin shrugged, but neither confirmed nor denied what Dillon had said.

Dillon shook his head and sighed. "You're a crafty old devil, I'll give you that. I fell for it, too—hook, line and sinker. And by rights I should be mad as hell at you. At any given time, you could have gone to the stockholders and they would have bailed you out." Dillon leaned forward, resting his elbows on his knees. "Those people at the club would do anything you asked. That's how much they think of you."

Franklin carefully set his glass on the table beside the sofa. He too leaned forward and propped his elbows on his knees. "There was a time in my life when I would have done that—gone straight to the stockholders and asked for the money. But that time has passed. You're not the only one in this family with pride, you know.''

Dillon ducked his head and stared at the can in his hands.

Franklin cleared his throat. ''People change. Even stubborn old fools like me. Sometimes voluntarily, sometimes because of circumstances. The day you left, I began to realize what's really important in life. Money can be made or lost at the drop of a hat, but family— the love and respect of an only son ... or a wife—can't be bought. It can only be earned, over a lifetime of giving and caring. And without those things from your family, nothing has much meaning. So you see, I really couldn't take the easy way out this time. I couldn't afford to, with so much at stake.''

As understanding began to dawn, Dillon raised his head and looked at his father. He swallowed hard, and when he was able to speak, his voice was choked with emotion.

''This time you won, Dad. This time we both won.''

''BUT WHAT ARE WE celebrating?'' Adrienne asked, puzzled by her uncle's insistence that they go out to dinner. They certainly couldn't afford to splurge for no good reason.

Louie shrugged as he hustled her out the door. ''For one thing, the grapevine did its job, and thanks to you, the bank loan for Twin Oaks has been paid off.''

"And another thing," Kristen piped up, following close behind. "You got the highest grade in your class on that term paper."

Since her daughter and uncle seemed really excited about their surprise outing—they'd insisted she put on her newest dress, and they had both donned their Sunday best—she'd gone along with them.

Several minutes later, when her uncle turned the car down the street that led to Twin Oaks Country Club, a flutter of suspicion caused her stomach to tighten. Adrienne twisted her head to glare at her uncle.

"Why are we going to the club?" she asked.

When several seconds passed and he didn't answer, Adrienne's eyes narrowed and she reached over to touch his arm. "What are you up to?" she demanded.

"We're going to dinner," he finally said, the set of his jaw determined.

"We can't go to the *club* for dinner. We're not members," she added desperately. Besides, she thought, there was a good possibility that Dillon was there, and just the thought of facing him made her grow weak.

Louie shrugged. "Stop worrying so much. Everything's under control."

"Yeah, Mom," Kristen called out from the back seat. "Chill out."

When Louie pulled beneath the portico and shut off the engine, Adrienne felt frozen to the seat. Beyond the double doors was everything she'd tried to forget. Just seeing the familiar building and grounds reminded her of Dillon.

Louie helped Kristen into her wheelchair first before he turned his attention to Adrienne. When he opened her door and took her arm to help her out of the car, she wanted to snatch it loose from his firm grip and demand that he take her home.

"Now, darlin', don't be stubborn. Come along."

Giving him her most scathing look, she finally succumbed to his gentle pressure and slid out of the car. "This is ridiculous," she muttered. "We can't go in there."

Louie ignored her and pulled her along with him as he pushed open the front door of the clubhouse.

Except for the music coming through the speakers in the ceiling, the foyer was as quiet as a tomb. Adrienne frowned, growing more uneasy with each step they took. Because it was dinnertime, there should have been waitresses scurrying to and fro, and the sounds of clinking dishes and people talking.

As they entered the main dining room, Adrienne glanced around and almost stumbled. It was empty. No people, no staff.

"What is going on?" she whispered.

"This way, darlin'," Louie urged, nudging her forward. It was when they reached the ballroom doors that Adrienne finally heard the murmur of voices. Before she could comment, Louie pushed them open.

She had only a second to register the fact that the huge room was packed with people before every eye in the room was on her and a collective shout of "Hooray!" went up from the crowd.

Adrienne turned to her uncle for an explanation, her insides quivering with confusion.

He nodded, grinning from ear to ear. "They're all here for you—in honor of what you did. By putting the word out, enough money was collected to pay off the bank loan."

"But how...who told them it was my idea?" she demanded.

"I did."

Adrienne would have recognized Eva's voice anywhere. "Eva! How could you?"

The older woman pursed her lips. "It needed to be done *and* you're too nice a lady not to get credit."

"Oh, Eva." She shook her head. "You're something else!"

Eva grinned. "That's what my husband tells me all the time."

Adrienne sighed and glanced back toward the crowd. She recognized members and employees, and felt her cheeks grow warm when she realized everyone was gazing expectantly at her.

When she spotted Franklin, Myrna, Mitchell Kelly and his wife making their way toward her, she felt a wave of happiness flood over her. It was wonderful to see Franklin back where he belonged.

Where was Dillon? she wondered, searching the throng. Was he angry about what she'd done? Was his absence a sign that he hadn't approved?

Smiling, Franklin stepped up and hugged her. Myrna followed suit.

"Well, young lady," he said jovially, "I think everyone here would agree that we all owe you a debt of
thanks." Franklin chuckled. "Wish I could have seen
the look on Jamison's face when Dillon handed him
that check. Dillon said he turned as pale as a ghost and
looked like he was going to throw up any minute."

Adrienne felt tears sting her eyes at the mention of
Dillon.

"Anyway," he went on, "I don't think we'll have to
worry about Jamison causing any more trouble. I even
heard that some of the members are closing out their
accounts at his bank."

Franklin placed his fingers beneath Adrienne's chin,
gently forcing her to look up at him. "Mitchell told me
that Dillon had already decided to go to the stockholders himself. If he'd had another month, he would have
won, doing things his way. But the important thing is
that he didn't buckle under the pressure. He hung in
there with the tenacity of a bulldog." He paused, his
eyes full of compassion. "You and my son did good.
Real good. You make one hell of a team."

Adrienne heard the pride in Franklin's voice and she
wondered if Dillon knew how his father felt about him,
how much he loved him. She hoped so, for both their
sakes.

A tear escaped down her cheek and she swallowed.
She felt someone squeeze her shoulder and turned her
head to see her uncle smiling in encouragement. Then
she felt a hand clasp hers, and when she looked down,

she saw Kristen looking up at her, her face shining with adoration.

Another tear escaped. Dillon's conspicuous absence from the celebration could only mean that she'd lost him for good. Even though she felt as if her heart was breaking all over again, she took comfort that her family was there for her, supporting her with their unconditional love.

Adrienne lifted her chin and cleared her throat. With everyone gathered in her honor, now was not the time to break down or mourn her loss. Later, in the privacy of her own bedroom... She pasted on a smile. She couldn't disappoint everyone.

"If it's okay, I'd like to propose a toast," she said quietly to Franklin.

Within minutes, glasses of champagne had been passed around, and a semicircle of employees and members formed around her. She raised her glass toward the crowd.

"To Twin Oaks and its continued success, and to—"

When the crowd suddenly parted and Dillon appeared, the rest of her words froze in Adrienne's throat. Her heart began to beat erratically, but there was nothing in his expression to tell her what he was thinking.

"Sorry to interrupt," he said, giving her a cursory glance. "But I have a toast of my own to propose first." With a look of arrogant confidence that baffled her, he smiled first at her uncle and Kristen, then at Myrna and Franklin.

Dillon held up his glass. "I'd like to toast the members and the employees. A finer group of people can't be found." He took a sip, then directed his gaze toward his father. "Second, I'd like to propose a toast to my father, who has always tried to instill in me certain values that at times I was too mule stubborn to comprehend. No man is an island. People need other people. And most of all, a son never grows too old to need the love and respect of his father."

Dillon finally turned his gaze on Adrienne. His eyes bore into hers like a laser, cutting to her very soul.

"I'd also like to thank a certain, very special lady, one who taught me that sometimes you have to consider people's personal circumstances in order to do business, and that not all interference—especially when it's done out of love—is wrong."

Adrienne watched in stunned fascination as he lifted his glass toward her, then drained it in one swallow.

As the crowd grew quiet, Dillon continued, "And now, if everyone will excuse us, the lady and I have some urgent business to discuss."

Before she could react, Dillon grabbed her hand and pulled her along behind him through the crowd and out of the ballroom. Keeping a firm grip, he headed straight for one of the smaller dining rooms.

The moment they entered the room, a wonderful blend of aromas assaulted her and she breathed in deeply. Spicy food and roses.

Roses! They seemed to be everywhere, she thought. The tiny room was lined with huge sprays of the beautiful crimson flowers. Along the only wall that wasn't flanked by roses was a rectangular table, which held silver chaffing dishes. In the center of the room was a table covered with white linen and set for two with the club's finest china. Completing the picture were candles and a bucket of champagne on the side.

It was every woman's romantic fantasy come true, she thought as she turned to him.

"Dillon, I—"

He shook his head. "Please." He squeezed her hands. "Don't say anything yet." He closed his eyes for a moment, and when he opened them, Adrienne saw pain reflected in their depths. "These weeks without you have been the worst kind of hell I've ever lived through."

"For me, too," she whispered.

"There's something else as well. You were right about my feelings for my father. I hadn't let go of the past. But I have now," he added.

"I kind of gathered that from your toast. By the way..." her eyes narrowed "...just whose idea was this—this celebration?"

Dillon grinned. "Eva let the cat out of the bag about what you'd done, but Uncle Louie and Kristen, with a little help from my father and mother, did the rest." He paused. "With a lot of encouragement from me, I might add."

Dillon let go of her hands to cradle her face. The love glowing from his eyes was like a shining light of hope at the end of a dark tunnel of despair. She felt paralyzed, as if the slightest movement she made might cause the wonderful magic of the moment to disappear forever.

"I love you, Adrienne Hamilton," he whispered. "I love you with all my heart and I want you to marry me."

Adrienne was conscious only of Dillon's gentle touch and the steady rhythm of her pounding heart. With a cry of joy and tears of happiness running freely down her cheeks, she finally found her voice to answer him. "Oh, Dillon, I love you, too, and yes, I'll marry you."

Her words were smothered by his hungry mouth, and every nerve in her body seemed to leap in response. She groaned and opened her mouth to give him entrance, and then groaned again when his tongue slid against her own and started in an erotic battle of give and take.

Suddenly conscious of a weak feeling in her knees, she looped her arms around his neck and hung on for dear life. When he pulled her to him more firmly, molding her body against his own, she wondered if anyone had ever fainted from experiencing such pure joy.

Dillon finally broke away with a gasp. "Oh, God, honey, I thought I'd lost you forever."

"I was miserable—" A noise at the door caught Adrienne's attention. She peeked over Dillon's shoulder, then frowned. "Okay, you two. How much longer did you plan to watch?" she asked her daughter and her uncle.

With a groan of frustration, Dillon loosened his hold on her and turned around.

Both Louie and Kristen had the grace to look embarrassed.

"We weren't really spying on you, Mom. But did you say yes?"

"Of course she said yes." Louie glared at Adrienne. "You did, didn't you?"

Adrienne laughed and nodded. Dillon shook his head and chuckled.

Louie and Kristen grinned at each other, then a conspiratorial look passed between them.

Louie cleared his throat. "In that case, we're leaving. And we won't bother waiting up, so just take your time coming home."

"Good night, Mom."

Adrienne continued to stare after them for several moments. A smile tugged at her lips when she heard Kristen ask her uncle if he thought she could be a bridesmaid at the wedding. Then their voices faded.

Dillon released her only long enough to step over and firmly close the door.

Adrienne shook her head. "Remind me to have a little talk with my uncle and my daughter."

Dillon laughed and caught her up in a fierce hug. "We'll both have a talk with them, but later...much, much later." He lowered his head, and when his lips touched hers, she forgot about everything, everything but the man she loved. She was finally where she belonged, she thought with a sigh of satisfaction. She was in Dillon's arms.

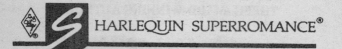

HARLEQUIN SUPERROMANCE®

COMING NEXT MONTH

AVAILABLE NOW:

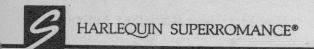

**Relive the romance...
Harlequin and Silhouette
are proud to present**

by Request™

A program of collections of three complete novels by the most
requested authors with the most requested themes. Be sure to
look for one volume each month with three complete novels by
top name authors.

In June: **NINE MONTHS** Penny Jordan
Stella Cameron
Janice Kaiser

**Three women pregnant and alone. But a lot can
happen in nine months!**

In July: **DADDY'S
HOME** Kristin James
Naomi Horton
Mary Lynn Baxter

**Daddy's Home... and his presence is long
overdue!**

In August: **FORGOTTEN
PAST** Barbara Kaye
Pamela Browning
Nancy Martin

**Do you dare to create a future if you've forgotten
the past?**

Available at your favorite retail outlet.

HARLEQUIN®   Silhouette®